Praise for
the Bram Stoker Award–winning novel *Crota*

"Convincing and fascinating. . . . How could you resist a book written by someone named Owl Goingback? *Crota* is not a tale to be read late at night. It's a chiller."
—*San Francisco Examiner*

"Goingback keeps the action brisk."   —*Publishers Weekly*

"Engrossing. . . . Goingback proves he has a talent for creating heart-stopping scenes that meld realism and fantasy. . . . Claustrophobically frightening. . . . Goingback utilizes his heritage well as he turns an Indian myth into a monster of a tale."   —*South Florida Sun-Sentinel*

"An extraordinary visionary novel."   —*The Anniston Star*

"One of the best un-put-downable novels that has passed through my hands in a long time. Goingback has excelled. Excitement on every page."   —Andre Norton

"Wow! I devoured *Crota*. What a terrific read."
—*Halifax* magazine

"Owl Goingback is one of the most interesting new writers working today. A natural storyteller who will be spinning his tales for a long time to come." —Martin H. Greenberg

Darker Than Night

"This book scared the pants off of me."   —Terry Brooks

"A chilling tale. . . . Mr. Goingback creates a story line that rivals the best of the genre's masters. . . . One of the year's best horror novels."   —Harriet Klausner

"Owl Goingback writes . . . the elemental scare, the campfire tale, that's all too rare these days."   —Gothic.net

Evil Whispers

BREED

OWL
GOINGBACK

Louise—Tael ~~Re~~ Reserved
Jane—Round—Nervous

Ⓞ
A SIGNET BOOK

SIGNET
Published by New American Library, a division of
Penguin Putnam Inc., 375 Hudson Street,
New York, New York 10014, U.S.A.
Penguin Books Ltd, 80 Strand,
London WC2R 0RL, England
Penguin Books Australia Ltd, Ringwood,
Victoria, Australia
Penguin Books Canada Ltd, 10 Alcorn Avenue,
Toronto, Ontario, Canada M4V 3B2
Penguin Books (N.Z.) Ltd, 182–190 Wairau Road,
Auckland 10, New Zealand

Penguin Books Ltd, Registered Offices:
Harmondsworth, Middlesex, England

First published by Signet, an imprint of New American Library,
a division of Penguin Putnam Inc.

First Printing, August 2002
10 9 8 7 6 5 4 3 2 1

 REGISTERED TRADEMARK—MARCA REGISTRADA

Printed in the United States of America

PUBLISHER'S NOTE
This is a work of fiction. Names, characters, places, and incidents either are
the product of the author's imagination or are used fictitiously, and any
resemblance to actual persons, living or dead, business establishments,
events, or locales is entirely coincidental.

For Nancy

And for my fellow members of
the Central Florida Muzzleloaders.
May your powder always be dry.

ACKNOWLEDGMENTS

Special thanks go to Garrett Peck, Sandy Craig, and Karen Harvey, for introducing me to the ghosts and hauntings of St. Augustine, Florida. And to the wonderful people at the St. Francis Inn, and Tour Saint Augustine, for their warm friendship and hospitality.

CHAPTER
1

The historic city of St. Augustine, Florida, was quiet at three o'clock in the morning, the night lying heavy and dark over ancient buildings and cobblestone streets. The gift shops and restaurants along St. George Street had closed their doors hours earlier, and all the bars in the old section of the city had extinguished their neon signs and turned out their drunks. The last of the tourists had made their final rounds for the evening, either on foot or in one of the many horse-drawn carriages, and had gone off to slumber in the pricey bed and breakfasts and inexpensive motels.

All of the streets in the old section of the city were deserted, except San Marco Avenue, along which a small white sedan moved south. The vehicle turned right onto Orange Street, slowly driving past the remains of the archaic City Gate. The two towering stone pillars that once served as gateposts looked like giant tombstones in the glow of the car's headlights, and served as a reminder that St. Augustine was once a walled city.

Driving past the gate, the sedan proceeded west on Orange Street for another two blocks, turning into an empty parking lot behind the Old Drugstore. Bringing the car to a halt, the driver turned off the engine and headlights, but made no move to exit the vehicle. Instead, she rolled down the window and sprinkled a pinch of tobacco on the ground.

Few people knew that the Old Drugstore, and its adjacent parking lot, was built over the top of an Indian burial ground. The desecration of a Native burial place was not something the city leaders wanted to mention in the tourist brochures, despite the fact that the elaborate headstone of Chief Tolomato stood on display inside the drugstore, supposedly standing in a spot directly over the location of his grave.

Satisfied that the pinch of tobacco would ward off any evil spirits, even those unhappy about a Nissan sedan parking over their remains, the driver rolled up her window and exited the car. She was joined a few moments later by two other women, who climbed out the opposite side of the vehicle. Like the driver, the two women were dressed mostly in black, their fingers adorned with an excess of silver rings and gemstones.

The driver's name was Maria Sanchez and, at forty-five, she was the oldest of the group, but only by a few years. She was also the leader of the ebony-clad trio, a teacher. But Ms. Sanchez was not an instructor in the Florida school system. She did not challenge the minds of elementary school children, nor did she lecture at any university or trade school.

As a matter of fact, she had never even finished high school. Instead, she had spent more than thirty years of her life studying all aspects of the occult and supernatural, rising up through the ranks of Wiccan and various covens, applying what she knew to help others, for a fee.

The occult had been good to Maria Sanchez, and she had earned a considerable fortune by reading tarot cards for elderly blue-haired ladies, and working love spells for the hopelessly lonely. She had saved enough money to buy a modest house in Cassadaga, Florida, a town renowned as a Mecca for spiritualists and followers of the occult. There she had hung out her shingle, advertising her special talents.

Two of her most promising students, Jane and Louise Fowler, had been with her for more than a year, long enough to learn all of the basics and move up to the next level. The two sisters had come to Maria after years of unsuccessfully trying to study on their own. The occult was simply not something you could master from a book purchased at the local mall. Nor could you learn it on the Internet, despite what many might have you believe. To walk the true path you had to have a devoted teacher—at least that was what Maria Sanchez had told the sisters when they paid a visit to her Cassadaga home. They needed a teacher who, for a moderate price, could guide them along on their journey to all things spiritual.

Shortly after their first meeting, Jane and Louise had moved to Cassadaga so they could study under Maria on a full-time basis. The sisters were well-off financially, thanks to the generosity of a deceased grandmother, so they didn't need to hold steady jobs. Instead, they were able to dedicate their time fully to the teachings of their leader. Still, after more than a year, they were both mere beginners with powers yet untested. They were also without the aid of a spiritual helper, someone from the other side to watch over the sisters and guide them in their journeys.

Looking around to make sure no one else was in the area, and they weren't being watched, Maria reached back into the car and removed a small leather shoulder bag from the backseat. She closed the door and locked the car, turning to favor her students with a nod and a slight smile.

"Are you ready, ladies?" she asked, sensing the eagerness of the sisters. Louise was the oldest of the two, tall, straight as a scarecrow, and somewhat reserved in her demeanor. She rarely spoke, unless spoken to, quite content to remain silent and let others do the talking. Jane, who was three years her junior, was shorter and round, filled with nervous energy, and in possession of a quick tongue that sometimes got her into trouble.

"I'm ready," Jane said, anxious to get started. "Is this our last stop?"

Her mentor nodded. "Yes. The last one. At least for tonight."

"Good," Jane replied. "I'm starving. I wonder if there's anyplace around here to get a bite to eat?"

Maria frowned, but did not scold the young woman. Jane had yet to realize that the quest for magic was far more important than food. "You're always hungry. We will eat later, after we have finished. Now let's get started. It will be morning soon, and we want to be finished before daylight."

"Maybe we can have breakfast at Denny's when we're done," Jane said, never knowing when to quit. "I could go for a grand slam."

"If you don't be quiet, I'll give you a grand slam," Louise whispered, growing weary of her sister's chatter.

Maria led the others past the drugstore to Cordova Street. They turned right at the street, walking slowly by an old two-story house. In front of the house was a towering live oak tree, with a palm tree growing out of the center of the oak. The trees were called "the lovers' tree," and were another one of the many oddly interesting sights to be found within the boundaries of the old city. There was a legend that went along with the trees, something about young lovers being united forever, but Maria had forgotten it.

The trees were significant, because they reflected the strangeness of St. Augustine, a city that seemed to be trapped in some kind of time warp, a place where the past still lived. The three women paused to study "the lovers' tree" for a moment, then continued on, stopping a short distance later when they reached the front of the Tolomato Cemetery.

Mounted on a metal post, next to the front gates of the cemetery, was a sign that read:

During the First Spanish Period, prior to 1763, this site was occupied by the Christian Indian village of Tolomato, with its chapel and burying ground served

*by Franciscan missionaries. The village was abandoned
when Great Britain acquired Florida. In 1777, Father
Pedro Camps, pastor of the Minorcan colonists, who
had come to St. Augustine after the failure of Andrew
Turnbull's settlement at New Smyrna, obtained permission from Governor Patrick Tonyn to establish this cemetery for his parishioners. Father Camps was buried here
in 1790; ten years later his remains were re-interred in
the "new church," the present Cathedral. The first
bishop of St. Augustine, Augustin Verot (d. 1876), is
buried in the mortuary chapel at the rear of the cemetery. The last burial took place in 1892.*

In all honesty, not many people were actually "buried" in the Tolomato Cemetery. The Spanish settlers
did not consider the New World to be holy ground,
so their bodies had been placed above it in stone
crypts, with the hope that one day their remains
would be returned to Spain for a proper burial. As
for the heretic Protestants who lived in St. Augustine
during the time of Spanish rule, their remains had
been buried outside the city walls in the nearby Huguenot Cemetery.

Due to its historical importance as one of the oldest
cemeteries in Florida, the Tolomato was no longer
open to the public. Two metal gates were kept locked
to guard against trespassers and vandals. There was
also a low stone wall, and a metal fence topped by
three strands of barbed wire, that enclosed the graveyard on all sides. Oddly enough, the top of the wire
fence, with its strands of pointy barbed wire, leaned
inward as if to keep something inside the cemetery,
rather than to keep intruders out.

The fact that the Tolomato Cemetery was kept
locked did not bother the women, because they

would not have to enter the grounds to accomplish their goals. Maria and her companions were looking for spiritual entities to serve as guides, and there was no better place to look for such things than in a cemetery, especially a cemetery as old as those that existed in St. Augustine. Not even the town of Cassadaga had such graveyards.

Maria looked up and down the street, making sure no one was watching. In a tourist town like St. Augustine, three women standing in front of the Tolomato Cemetery might not look very suspicious. Still, the hour was quite late, and why draw unwanted attention when you didn't have to? Explaining to a bored policeman what they were doing was something she could live without.

Satisfied they were alone, Maria reached into the leather bag she carried and removed three white candles, along with an equal number of small quartz crystals. Keeping a crystal and candle for herself, she handed the others to Jane and Louise, explaining that they were going to repeat the same ceremony they had already performed that night at two other local cemeteries. Removing a butane lighter from the bag, she lit all three candles. With candles grasped in their right hands, and crystals held tightly in their left, the women turned to face the graveyard. It was a calm night, so the tiny flames of the candles were in no danger of blowing out.

Maria Sanchez stood silent for a moment, feeling the atmosphere around her. She then recited an ancient incantation, asking the spirits of the Tolomato Cemetery to come out of their graves and join them. The others remained quiet as the words were spoken, though Jane shifted her weight back and forth slightly to ease the discomfort of standing. Maria gave her a harsh glance to still her movement, but it went unnoticed in the darkness.

Another minute passed. Then Maria said, "There. That's it. The incantation is complete. Three times the ceremony. Three times the power."

Jane looked around, obviously disappointed. "But I don't see anything. You said we would be able to summon spirits tonight, but nothing happened."

"Spirits are not puppy dogs," Maria snapped. "You can't expect to whistle and have them come running. They will come to you only if you are worthy of their attention, and they will show themselves only if they want to be seen."

Truthfully, in all her years spent studying the occult, Maria had never seen a spirit, but she did sometimes have feelings. Slight tingles that let her know when a visitor from the other side was near.

Despite her lack of spectral encounters, Maria was confident in the incantation she had just recited. The ceremony had been taken from the personal journal of one of Cassadaga's most renowned mediums. She had been gifted the journal by the medium's wife, a few days after he had died of a self-inflicted gunshot wound.

"We have performed the ceremony at three different cemeteries tonight," she continued, "so the triad is now complete. The gates to the spirit world are open, and it is only a matter of time before you get your guides. Be patient, and be alert. The spirits will let you know when they are around."

The sisters smiled, apparently satisfied with their

teacher's explanation. Maria started to tell them that it was okay to blow out their candles, when a gust of wind sprang up suddenly and blew out all three flames. The sudden gust was followed by a loud metallic ping, all three women jumping back as the chain holding the cemetery gates closed split in half and clattered to the ground.

"Look at that!" Louise said, her voice an awed whisper.

Maria stared at the chain, astonished by what she had just seen. No sooner had the chain hit the ground than the metal gates of the cemetery swung open.

"Holy crap!" Jane exclaimed, forgetting her manners.

"Shhh . . ." Maria said, warning her to be quiet. "This is what you wanted. This is why you're here. The spirits must have heard our words, and are welcoming us into their domain."

"Forget that shit," Jane said. "I'm not going in there."

Maria wheeled on her. "You said you wanted to be a master of the occult. A person with powers. Well, here's your chance. The spirits are calling you. Are you going to just ignore them?"

"You're damn right I'm going to ignore them," Jane replied, obviously frightened. "I don't mind a spirit paying a friendly visit to my home, but I'm not going to go traipsing around in a cemetery at night. You want to answer their call, then you go right ahead. Be my guest."

Maria was angry, and she was also a little afraid. She didn't want to go into the cemetery either, especially not by herself. Not at night. She also didn't want to lose the power she held over the other two women. They had always looked up to her, respected her. She was in danger of losing that respect now, especially if she showed fear about entering the cemetery.

"All right. Be that way. I'll go by myself. But don't come crying to me later because you have no spirit guides to help you in life. And don't ever expect me to waste my time on you again. You just stand there and miss out on everything we've worked so hard to accomplish."

Her words must have sunk in, because Jane suddenly looked browbeaten. "I'm sorry," she said, lowering her gaze. "I'll go with you."

She stared at Jane for a moment longer, then nodded. "Good. We'll all go. Three of us. Three, the magic number."

Maria collected the candles and crystals from the two women, placing the items back into her bag. She left the bag sitting just inside the front gates as they entered the Tolomato Cemetery. Maria Sanchez didn't know what she was looking for, but her feelings told her that something big was about to happen.

Following the narrow path that led from the front gates to the rear of the cemetery, the women passed several stone crypts and the bust of Augustin Verot. A strange silence seemed to hang over the area, and Maria found herself straining to listen for sounds. Except for their footfalls, and the sound of Jane's heavy breathing, the night remained eerily quiet.

They were less than fifty feet from the white mausoleum that stood at the back of the cemetery, when Maria was overcome with a feeling of intense fear.

She looked around, startled, but there was nothing to be seen. There were only the graves, and the darkness.

Maria stopped. The sisters also stopped, standing a few feet away. Jane started to say something, but she motioned for her to keep quiet. Standing there among the ancient graves, she listened to the night around her, trying to find a source for her feeling of fear. She willed the little voice inside her head to go quiet and calm, hoping her magical powers would now come to her aid.

The feeling grew stronger, almost choking her. The other women must have felt something too, for they began looking around nervously. Perhaps the feeling was caused by restless spirits who looked upon their presence in the cemetery as an intrusion. Maybe it was nothing more than lingering psychic fingerprints, left behind by those who had suffered terrible hardships in the New World.

She tried telling herself that it was just her imagination, and what she felt was the result of being in a spooky cemetery late at night. But the feeling had a sense of darkness to it, as if evil was touching her heart.

Suddenly, from the rear of the cemetery, there appeared a great blackness, darker than the night around it, rising out of the ground like a billowy cloud of smoke. At first she thought it was only a trick of the eyes, but the others must have seen it too. One of the women gave a startled little gasp, small and squeaky, like the cry of a mouse.

The blackness flowed from the farthest corner of the cemetery, moving past the ancient gravestones and crypts, blocking out the soft glow of a distant streetlight, and gaining speed as it rolled toward the frightened women. Maria could not help but wonder what manner of evil had been awakened with their incantation. What nameless thing had they accidentally summoned from the great void of the spirit world?

Reaching the mausoleum, the blackness moved down the narrow lane toward them. Maria tried to think of a spell she might use to protect them against the approaching darkness, but no such spells came to mind. Crystals and incantations seemed foolish child's play against the thing that now moved through the Tolomato Cemetery, seeking out those who had summoned it. Against such an evil she would be no match, no matter how many magical words she could recite.

The women watched in horror as the thing they had accidentally summoned changed shapes, transforming from a rolling cloud of blackness to a monster that resembled a maddening cross between an octopus and a giant spider, to the dark figure of a man with tentacle arms, and back again to a shapeless mass of darkness. This was no helpful spirit, coming to serve them as a guide. It was a thing of pure evil, conjured from the very bowels of hell.

Knowing that the three of them were outmatched, and in great danger, Maria could think of only one thing to say to her students: "Run!"

Turning on her heels, Maria sprinted for the front of the cemetery. The other women did not need to be told twice, for they too ran for their lives. Louise moved like a comical stick figure, all elbows and knees, a grimace of fear pulling at the corners of her mouth. Her sister, Jane, held her skirt with both hands as she pumped her short, thick legs high in the air. The plump woman spoke as she ran, a single word repeated over and over again, keeping time with the heavy sounds of her footfalls: "Oh, oh, oh, oh, oh, oh, oh. . . ."

They neared the front gate, and Maria was struck with the sudden maddening thought that the double gates would swing shut in their faces before they could escape the confines of the cemetery. She had seen the chain magically split in half and fall to the ground, had watched in awe as the metal gates swung open by themselves. Surely, if the thing pursuing them could unlock and open the gates to invite them in, then it could easily close the gates to keep them from getting out.

But the gates did not close as they reached the front of the cemetery. The metal bars did not spring shut to block their exit. Louise reached the gates first, not even bothering to look back as she fled from the Tolomato. She ran out into the street, stumbled and nearly fell, but kept her footing as she turned left, racing for the nearby parking lot. Maria did not call after her; Louise knew where the spare key for the Nissan was kept, and was no doubt hurrying to start the car.

Surprisingly, Jane reached the gates second, a full ten feet ahead of Maria. The fear of things far worse than death had empowered the short, portly woman, enabling her body to perform a feat that would have been nearly impossible any other time. She glanced backward as she reached the gates, and the look of terror on her face told Maria that they were still being chased by the thing they had summoned.

Maria was confident they would be safe once they got out of the cemetery; at least she hoped they would be safe. She was praying the evil spirit had its limitations, and could not venture beyond the cemetery walls. Ghosts rarely left the places they haunted, confined by rules mortals did not understand.

She was almost to the front gates, just a few feet away from possible safety, when she tripped over something in the darkness and went sprawling. She didn't have to see the item to know that it was her leather shoulder bag, the bag she had set just inside the front gates for safekeeping when they entered the cemetery.

With a startled cry, and a painful jolt, Maria Sanchez hit the ground. Crawling, nearly mad with fear, she tried to get back to her feet and continue running. She almost made it, but an ebony tentacle grabbed her around the legs and snatched her back inside the cemetery, dragging her toward a thing of darkness.

She screamed in terror, a high-pitched cry that was cut short. A fatal silence followed, interrupted briefly by the distant sound of a car engine revving, and the squeal of tires as a small white sedan sped out of the parking lot.

CHAPTER
2

Detective Jack Colvin wasn't out looking for bad guys when he turned off of U.S. 1, following King Street to the old section of St. Augustine. Nor was he investigating clues to a recent crime. Instead, he was enjoying a well-earned day off, hoping to spend the morning hours sketching a few landscapes before the tourists flooded the area.

Jack sketched for his own enjoyment, simple pencil drawings, or pen and inks, of the city's historic homes and buildings. In the past ten years he must have done close to a thousand drawings; they adorned the walls of his two-bedroom home, and took up space in the closets and various desk drawers.

Since he was never able to completely separate himself from his work, he often used the time that he sketched to think about the details of a particular case. Sitting under a shade tree, pad and pencil in hand, he sometimes came to conclusions he would never have considered while confined to his stuffy office at the police station.

Not that he was working on any cases at the moment. Things had been rather quiet in the old city, and his casebook was clear. Still, he enjoyed his artist sessions, because it gave him a chance to be alone with his inner thoughts. Being a thirty-six-year-old bachelor, with no special lady in his life, he had been having a lot of inner thoughts. The little voice inside his head was telling him that maybe it was time to find someone to share his life, settle down, perhaps even start a family.

Parking his car on Granada Street, he put a dollar's worth of quarters into the meter, and then walked slowly north past the Lightner Museum and Flagler College. The elaborately ornate buildings that housed the museum and the college had once been luxury hotels for the superrich. Built by railroad tycoon Henry Flagler in the late 1800s, they had been designed to lure the wealthy from the North, turning the city of St. Augustine into the Newport of the South.

Sadly, old Henry's plans had failed, for the Rockefellers and Vanderbilts had set their sights farther south, seeking even warmer weather and finding it in the tropical retreats of Miami and Key West. The buildings remained as a reminder of what could have been, glistening towers of red and white stone that spoke of faded glory and a forgotten era. Some say that the ghost of Henry Flagler still walks the halls of Flagler College; others say that it is the ghost of his insane second wife, Ida Alice, that haunts the building and grounds.

After passing the college, Jack walked a block east to what could probably be considered the heart of the old section. St. George Street wasn't a strip mall, but it came damn close to being one. Lined with gift shops, souvenir stands, clothing stores, and restaurants, the pedestrian-only thoroughfare was where most of the visiting tourists bid farewell to their hard-earned money. Many of the buildings along the street were indeed quite old, but St. George did not possess the quiet charm that existed in other sections of the historic city.

It was still early, so most of the gift shops along St. George had not yet opened for business. The tourists were also still relatively few in number, outnumbered by the locals, who were grabbing quick cups of coffee, and morning newspapers, before heading off to work. The peace and quiet wouldn't last long, however, because it was Saturday and the narrow avenue would soon be filled with throngs of people shopping for bargain souvenirs.

There used to be a lot of artists and street musicians set up along the street, but the city had passed a law forbidding public performance of any kind on St. George. Jack didn't have to worry about violating the local law in his artistic pursuits, because he would never dream of setting up to showcase, or sell, any of his drawings. Not that he was afraid of being arrested—he just didn't think any of his sketches were good enough to sell. Nor did he like people looking over his shoulder while he worked.

The detective stopped walking when he reached the old City Gate at the north end of St. George Street, thinking about his choices for possible sketches. In front of him was the Huguenot Cemetery and the visitor information center, while in the distance loomed the Castillo de San Marcos, the massive gray stone fortress that stood watch over the harbor.

The Castillo had been built by the Spanish in the 1600s, and was constructed entirely of coquina, a native shell rock mined on Anatasia Island. Over the years, the military structure had seen its fair share of violence and suffering. It had stood strong against invasions of bloodthirsty pirates and heathen English, offering a safe haven for the soldiers and citizens of St. Augustine.

In later years, under American rule, the fortress was renamed Fort Marion and served as a military prison to house members of various Indian tribes, victims of a westward expansion that had stolen their land. Entire families had been imprisoned at the fort, suffering from sickness, malnutrition, and the relentless heat and humidity. On the harbor side, a bullet-ridden wall still marked the spot where the firing squads of three different nations had executed helpless prisoners. The holes stood as a silent testimony to the bloody history of St. Augustine.

He thought about doing a quick sketch of the Castillo, but decided against it. He had already done quite a few sketches of the old fort, from several different angles, and really wasn't in the mood to do another one. Besides, he found the fortress depressing, and the last thing in the world he wanted to think about on his day off was imprisonment.

Walking west along Orange Street, he made his way slowly toward another one of the city's interesting buildings. Like many of the structures in the historic district, the Old Drugstore appeared to be in danger of falling down. The rustic two-story wooden building sat on the corner of Orange and Cordova, its sagging frame of weathered pine standing out in sharp contrast to the newer buildings surrounding it. Jack could almost hear the termites and carpenter ants chewing as he stood gazing at the old building, wondering how many more years it would be before it crumbled into dust.

For some strange reason he had never done a drawing of the Old Drugstore, even though he knew it would make an interesting sketch. He thought about opening his pad and taking a seat on a bench across the street from the drugstore, but shook his head and changed his mind. He just wasn't in the mood to sketch another historic building. He wanted something different to draw, something that would give him a challenge and release the creative juices. He wanted to be quietly melancholy, before the hot Florida sun had a chance to chase away the grayness of the day.

Luckily, he didn't have far to walk to find the ideal place to be moody. Just past the Old Drugstore, on Cordova Street, was the Tolomato Cemetery, and he could think of no better place to conjure somber thoughts and feelings than at a graveyard. Older cemeteries were even better for inspiring the artist within him, because there was a feeling to them that was nearly impossible to describe. They were special places, calling out to the creative, and to those with open minds, promising to share dark secrets with anyone who dared to linger beneath the shade of their towering oak trees.

Jack decided to sketch the cemetery from across the street, sitting on an elevated ridge of ground that was part of the original earthen works that once encircled the Spanish settlement. He had just stepped off the sidewalk to cross the street, when he noticed that the front gates of the Tolomato stood open. He had never seen the gates open before, and wondered if a grounds crew was working inside the cemetery. If so, then maybe they wouldn't mind if he walked around for a few minutes. He would love to get a closer look at some of the burial sites, maybe even do a few quick sketches.

There were no sounds of power mowers, or hedge trimmers, coming from within the tiny confines of the cemetery, so maybe it wasn't a grounds crew that had opened the gates. Nor did he see a city truck, or any other vehicles, parked in the area.

If it wasn't a grounds crew, then maybe the front gates had been opened by a member of the Historical Society. The St. Augustine Historical Society had considerable power within the old city, and were responsible for maintaining a number of historic sites. They were also responsible for the publication of papers and books about the town, as well as raising funds to restore many of the older homes to their original condition.

Jack thought it might be a member of the Historical Society who had opened the front gates, but then he spotted the broken chain on the sidewalk. The only person who would do such a thing would be someone who did not have permission to enter the cemetery: a vandal or trespasser in search of mischief, or a tourist in search of an illegal souvenir.

Whoever cut the chain to enter the cemetery must have been in quite a hurry when they departed, for they had left the gates standing wide open. He wondered if it had been a couple of college kids out for thrills: some idiot trying to prove his bravery to his drunken buddies, or trying very hard to impress a girl. Maybe a young couple had broken into the graveyard, but they had gotten scared and ran away. The Tolomato Cemetery was spooky as hell at night, especially to those who believed the local legends about its ghosts.

"So much for a peaceful morning of sketching," he said, frowning. Even though he was off duty, he still carried his badge. He was also armed, a 9mm Glock tucked securely into the shoulder holster concealed beneath his jacket.

Just inside the front gates, he spotted a leather shoulder bag on the ground, apparently dropped by whoever had broken into the cemetery. He suspected the bag might contain a hacksaw, or burglar tools, and was surprised to discover its contents consisted of three white candles, three plum-sized quartz crystals, a butane lighter, and several tied bundles of dried herbs. He sniffed one of the bundles, decided it was made of cedar and sage, and dropped it back into the bag.

A cedar and sage smudge stick, the kind sold in New Age shops. New Agers. Wanna-be witches. College girls with purple hair and body piercings. The hippies of the new millennium. He had had a few run-ins with such people in the past, arresting them on possession of illegal drugs, or putting a stop to ceremonies that always seemed to take place on private property. Such things weren't really a problem in St. Augustine, because New Agers were few in number. Usually, it was just a couple of college kids trying to invoke a higher spirit to help them with their term papers, or using a ceremony as an excuse to get stoned and naked.

Setting the bag aside, he made his way slowly toward the rear of the property. He was pleased to see that none of the headstones had been toppled, nor had any of the graves been disturbed. There wasn't even any graffiti painted on the side of the mausoleum, which had once happened several years earlier.

Walking slowly back toward the front gates, he discovered a silver ring on the ground, just a few feet away from the main path. The ring was large and ornate, with two carved snakes circling an oval blue stone. It was obviously quite valuable, and he wondered what it was doing in the graveyard. Maybe the person who had cut the chain, and opened the front gates, had also been the same person to lose the ring.

"Serves them right."

He started to pick up the ring, but then decided not to touch it until after he had finished looking around. The ring might turn out to be evidence in a crime, so it wouldn't do to go handling it. It was bad enough he had picked up the leather bag. Pulling a half-full pack of Winston cigarettes from his jacket pocket, he set the pack beside the ring to mark its location. It would be easier to find the bright red cigarette pack, than it would be to try to locate the silver ring again.

He had just set the cigarettes next to the ring when

he spotted something on the ground about thirty feet off to his right. At first he thought it was a discarded plastic trash bag, or maybe one of the larger black bags used for leaves and lawn clippings. But as he walked over to the object, he discovered that the tattered material was cloth and not plastic.

The shredded fabric was thick and heavy, black in color and probably wool, much too heavy to be the remains of a scarf or shirt. Attached to one of the pieces was a large plastic button, the type commonly found on women's dresses. The remains of the dress lay near one of the ancient gravestones, its frayed edges flapping in the morning breeze.

Beyond the dress were a few thinner pieces of shredded material that might have once been a pair of dark blue panties. And there was a pair of women's shoes beyond that.

Alarm bells sounded inside the detective's head when he spotted several dull brown stains on the tattered dress that might be blood. Contrary to what was depicted on television cop shows, bloodstains were not always bright red, and often ranged in color from reddish-brown to black, and could even appear green, blue, or grayish-white, depending on the actions of sunlight, heat, wind, and weather.

"Son of a bitch."

The situation had just gone from a simple case of breaking and entering, to a potential crime scene. Squatting down beside the dress, Jack pulled a white handkerchief from his back pocket and gently touched it against one of the brown stains. The blood was still wet, which ruled out the notion that the dress might have been taken from one of the graves.

Not that he had ever suspected the dress came from a grave. Its styling was rather modern, something that might be found on a rack at Sears, or JC Penney's, and there hadn't been a burial in the Tolomato for over a hundred years.

Pulling a pencil from his jacket pocket, he carefully lifted the tattered fabric off the ground. Beneath the dress was a scattering of small pieces of bone, and several human molars. There were also what looked to be pieces of skin, varying in size from a few centimeters to an inch or two in length. The bones were still wet with blood, as were the molars, due in part to the dampness of the surrounding grass and being covered by the fabric, and the pieces of skin were soft and pliable to the touch.

No doubt about it, he was definitely looking at a crime scene. Someone had dumped human remains on the grounds of the Tolomato, remains that might have come from a homicide victim. The bones, teeth, and skin were still fresh, and had probably been removed from the victim's body within the past six hours. Unhooking his cell phone from his belt, he called the station to report his findings and request additional help.

Rarely was a homicide detective the first person to arrive at a crime scene. More often than not, it was some rookie cop who didn't know the first thing about securing the scene, allowing valuable evidence to be destroyed, trampled, or misplaced. But Jack knew exactly what steps had to be taken, starting with securing the scene before anyone else could enter the area.

Standing up, he walked back toward the front of

the Tolomato, choosing a course not likely taken by the perpetrator. The perp had probably walked along the central path, leading from the front gates to the mausoleum, so Jack avoided that route, fearful of destroying any trace evidence that might have been left behind.

Since he did not have a role of barrier tape in his back pocket, his only way of securing the cemetery was to close the front gates. Knowing the metal bars could have valuable fingerprints on them, he used the toe of his shoe to move the gates.

He closed the first gate, and started to close the second, when he spotted the broken chain lying on the sidewalk. Suspecting the chain might also have fingerprints on it, and not wanting anyone to disturb those prints, he slipped a pencil through one of the links and carried it inside the cemetery.

Upon closer examination, the detective noticed that one of the links in the chain had been pulled apart, rather than cut. That meant the perp had used some kind of pry bar to break the chain, rather than cutting it in two with a hacksaw or bolt cutters.

Setting the broken chain on the ground just inside the entrance, Jack closed the second gate. He then opened his sketch pad and wrote the words CRIME SCENE—DO NOT ENTER in big letters on the first page. Tearing the page from the pad, he stuck it between one of the metal bars and the wire fence, adjusting the sign so it could be read by anyone approaching the front gates. The second page of the sketch pad would be used for taking notes, and he would use several more pages after that to make preliminary sketches of the crime scene.

Looking around, Detective Colvin decided he had done all he could to secure the area. He could not properly safeguard a crime scene by himself; all he could do now was wait for the cavalry to arrive.

CHAPTER
3

[handwritten: S̄ SĀBRA ∂KNee]

Ssabra Onih saw the sailboat coming and urged her little Ford Escort to even greater speed, hoping to get across the Bridge of Lions before the drawbridge was raised for the boat. It was going to be a close race, and she knew it. The sailboat was closing in on the bridge, seeking passage from Matanzas Bay to open waters. One of those big yacht things, with three masts, the kind owned by rich people who loved showing off to the neighbors. The captain of the boat had probably timed his sail to coincide with morning traffic, just so he could be the center of attention.

Glancing over her shoulder, she shot out into the left lane of traffic, passing two elderly women in a slow-moving Oldsmobile. Whipping back to the right, she made it around a white delivery truck that was holding up traffic in the left lane. A second or two later she made it over the drawbridge before the light turned red.

Leaving the bridge behind her, she drove west on Cathedral Place into the heart of the historic district. It was Saturday morning and the tourists were already circling the old plaza like vultures, searching for free parking places. Not that traffic was any better during the week; finding a parking place close to where you wanted to go was always a matter of timing and dumb luck.

She turned left at Cordova, and then right on Bridge Street, driving behind the Lightner Museum. Taking another right, she turned into the tiny parking lot behind the building occupied by First City Tours. Parking in an empty slot, she grabbed her costume off the passenger seat and entered through the back door.

Ssabra had moved to St. Augustine almost five years earlier, at the age of twenty-three, following the death of her fiancé. Alan's fatal accident had left her with a world of painful memories, and she was unable to face friends or family members without feeling the loss. Her estranged father, a full-blooded Cherokee who had given Ssabra her unusual name, might have suggested she try to heal her heart through traditional methods, but she had never been very much in touch with her Indian heritage. Instead of seeking solace in a sweat lodge, or through prayer ceremonies, she had decided to leave the hurt behind and relocate to Florida.

Working as a waitress her first nine months in the old city, a job she absolutely hated, she was lucky enough to meet the right people and get hired as a tour guide. In addition to giving day tours to retirement groups and grade schoolers, she also gave ghost tours at night. The ghost tours had been started several years earlier, after the owners of First City Tours received numerous requests for information about St. Augustine's "haunted" sights. The nightly ghost jaunts proved to be an instant hit, and now brought in more income than all the other tours combined.

Ssabra enjoyed the ghost tours because they were a lot of fun, and she could really get into her role as a spooky storyteller. She also got to dress up in an eighteenth-century-style costume, and carry a lantern for effect. And it was far cooler in the humid summertime to lead a tour at night, than it was to walk around in the heat of the day.

She had just entered the tour office when Claire Jones rushed up to her. Claire was a few years younger than Ssabra, short and slightly rounded, with flaming red hair and green eyes. She was also a tour guide, but had only been with the company for a few months. She sometimes got her dates and facts wrong, but her bubbling enthusiasm always made up for her goofs.

"Did you hear the news?" Claire asked, excited and apparently eager to spread some juicy bit of gossip.

"What news?" Ssabra hung her costume in the closet.

"About the Tolomato Cemetery. Something happened there last night. Police are all over the place."

"What happened?" Ssabra asked, troubled. The Tolomato Cemetery was one of the most popular stops on the ghost tour. If something had happened, the police might have the area sealed off. It would be a big disappointment to her customers.

"I'm not sure. Something big. I've heard the police found a body. . . ."

Ssabra smiled. "A cemetery would be a good place to find a body."

"No. No. No. Not like that. Not a body in the ground. I heard they found one that had been dug up. Some people are even saying that there was a murder."

"And where did you hear all this?"

"I heard it before I came to work."

"Where?"

"I heard some of the customers at Fernando's talking about it." Fernando's was a little coffee shop, just north of the plaza, that catered more to the local crowd than to tourists, the perfect spot to grab a hot cup of coffee, a fresh muffin, and an earful of gossip.

"And who told you this bit of news?" Ssabra asked, raising an eyebrow.

Claire swallowed and looked around the room, obviously not wanting to reveal the source of her information.

"Who told you?" she asked again.

Claire turned back toward her, but didn't look her in the eyes. "Siler told me."

"Siler?" Ssabra laughed. "You know better than to believe anything that old man has to say."

Siler Lock was an elderly black man who used to work as a tailor before retiring. He now spent his mornings sipping coffee with the locals, and spent most of his afternoons fishing along the Intercoastal Waterway. He was a good-hearted old man, but he just loved to gossip. He was also quite a flirt with the ladies.

"He was telling the truth," Claire argued. "I saw the police cars myself. I drove past the Tolomato on my way over here. They had the cemetery roped off."

"Did you see any bodies?"

"No."

"How about an ambulance? Or a hearse?"

"No, but—"

"Then I wouldn't go screaming murder, if I were you. Besides, it's bad for business. You go talking about a murder and half the people signed up for tonight's ghost tour will cancel on us. I don't know about you, but I like getting paid. So keep quiet about this, even if old Siler is right."

Claire nodded, then hurried off to tell one of the other employees about what she had heard. Ssabra smiled and shook her head. The young woman lived to gossip, and a possible homicide in the town's cemetery was definitely something to talk about.

Ssabra didn't have time to dwell on what may, or may not, have happened at the Tolomato Cemetery the previous evening. She had two groups of senior citizens signed up for tours that afternoon. Seniors were far easier to manage than an equal number of overactive schoolchildren, but they did need special consideration. Many of the streets in the old section of St. Augustine were still cobblestone, which could create quite a problem for those in wheelchairs or using a cane. She also made a conscious effort to speak slower, and louder, aware of the fact that some of them might be a little hard of hearing. Finally, she stopped for breaks more often with seniors, especially during the brutally warm summer months.

Grabbing a quick cup of coffee to clear the cobwebs from her head, she headed out the front door to meet with her first tour group of the day.

CHAPTER
4

While Jack Colvin waited for the boys from the crime lab to show up at the Tolomato Cemetery, he took another walk back through the grounds looking for clues and evidence. He was more thorough on his second round, because he was now dealing with a homicide and not just a simple case of trespassing or vandalism. Starting with the spot where he had found the remains, he walked in an outward spiral until he covered all of the cemetery. Still, he found nothing that might be a clue left behind by the perpetrator, at least no physical evidence that could be seen by the naked eye.

After walking through the cemetery a second time, and finding nothing, he returned to the starting point. Opening his pad of paper, he made a quick sketch of the crime scene, wanting to record as many little details as possible before they were lost to the elements. Afternoon thunderstorms were not uncommon in Florida, even in the middle of September, so he wanted to record the scene in detail in case it did rain later that day.

Sketches of crime scenes were often as valuable as photographs, because they provided a detailed image of the scene at the time of the drawing. Crime scenes changed with the passage of time, especially those occurring outdoors, so sketches and photographs were always given the highest priority.

Jack drew a quick sketch of the tattered clothing, and shoes, and the area surrounding them, leaving a space on the left side of the page blank for notes. In that blank space, he wrote his full name and police rank, the date, time, crime classification and case number, and the address where the scene was located. He also listed landmarks, and compass directions, as well as the critical features of the crime scene.

His right hand was already starting to cramp by the time he jotted down all the information that needed to be included with the first sketch. Flipping the page, he started to make another sketch of the scene from a different direction, but was interrupted by the sight of two vehicles stopping in front of the cemetery.

The cavalry has arrived.

Closing his sketch pad, he stood up and started walking toward the front gates. The first vehicle to arrive on the scene was an unmarked blue patrol car, which he immediately recognized as the car always driven by fellow detective, and good friend, Bill Moats.

Detective Moats was a quiet, soft-spoken man a few years older than Jack and a few pounds heavier, with beautiful silver-gray hair and a thick mustache. He was the last of the true Southern gentlemen, born and raised in the blue-blood society of Charleston, South Carolina, where horse racing and formal balls were still a way of life. His ancestors had been noted politicians, judges, and military leaders, and they had fought against the dreaded Yankees under Stonewall Jackson and Jeb Stuart.

Moats was the senior of the two men, in years and experience, but he often allowed Jack to be the lead detective when the two of them worked a case together. They made a perfect team, looking at the evidence from different angles, each uncovering clues that the other might have missed. And where Jack excelled with crime scene investigations, Bill was a critical thinker and would often come up with new leads by going back through the files.

The second vehicle that stopped in front of the gates was the white Chevy van used by the Crime Scene Investigation Unit, and contained all the equipment needed to process the scene: cameras, molds for making plaster casts, evidence collection kits, fingerprinting equipment, etc. The CSI unit was made up of specially trained civilian and police officers, two of which arrived in the van.

"Good morning," Bill shouted, seeing Detective Colvin walking toward the front gates. "You just couldn't take a day off, could you?"

Jack grinned. "You know how it is—my life is my work." Using the toe of his shoe, he pushed open one of the gates.

Detective Moats climbed out of his car and gave orders to the two men getting out of the van, instructing them to seal off the entrance to the cemetery with barrier tape and then start taking photographs. He grabbed a second role of barrier tape for himself, probably wanting to set up another barricade around where the remains were found.

It was a good idea to get both barricades in place before any sightseers showed up. Once word got around about the homicide, every cop at the station would want to come down and take a look. Fellow officers visiting the crime scene could be a problem, and they were often as destructive as civilians when it came to fragile evidence. The double barricade would be a deterrent to them.

"I've already called the medical examiner's office, and he should be here in a few minutes." Bill stopped just inside the front gates and looked around. "Who found the body?"

"I did," Jack replied. "But there isn't a body."

Bill looked confused. "No body?"

"No. Just a handful of remains: bone, teeth, skin, clothing. That sort of thing."

"Are you sure you're dealing with a homicide? It's not something someone dug up from one of the graves?"

Jack shook his head. "The remains didn't come from a grave. The clothing is too modern, and two of the molars have had dental work. The remains are also fresh, and look like they were removed from the victim within the past six hours."

"I think you had better show me."

He led the other detective to the spot where the clothing and remains had been dumped, again following a path not likely used by the perpetrator. Bill studied the crime scene in silence for a few minutes, then turned to face his partner.

"You're right. It's a homicide, but I don't think it happened here."

"Neither do I," Jack agreed. "There's no blood to speak of on the grass. Only a few drops, and that probably transferred from the clothing."

"You want to be lead detective on this one?" asked Jack. "I mean, it was supposed to be my day off, and I don't want to go stepping on your toes."

Bill smiled. "You found it, so it's your baby. I'm just here to assist. Tell me what you want done, and I'll get started."

"Well, since you put it that way: the first thing I want to do is put a barrier around the remains. I don't want anyone walking through this area until after CSI has had a chance to look it over, not even the medical examiner. Once they have taken a good look at the crime scene, then we'll let the ME examine the pieces.

"I also want to rope off the main path that leads from the front gates to the mausoleum. Odds are that's the path the perp used last night when dumping what was left of his victim. I found an ornate silver ring lying near the path. I've marked its location with a pack of cigarettes. I want it photographed, bagged and tagged. The ring may contain an inscription, or a jeweler's mark, that might help us trace it to its owner."

"Bag and tag the ring. Got it." Bill nodded, a slight smile touching the corners of his mouth. "You didn't pick it up, did you?"

Jack coughed. "I didn't touch the ring, but I did

handle the leather bag sitting just inside the entrance. I didn't know I was dealing with a homicide at the time."

"Okay. You're excused."

"Thanks, Dad." Jack laughed. "After the CSI boys get the front of the cemetery sealed off, and have a look at the crime scene, I want them to start taking pictures. I also want them to dust the front gates and the chain for fingerprints."

"Those gates are probably loaded with prints. This place is popular with the tourists."

"Yeah, I know it is. We probably won't get anything we can use, but I still want to check for prints anyway. If we can find a matching set on the gates and the chain, then we might be able to narrow down our list of suspects. Have them check the bag too."

"In the meantime . . ."

"In the meantime, after we string some barrier tape around the remains, and block off the main path, I would like the two of us to do a thorough search of the grounds, just in case I missed anything earlier. It would probably be best if we used a grid method, searching one section at a time."

"That's going to take time." Bill looked around at the cemetery. "I had better call the station and get a couple more bodies out here. I'm sure I can get some of the traffic cops to quit hanging around Dunkin' Donuts long enough to give us some help."

"Probably a good idea," Jack agreed. "But when they get here, tell them to keep their damn hands in their pockets. I don't want them touching anything."

"Got it." Detective Moats used his cell phone to call the station to request a few more officers to help out with the investigation, while Jack spoke with the CSI officers about how he wanted them to proceed. The two detectives then strung barrier tape around the clothing and remains, and along the main path, sealing off the areas. After that, they divided the cemetery up in a square grid pattern, using gravestones and imaginary lines for boundaries, and started searching each section carefully. Two patrol officers arrived on the scene about twenty minutes later, and they were put to work searching the opposite side of the cemetery. Much to Detective Colvin's amusement, Bill made a point of telling the officers to keep their "damn" hands in their pockets as they searched for clues and evidence.

The medical examiner arrived at the cemetery about an hour later. The fact that he was still wearing golfing attire under his white lab coat suggested he might have been out teeing off on a few holes, which would explain why he hadn't answered his pager when first called.

Working with the CSI officers, the medical examiner started carefully going over the human remains, and tattered articles of women's clothing. As each item was examined, it was carefully bagged and labeled for further study back at the laboratory.

The dress was the first item to be examined, with extra care taken in regards to the bloodstains. A couple of the stains were still slightly wet, and quarter-inch cotton squares were dipped into the blood using forceps, and then put into glass test tubes. The test tubes were left unstopped so the cotton squares could air dry.

Several strands of hair were also discovered clinging to the dress. There was no way to determine in the field if the hair fibers had come from the victim, the perpetrator, or from both of them. That was something they would try to determine under a microscope, back at the lab.

After they had collected hair and blood samples, the dress was carefully lifted off the ground and spread out on a large sheet of brown paper, allowing it to air dry. Once dried, it was carefully folded and sealed in a large paper bag. The blue panties and the leather shoes were also examined and then sealed in paper bags.

With the clothing out of the way, the medical examiner could focus his attention on the human remains that had been under the dress. The pieces of skin and bone were collected first, with the examiner placing each fragment in a separate glass container.

The last items to be collected were the teeth, three in all, with two of them containing modern fillings. Teeth were especially significant in determining the age of a victim, based upon the changes they undergo during aging.

Once all of the remains had been properly stored for transportation back to the medical examiner's office, the CSI officers gathered several soil samples from the spot and placed them in cardboard boxes. The samples would be examined in detail back at the lab, looking for trace elements such as hair or fiber. Chemical analysis would also be run on the soil to see if it contained blood, semen, or other liquids.

The medical examiner's job was done once all the evidence had been tagged and bagged. Taking charge of the remains and clothing, he bid the others farewell and headed back to his office, promising he would be in touch as soon as all the tests were run. With the ME's departure, the two crime scene investigating officers resumed the task of trying to lift fingerprints off the front gates, broken chain, and the leather shoulder bag. They also collected the ornate silver ring for evidence. Jack and Bill finished up with their grid search of the cemetery, allowing the two patrol officers to head back to the station.

There wasn't much else they could do for the day, except canvass the neighborhood in search of clues. The Tolomato Cemetery was flanked by houses, so maybe someone in the area had seen or heard something during the night. There was also a green Dumpster that sat just on the other side of the fence, behind the Old Drugstore, that warranted a quick search. The perp might have dropped something into the Dumpster on his way to or from the graveyard: gloves, a pry bar used to break the chain, or maybe a container used to carry the clothing and remains.

The two detectives were on their way to check out the Dumpster when a television news truck pulled up in front of the cemetery. Word had obviously already gotten out about the homicide.

"Looks like we've got company," Bill said, pointing at the truck. "Somebody at the office must have loose lips."

"Maybe it's a slow news day, and they were listening to police broadcasts."

"I didn't say anything over the radio. Did you?"

"Not me," Jack replied. "I used my cell phone."

"Well, somebody must have said something over the air." Bill stopped and pulled a pipe and pouch of tobacco out of his jacket pocket. "Why don't you go have a look in that Dumpster. I'll play public affairs officer for the day."

"You're going to give them a statement?"

The older detective nodded. "We might have need of the press later on, so I had better give them a tidbit or two now to keep them happy. They're going to find out everything anyway, so I might as well be nice. I'll tell them that human remains were found, but it has yet to be determined where they came from. It's also undetermined at this time if it was a homicide, or an attempt at an illegal burial."

"Sounds good to me."

"I thought you'd approve." Bill smiled.

"Okay, you deal with the press, and I'll go look through the Dumpster." Jack looked around, suddenly realizing what he had just agreed to. "Wait a minute. You get to kick back and chat with the media, while I go rooting around in a trash bin. I think you just tricked me."

Bill laughed. "I did indeed."

"Damn. There's probably all kinds of nasty stuff in that Dumpster. What a way to spend my day off"—Jack glanced at his watch—"and the day is only half over."

CHAPTER
5

It was already dark by the time Ssabra finished with her afternoon tours. After arriving back at the office, she changed into the costume she always wore for the ghost tours: a dark blue dress with layered petticoats, the kind that were typically worn during the 1800s, and a matching scarf and bonnet. Her shoes were modern, but the dress was so long no one could see them. Once dressed, she put a new candle in her lantern and headed out the door.

First City Tours ran two different ghost tours at night. The eight o'clock tour covered the northern end of the old city, and included stops at the Huguenot Cemetery, the Tolomato Cemetery, the Casablanca Inn, and several spots along St. George Street. The nine o'clock tour focused on the south side, with Flagler College, the St. Francis Inn, and the old armory being key points of interest. The tours normally took a little over an hour to conduct, with twenty to thirty people in each group.

She would be leading one of the eight o'clock groups, which meant she had approximately twenty minutes to get back over to St. George Street, where customers would be signing up to take the tour. She wasn't pressed for time, because it wasn't that far of a walk, but she did need to get her butt in gear.

Ssabra arrived at the north end of St. George Street in record time, with a few minutes left to spare. It was amazing how fast she could move when she wanted to, despite being hampered by a long dress and several layers of petticoats. It was even more amazing how many people were already standing in line behind the Mill Top Tavern, waiting to sign up for the tours. It was obviously going to be another busy night in the haunted city.

Checking in with the girls manning the sign-up sheets, she was given a group of around twenty-five people to take out on tour. As was often the case, her group for the night was a mixture of tourists and locals: couples, families, young and old, even a few repeat customers who had taken one of her ghost tours earlier in the week. She didn't mind the variety; as a matter of fact, the diversity of her group would help to make the night more interesting. She could be factual and informative for the adults, while playing the part of the spooky storyteller for the little ones. She always delighted in making children snuggle closer to their parents for protection.

Moving her group away from the sign-up table, she double-checked to make sure everyone was wearing a ghost sticker. The stickers were given to tour customers when they paid their money, and served as a means of identifying who was in the group. It was not unusual to have someone try to slip into the group during the tour, and the lack of a ghost sticker was an easy way to identify them.

Usually, she didn't have much trouble getting rid of a nonpaying outsider. The others in the group had paid their money, and they were not about to have someone tag along for free. They would tell the party crasher to get lost. It was amazing how protective a group could be of their tour and their tour guide.

Counting heads and checking stickers, she introduced herself to the group. "Good evening, ladies and gentlemen, boys and girls. My name is Ssabra Onih, and I will be your official guide for tonight's ghost tour."

Slipping into character, she favored the crowd with a slight smile and lit the candle in her lantern. "I hope that none among you are faint of heart, for I promise you an evening of spooky delights. We are going to visit the haunted places of North America's oldest city, walking hand in hand with its ghostly residents.

"I must warn you that this is a walking tour, so I hope you're all wearing comfortable shoes. Also, we will be crossing several streets where there's traffic, so I ask that none of you cross before I do. It wouldn't do to have any of you run over by a speeding car. If that happens, you just may end up as one of the many ghosts of our lovely city."

Finished with the introduction, she gathered her group together and led them south along the crowded avenue. The first stop of the evening was the Pellicer-Peso de Burgo house at 49 St. George

Street. After everyone gathered in a semicircle around her, she told the story of the hauntings that were associated with the original building.

"The building you see behind me is called the Pellicer-Peso de Burgo house. It is a reconstruction of a Minorcan duplex, and was built by the Historic St. Augustine Preservation Board in 1974. It is now a museum run by the city of St. Augustine.

"Prior to the Minorcan duplex, this site was occupied by a print shop and stationery store. The business was located on the ground floor, with a private residence above that. The business and residence were both owned by the Paffe family, some of the wealthier citizens of old St. Augustine.

"The haunting that I want to tell you about, the one associated with this site, took place in 1927, around the same time that a vicious hurricane was battering the east coast of Florida. Mrs. Paffe was quite elderly, and she lived in the upstairs residence with her grandson. The poor woman was also ill, and a nurse had been hired to take care of her.

"One night, when the winds of the hurricane were blowing strongly against the shuttered windows, the nurse went into Mrs. Paffe's bedroom to check on her, only to find a nun kneeling beside the bed, obviously praying for the elderly woman. Finding it odd that someone else would be in the room, the nurse went to the grandson's room to inquire about the nun.

"The nurse was quite surprised when the grandson told her that the nun was actually a spirit, and often appeared to comfort his grandmother when she was afraid. The elderly woman was terrified of storms, especially hurricanes, so the nun had obviously come to help ease Mrs. Paffe's fears.

"The nurse was a little skeptical of the grandson's story, so she walked back to the bedroom of Mrs. Paffe. But the nun was no longer at the bedside of the elderly woman, nor had she gone down the stairs and out the front door. She had simply vanished. The nurse was surprised to find that the nun had disappeared, and began to wonder if she really had seen a ghost.

"A few nights later the nurse went to check on Mrs. Paffe, only to find a strange man standing in the room. The man was young, tall, and dark-haired, dressed in an odd-looking uniform, like those the Spanish soldiers used to wear in the 1700s. Thinking that the soldier must be a family friend, and had come to pay a visit on the elderly woman, the nurse left the room and went to see Mrs. Paffe's grandson.

"When the nurse told the grandson about the Spanish soldier, he became quite upset and ran down the hallway into his grandmother's bedroom. But he was too late. The soldier had gone, and he had taken with him the spirit of the sick woman. Mrs. Paffe was dead.

"It seems that Mrs. Paffe had told her grandson about the nun who always came to visit her when she was sick or afraid. She had also told him about the Spanish soldier who would one day come to escort her spirit to the other side. The soldier had indeed come that night, carrying Mrs. Paffe's soul to the great beyond."

She stopped speaking and fell silent, allowing her

story to sink in. There were several smiles among the members of the group, and a few nodding heads. But for the most part, her listeners were happy to just stand quietly in front of the de Burgo house, searching its windows and doors for any signs of a ghost.

"And now, if you will all follow me, we will move on to our next location."

The tour guide had planned on taking her group to the Casablanca Inn, and telling them the story about the ghost who still signaled to ships in the harbor, but another group had gotten there ahead of her. Not wanting to risk getting the two groups mixed up, which could easily happen, she decided to lead her people north to one of the old cemeteries.

Ssabra turned to her group and smiled. "It looks like someone beat us to the Casablanca Inn. That's okay. We can come back to it later. Right now, I want to take you to one of St. Augustine's oldest cemeteries. Make sure you all stay together; I wouldn't want anyone to get lost along the way. I also want you to keep a sharp watch, for where we are going ghosts have been seen on many occasions. Several people have even captured them on film, so make sure you have your cameras ready."

There was general laughter among the group, but she noticed that two of the children moved a step closer to their parents. A young woman also snuggled against her boyfriend, perhaps pretending to be afraid. He didn't seem to mind, as he put his arm protectively around her shoulders.

Leading the tour group north past the old City Gate, they arrived at their destination. The Huguenot

Cemetery was the burial place for the city's early Protestant residents. Since St. Augustine had originally been under Catholic rule, the cemetery had been built outside the city walls. No way the good Catholics were going to let heretics be buried inside the city.

The half-acre burial ground was established in 1821, the same year that a yellow fever epidemic swept through the area. Many of those buried in the cemetery had fallen victim to the deadly disease; some had even been buried side by side in unmarked mass graves. Because of the mass graves, no one knew for sure just how many people were buried in the Huguenot.

Telling stories about the yellow fever epidemic, and early burials, cast a somber spell over the tour group. Many of them gazed thoughtfully at the cemetery, perhaps wondering about the hardships and suffering of the permanent residents. Standing there in the darkness, it was easy to imagine restless spirits wandering among the gravestones.

But with tragedy sometimes came comedy. Ssabra also told the story about the Honorable Judge John B. Stickney, who was said to still haunt the tiny cemetery, even though his body had been dug up and sent elsewhere. According to the legend, a couple of drunken grave robbers had stolen the judge's gold teeth when his body was being removed for reburial up North, and his spirit still haunted the cemetery in search of his shiny molars.

Ssabra had just turned to point out the headstone of Judge Stickney, when she heard someone speak.

"Osiyo."

Thinking someone might have a question, or a comment to make, she turned back to face her group. "Yes? Did someone have a question?"

A few of the people in the group looked at each other, but no one spoke up. "I'm sorry. My ears must be playing tricks on me."

"Maybe you heard a ghost," a little boy said, stepping away from his mother.

"Could be." Ssabra laughed. "And if I see one tonight, I'll show you just how fast I can run."

She must have overheard one of her tour members saying something to another, and had mistaken it for a question directed toward her. Finished with her stories about the Huguenot, Ssabra led the group down the street to the Tolomato Cemetery.

The Tolomato looked just the way it always did at night, spooky and dark. A narrow rectangle of land where ancient headstones and crypts stuck out of the ground like old bones, and where towering oak trees wore long gray beards of Spanish moss. It was always quiet at the graveyard, but it was never completely silent, for even the slightest hint of a breeze made the dried fronds of the palmetto trees whisper to each other.

The police had left the area earlier in the day, taking their bright yellow barrier tape with them. The gates were again closed, secured with a brand new chain and padlock. Whatever had happened there that morning, be it human remains being found or even a murder, the investigation was obviously over.

Gathering her group together on the sidewalk in front of the entrance gates, Ssabra recited several ghost stories about the Tolomato. One of the stories

she told was about the two boys who had spent the
night in the cemetery, back when doing such things
wouldn't get them arrested, and how they had awakened to see a ghost floating across the grounds
toward them. Terrified out of their wits, both boys
fled for their lives. Later they learned that the ghost
they had seen was that of a young woman who had
died one week before her wedding day, and whose
last request was to be buried in her white bridal
gown.

The boys were not the only ones to see the phantom bride, for she had been sighted numerous times
over the years. Some even claimed to have photos of
the woman in white, proof positive that life did exist
beyond the grave.

Ssabra spoke slowly as she recited her ghostly
tales, choosing her words carefully, drawing her listeners into the story. As she spoke, several members
of the group crowded closer to the fence, obviously
hoping to see a spirit or two wandering among the
graves. Others took flash photos, and videotape, hoping to catch something on film that wasn't visible to
the naked eye.

Finished with the ghostly stories about the Tolomato, they moved on to several other places in the
old city that were supposed to be haunted. They paid
a visit to Fay's house, which was said to be inhabited
by the ghost of a mean old woman who had chain-
smoked cigarettes when still alive. Some claimed that
Fay still chain-smoked in death, for the glowing tip
of a cigarette was often seen in the second-floor window of the old house. They also stopped by the Old
Spanish Bakery, where the spirit of a young woman

had been seen on numerous occasions hanging laundry over a wooden fence.

The walking tour took a little over an hour and a half to complete, and finished back on St. George Street, not far from the spot where they had started. Thanking her group, Ssabra bade them a fond farewell and sent them on their way. Some members of the group headed back to the cemeteries for another look, hoping to see a real ghost. The others wandered off to explore the city's various nightclubs.

Since the evening was still fairly young, Ssabra decided to grab herself an ice-cream cone before heading back to her car. She enjoyed the ice cream while sitting on an empty park bench, watching the tourists move slowly along St. George Street. After the ice cream, she was still in no hurry to go home and decided to wander around for a little while. St. Augustine was a fairly safe place to walk at night, even for a woman by herself. For one thing there were usually other people out and about until the wee hours of the morning.

Choosing streets less crowded, she walked along looking at the majestic old homes. Ssabra wished she had enough money to purchase one of the old Victorian homes in the city, turning it into a bed and breakfast, but those homes were well beyond her price range. Even the ones that needed extensive remodeling usually sold for a minimum of two hundred and fifty thousand dollars.

It was a little after eleven p.m. when she decided to call it a night and go home. She was on the north side of the old section, walking past the Huguenot Cemetery, when she detected the faint odor of pipe tobacco. Curious, she turned around to look for the source of the aroma, but there was no one else in the area. Perhaps the smell of pipe tobacco had been carried from farther up the street. There was a little tobacco shop on St. George, so maybe a customer had lit up after making a purchase.

She sniffed again. The odor was still there, even more noticeable than before. Odd, but it smelled like it was coming from inside the cemetery. Curious about the aroma, she approached the stone wall that ran along the south side of the graveyard.

The Huguenot was quite dark, and it was hard to make out even the tombstones, but she didn't think anyone had gotten inside the cemetery. At least she didn't see anyone. Still, if there were someone there, she probably wouldn't be able to see them unless they were walking around. If they were standing still, sitting, or hiding in the shadows of an oak tree, they would be practically invisible. If someone had sneaked in, then they weren't too intelligent; for if she could smell the aroma of their pipe, then so too could the police.

She stood there for a few moments longer, searching for an intruder, but she didn't see anyone. The aroma of pipe tobacco had also faded. It had probably come from somewhere down the street, and she had been foolish for wasting her time around the old cemetery.

Turning her back on the Huguenot, she started back toward St. George Street. She had just taken a few steps, however, when she heard a man's voice, deep and rich.

"Osiyo."

Ssabra spun around, startled by the voice. She expected to find someone standing behind her, but no one was there.

"Who said that?" she asked, her eyes searching the darkness for the person who had spoken.

A chill danced down her spine. The voice had come from behind her as she turned away from the cemetery, which meant the voice had come from within the graveyard. She had been right earlier, in thinking that someone might have sneaked onto the grounds. Unlike the Tolomato Cemetery, there wasn't a high fence, or strands of barbed wire, guarding the Huguenot. It would be easy to scale the low stone wall on the south side to gain entrance into the cemetery.

But if someone was sneaking around inside the graveyard, then why were they making their presence known? The city authorities took a dim view of trespassers, especially when it came to the historic spots of St. Augustine. The police would arrest such people, making an example of them to warn others. The only possible explanation could be that the man was drunk. A sober vandal would not be so stupid as to light a pipe and speak to others.

Knowing she might be taking a risk, Ssabra felt compelled to warn the man of his foolishness. She should call the police and report him, but she didn't want to see anyone get into trouble, not when it could be avoided.

"You had better get out of there." She spoke loud enough to be heard by anyone who might be listening. "The police will have your hide for going in to that cemetery."

She waited a few moments for a reply, but there

was only silence. "Do you hear me? You had better get out of there before you get into trouble."

Ssabra turned and looked up and down the street, hoping someone else would come along. She didn't like hanging around the cemetery, speaking to the unseen man. He was probably just a drunk, but that didn't mean he wasn't dangerous. Unfortunately, the street was empty. She was alone.

Wishing she had her cell phone, or some pepper spray, Ssabra crept closer to the stone wall. She was thinking that maybe the man was sitting just on the inside of the wall, which would explain why she couldn't see him. He was probably just an old wino too drunk to walk, and had gotten into the cemetery to sleep it off. Still, she needed to get him out of there before the police found him.

Reaching the wall, she leaned over and looked on the other side, but there was no one there. At least she didn't see anyone. She was still peering over the wall, when she again heard the voice.

"Osiyo."

Ssabra jumped back. The voice came from directly above her. Startled, she looked up into the branches of a nearby oak tree, but she didn't see anyone. The branches were empty; there was no one there.

She was starting to get nervous. She suddenly remembered hearing the same word spoken earlier while leading the tour group. At the time she thought one of her group had asked a question, but now she knew otherwise. Someone inside the cemetery had been speaking to her, someone who could be heard but not seen.

"Enough of this." She turned away from the cemetery. "You can stay in there all night, for all I care. I'm out of here."

With those parting words, she hurried across the street, fleeing the darkness of the cemetery for the lights along St. George Street. She didn't slow down as she passed through the old City Gate. Nor did she look back toward the Huguenot Cemetery, fearful of what she might see. But had she stopped to look, she might have noticed a thin bluish wisp of tobacco smoke that drifted up from the lowest branch of an oak tree, dancing upon the night wind. And she might have heard the distinct laughter of a man who was well pleased with himself.

CHAPTER
6

Kevin Bess sat at a quiet little bar on Cordova Street, slowly nursing a bottle of Budweiser. The beer, and the muscle relaxers he had taken earlier, helped to ease the pain in his lower back, but did not entirely eliminate it. Nothing ever stopped the pain. It was with him all the time, twenty-four hours a day, seven days a week, a constant reminder of a fateful moment in time five years earlier.

He had been a carpenter, with a good paying job working for a local construction company. Employed and happy, he owned a nice little condo near the beach; he also owned a beautiful blue Harley Davidson. But everything changed one fateful Friday night when a Cadillac made an illegal left turn in front of him. He tried to avoid hitting the car, but the road was slick from an August thunderstorm, and he smashed into the vehicle at nearly fifty miles an hour. Kevin went airborne over the car, doing a less than graceful half gainer, slamming down on the hard street. He broke his left leg in three places, and crushed several of the vertebrae in his spine.

The driver of the Cadillac was a retired judge, and still had clout in the legal system, so the accident was not charged to either party. Which meant the other guy's insurance company didn't have to pay for the damage to Kevin's bike, or the damage to his body.

He spent nearly a month in the hospital, with an additional six months bedridden at home. Unable to work, he lost his job with the construction company. He also lost his condo when he couldn't keep up with the monthly mortgage payments. He finally healed enough to get out of bed and walk, but there was now a weakness in his back that had never been there before. Going back to his old job was out of the question. No way he could swing a hammer, or carry lumber for a living. He had to settle for the small amount of money he received every two weeks from social security.

In addition to the weakness, there was also a great deal of pain in his back. Pain that always seemed to be with him, morning, noon, and night. Pain that took the beauty from his life, and made him see things with tired, bitter eyes. The bitterness had taken over his life, causing his girlfriend of three years to finally give up on him and move in with somebody else.

Kevin drank his beer, and then ordered another. He wasn't worried about getting drunk, because he wasn't driving. Not that he owned a car, or even a motorcycle. Such things were luxuries of the past. He had just enough money for beer, and to pay the rent on the decrepit, one-room apartment he now called his home. He wouldn't even have enough money for that if his older sister didn't help him out from time to time.

"Thank God for big sisters," he said, lifting the new bottle of beer the waitress had brought him. The waitress just frowned and walked away.

The employees of the bar didn't really like him hanging out in their establishment several nights a week, but they tolerated his presence. He always sat alone at a corner table, listening to what the other customers had to say but never attempting to join in on the conversation.

The bar had already announced last call for the evening, and most of the customers had gone home, when he finally decided to call it a night. Finishing the last of his beer, he laid a dollar on the table, grabbed his walking cane, and slowly stood up. The beer and medication had gone to his head, giving him a pleasant buzz that was almost pain free. Almost, for as soon as he stood up, a fiery twinge shot up his back, letting him know that things had not changed.

Using the cane to help support a leg that would never be completely healed, he hobbled out the front door and down the wooden steps to the street. He lived six blocks north of the bar, and it usually took him close to an hour to walk home, depending on how much booze and how many pills he had consumed during the evening. Pausing to light an unfiltered cigarette, he started down the street, his body quickly falling into a rhythmic gate that was part hobble and part drunken stagger.

He turned right on Cordova Street, passing several
Victorian homes that had been converted into bed
and breakfasts. Though lights burned in the ornate,
two-story buildings, it was doubtful if anyone was
still up at such a late hour. The temporary residents
were probably sound asleep on antique beds, and
feather pillows, dreaming of stock trades, bank merg-
ers, and what flavor jam they would put on their
croissants in the morning.

"Fuck them," he whispered under his breath.
"Fuck them all."

Hobbling past the bed and breakfasts, he came to
the Tolomato Cemetery. The cemetery stood empty
and dark, a place of dense shadows and eerie silence.
Kevin paused for a moment in front of the cemetery's
front gates, wondering about the people who were
buried inside. He wondered if being dead was any
easier than being alive, a thought that often crossed
his mind when passing the old cemetery. He had
pondered the same question on nights when the pain
got too bad for him to sleep, during the hours of
endless darkness when he would sit in his tiny living
room with a loaded pistol in his hand. One night,
maybe soon, he would learn the answer to his
question.

"You guys are the lucky ones," he said out loud,
his words slurring slightly. "All you have to do is
lay there and sleep. No more pain. You ought to
come out here, in the real world, and put up with
the things I have to put up with."

He smiled, swaying slightly on his feet. Finally,
here were some people who would listen to what he
had to say.

"That's right. You've got it easy. All of you. Why don't you come on out and join me? Come out and see what the real world is like. Come on. I dare you. I double dare you."

From somewhere in the distance a dog suddenly howled, its cry carried like ghostly music on the wind. Hushing his drunken banter, Kevin paused to listen. The dog howled twice more, then grew quiet, probably hushed by its owner.

Turning his attention back to the cemetery, he studied the row of graves closest to the front wall. The graves were quiet and undisturbed; no one had accepted his invitation to join him in the real world.

"Cowards."

Disappointed, he turned and started down the street, weaving a little more than he had earlier as the beers and muscle relaxers started to catch up with him. He wished he had a car to drive, but he didn't. Maybe he should call his sister and ask for a ride. She wouldn't be too happy to receive a phone call at two in the morning, but he was family. She would come to get him, even if it meant he had to listen to a lecture all the way home.

Deciding he would indeed call his sister, if he could find a pay phone, Kevin continued walking in the direction of his apartment. He had just reached the Old Drugstore when he heard a strange sound coming from behind him. It was an odd clanging noise, metal on metal, like a mechanic beating a wrench against an old car engine. Thinking that someone might be having trouble, he stopped and turned around. But the street was empty of people and cars, deserted except for the drunken cripple who stood listening in the darkness. Curious about the noise, he started retracing his steps.

He had only gone about half a block, however, when he located the source of the metallic clanging. The sound was caused by the front gates of the Tolomato Cemetery, and the metal chain that held them closed. The gates were jerking back and forth, as if being blown by a strong wind, straining at the heavy chain. But no wind blew; the night air was heavy and still.

The metal gates moved almost a foot one way, then slammed back in the opposite direction. Back and forth they went, slamming against the chain, looking as if someone was jerking the gates in an attempt to break free from the cemetery.

"What the hell?" He stepped off the sidewalk and moved out into the street, wanting to get a better view of what was happening. Even in the middle of the street there was no breeze to be felt, so it could not be the wind that moved the gates. Nor was anyone trapped on the inside of the cemetery, trying desperately to get out. He could see through the metal gates into the graveyard, and there was no one there. Still, the gates continued to bang back and forth, their motion growing more frenzied by the moment.

A sudden thought came to him, causing his alcoholic buzz to depart and sending a chill dancing down his spine. A few moments ago he had dared the dead to join him in the real world, and now it looked like someone was trying to take him up on the offer.

"Shit," he whispered, his mouth going dry. "Shit. Shit. Shit."

Then, as he stood there watching, the gates stopped their frantic movement. The night again grew quiet.

Kevin laughed nervously. "They must have given up."

His laugher quickly died, however, as a horrible odor rolled over him. It was the smell of old roadkill, of something lying dead and rotten in the hot Florida sunshine, the stench of a swollen possum on a back country road. The smell came from inside the Tolomato Cemetery, rolling thick and pungent out into the street, causing him to gag.

With the odor came something else, a sight much too terrifying to describe. He thought at first his eyes must be playing tricks on him, but it was no trick that he saw. Nor was it a result of too many Budweisers, and too many pills. Something large and black was moving across the grounds of the cemetery, making its way from the back of the graveyard to the front gates. A nearly shapeless mass of infinite darkness that seemed to swallow up everything in its path.

"Dear Jesus, what in the hell is that?"

It was like a low-lying cloud, a patch of fog hugging the ground as it rolled toward the front of the cemetery. Churning, billowing, expanding outward, only to shrink back on itself, it seemed to shimmer and change shape as it moved. As the rolling cloud of blackness drew nearer, it reached out to him with ebony tentacles.

Kevin blinked and shook his head, trying to comprehend what he was seeing. The patch of darkness grew more solid the closer it got to him, took on definition in the night. It looked like a giant black octopus, or maybe a spider.

That was it. The thing moving through the Tolomato Cemetery looked like a giant spider, a nightmarish, mutant spider that continually changed its shape and definition. One moment it was large and round, the next it was thin and narrow.

Suddenly, the thing changed shape again, transforming into a figure that was almost human. Almost, for the apparition had the body and head of a man, bearded and dressed in a flowing dark robe, but it had long black tentacles for arms. The tentacles stretched out toward the front of the cemetery, reaching for the frightened crippled man who stood in the middle of the street.

It was the thing's almost-human appearance that terrified him most of all, and he damn sure didn't trust the locked gates to keep it inside the cemetery. Instinct told him that bars and chains could not stop such a thing. Hell, guns and tanks probably couldn't stop it.

Deciding that a hasty retreat was the best plan of action, he stifled a cry and turned away from the Tolomato. He tried to put as much distance between himself and the nightmarish creature as he possibly could, but he could only hobble so fast. Even the added adrenaline rush of fear could not make his body move any quicker.

He had just reached the Old Drugstore when the thing reached the front of the cemetery, nearly ripping the metal gates off their hinges. Flowing out into the street, the multilegged beast of darkness scurried after its prey, its movements silent except for a muffled hooting sound.

Kevin turned and looked behind him, watching in horror as the monster moved out into the street, his bladder silently relieving itself of a night's worth of good beer. He prayed that the thing would go the other direction, but God must not have heard his prayer, for it came after him.

"Shit. Shit. Shit," he said, urging his body to even greater speed. He turned right on Orange Street, hoping to make it to Avenida Menendez. There was usually traffic on the Avenida, no matter what time of night it was. He would be able to flag someone down and get help.

But he had only made it a block when the thing caught him, a thin black tentacle wrapping around his right ankle. Kevin screamed, a fiery pain ripping up his leg. He turned to see the monster, and wished to God he hadn't. It was better not to see his attacker, for in its true form it was sheer madness to look upon. Such a thing had not been seen in the world of mankind for a long, long time.

His cane slipped out of limp fingers and fell clattering to the street. Kevin made no attempt to pick it up, for he knew the slender wooden shaft would not protect him. Nor did he attempt to cry for help, for fear had stolen his voice like a thief in the night. He could only stand and stare as the creature before him did a hypnotic little dance, slowly weaving from side to side as it studied him.

Another tentacle wrapped around his waist, slipping beneath the fabric of his jeans. Tiny teeth sliced like razor blades as the tentacle moved down his left leg, touching, tasting, feeding. Pieces of flesh were cut from the bone and swallowed by a hungry mouth.

A single tear ran down his left cheek as Kevin lowered his head and closed his eyes. More tentacles wrapped around his body, snatching his legs out from under him. There was a moment of sheer weightlessness as he was lifted into the air, followed by the indescribable sensation of having the flesh ripped from his bones. Darkness followed.

CHAPTER
7

Ssabra Onih had been a resident of Cypress Pointe for almost five years. Her second-floor, one-bedroom apartment was located on the backside of the complex, with a wooden porch that overlooked a retention pond and drainage ditch. The water in the pond was fairly clean, and might have been the perfect spot for an afternoon dip, were it not for the eight-foot alligator that called the place home. The overgrown lizard had moved into the area a few months after she did, and was a fairly common sight in the early evening hours.

The view from her bedroom window was not nearly as nice as the one from her porch, because her bedroom faced an identical apartment in the next building: an apartment occupied by an overweight man who liked to walk around on his porch wearing nothing more than a pair of Speedos. Such a sight could be very hard on the eyes, especially when her portly neighbor was bent over watering his plants, which was why she made sure to keep the blinds covering her bedroom window lowered at all times.

Arriving home from work a little before midnight, Ssabra popped a frozen dinner into the microwave and set the timer. She then slipped out of her historical costume, taking care to hang the dress on a hanger so it wouldn't get wrinkled. Wrapping herself in a faded yellow robe, she went into the bathroom to start a shower.

Not having a man in her life, her evenings were rather simple and pretty much routine: shower, followed by dinner in front of the television, then, if she wasn't too tired, she might have a glass of wine and curl up with a book for an hour or two before going to bed.

The frozen dinner would take less than ten minutes to cook, giving her just enough time to take a quick shower. Adjusting the temperature so it was hot, but not scalding, she discarded her robe and underwear and stepped under the water. Grabbing a bar of deodorant soap off the rack, she lathered up, washing away the dirt and memories of the day. She was just about to rinse off, when the lights in the apartment suddenly went out.

"Hey!" she yelled, even though there was no one to hear her cry. "What's going on?"

She stood quiet for a moment, thinking that the sudden blackout might be just a temporary thing. The apartment complex had been built back in the 1950s, which meant all the wiring was aluminum and old. It wasn't designed to handle the stress of multiple modern appliances and air-conditioning. Blackouts and temporary outages were not uncommon, especially in the hot summer months when everyone had their air conditioners running at full blast.

A few moments passed, and she realized that the power obviously wasn't going to come back on anytime soon. Turning off the water, she reached out and grabbed a towel to dry herself off. As she stepped out of the bathtub, she suddenly became aware of how cold it was in the bathroom.

"Brrrr . . . it's freezing in here. The stupid air conditioner must be acting up again. No wonder the power went out. It must have tripped a circuit breaker."

Ssabra discarded the towel and felt around in the dark for her robe, slipping it on over her still damp skin. Opening the bathroom door, she stepped out into the hallway, surprised to find that the lights still burned in the rest of her apartment. It obviously wasn't a power outage. She must have burned out a bulb in the bathroom. But how could that be? Her bathroom was lighted by three bulbs above the sink. All three of them would have to go out at once in order for the room to be dark.

She stepped back into the bathroom, and started to jiggle the light switch to see if all three light bulbs really had burned out at once, but stopped when she noticed that the light switch was down in the off position. Raising the switch, the lights above the mirror came on.

"What the heck?" she asked, looking at the lights and then down at the switch. There hadn't been a power outage, nor had a fuse blown. And none of the lights had burned out. Instead, the switch had been flipped off, but how had that happened?

Ssabra thought about it for a moment. Maybe she hadn't flipped the switch all the way up, and it had slid back to the off position. Perhaps the vibration of the shower door sliding closed had caused the switch to slip down. Or maybe something had come in contact with the light switch: a bug, perhaps.

She took a step back from the switch and looked around, fearful that she was now sharing the tiny bathroom with an overly large palmetto bug. She wasn't terrified of bugs, but she didn't like them either. And Ssabra damn sure didn't want to tangle with a cockroach from hell when she was still wet and half-naked.

Whatever the cause, the problems with the lights had been solved. Unfortunately, her relaxing shower had been interrupted, and she didn't feel like climbing back under the water to shampoo her hair. She would just have to get up a little earlier in the morning to finish the job.

There was nothing wrong with the bathroom lights, but the air conditioner was obviously on the fritz again. It was freezing in her apartment. As a matter of fact, it was so cold in the bathroom she could see her breath.

Ssabra exhaled, watching as a cloud of white mist drifted away from her lips. "This is ridiculous. I'm going to catch bloody pneumonia."

Clutching her bathrobe tightly at her neck, she hurried into the living room to check the thermostat. According to the temperature gauge, the air-conditioning unit was operating normally. It obviously *wasn't* operating normally, but there was little she could do about it except turn the air conditioner completely off. She would call the maintenance people in the morning to have them fix the problem.

Returning to the bathroom, she grabbed her discarded underwear and her hairbrush. The bathroom mirror was completely covered with a layer of condensation, due to the combination of a hot shower and a freezing bathroom. She was about to wipe the mirror off so she could see herself, when a tiny clear spot appeared on the glass. It was no more than the size of a dime, but, as she watched, it started to move slowly down the mirror to form a clear streak.

She assumed that the steak appearing on the mirror was being created by tiny water droplets racing each other down the glass, but when the streak reached the bottom of the mirror it turned right, traveled straight for a few inches, then started back up toward the top. Reaching the top of the mirror, the streak turned left, returning to the spot where it had started.

At first she thought it was just the condensation lifting from the glass, but then she realized that something strange was happening. A perfect oval had appeared in the steamy bathroom mirror. A few moments later another tiny clear spot appeared on the glass, a few inches to the right of the first. It too started to move, following a curving pattern from the top of the mirror to the bottom.

Much to her surprise, Ssabra suddenly realized that letters were forming on her bathroom mirror. First the letter *O*, then *S*, and an *I*. The letter *Y* next appeared, and then another *O* followed, forming a word, or perhaps a name.

"Osiyo." She said the word aloud, her skin breaking out in goosebumps. It was the same word she had heard earlier at the Huguenot Cemetery, spoken by a man she could not see. And now someone was writing it on her bathroom mirror, someone who could not be seen. It was as if someone were standing in front of the mirror, drawing the letters with an invisible fingertip.

Ssabra had no urge to reach out to see if she could feel the person who could not be seen. Nor did she want to remain in the bathroom for another second, not even to see if any other words would form on the mirror. A whole frigging book could magically appear, and she would not care.

Snatching the bathroom door open, she ran across the living room to her bedroom. She closed the bedroom door behind her, locked it, and picked up the telephone. She started to call 911, her fingers trembling so badly she could barely hit the right buttons, but then she stopped and put down the phone.

If she called the police, what would she tell them? *Hello, Police Department? Yes, this is Ssabra Onih. I need you to send a squad car over to my apartment right away, because I think I have the invisible man drawing things on my bathroom mirror.*

No. That probably wouldn't go over too well. It might even get her arrested for making a crank phone call. Telephoning the police was out of the question, but she needed to talk with someone, anyone, about the strange things happening in her apartment. She was scared, and she needed a reassuring voice on the phone, someone to convince her that she wasn't going crazy.

"Jenny," she said aloud. "I'll call Jenny Sanders. She'll know what to do."

Jenny Sanders worked at the restaurant where Ssabra used to work. They had been friends for years. She was around Ssabra's age, very levelheaded, and quite intelligent. She was also a great listener, which was another quality of a good friend.

Punching in the number from memory, Ssabra waited impatiently as the phone at the other end of the line began to ring. She shifted her weight nervously from one foot to the other, hoping her friend would pick up the phone, and that she had not gone out for the evening. As she waited, counting the rings, she kept an eye on the bedroom door. The door was locked, but she was still worried that the knob would begin to twist back and forth as someone tried to get into the bedroom. If the knob did start to turn, Ssabra was going to take her chances and climb out the bedroom window. The phone rang twice, then a third time. "Come on. Come on. Pick it up, Jenny. I know you're home. Pick up the phone."

The phone rang a fourth time, and then there was a sharp click, followed by the recorded voice of Jenny Sanders. "Hi. This is Jenny. I'm sorry, but I'm not home right now. Please leave your name and number, and I'll call you back as soon as possible."

"Damn." She waited for the beep, then said, "Jenny, this is Ssabra. Please call me back when you hear this message. I need you."

There was another click, and then Jenny's voice came on the line. Her real voice, and not just a recording.

"Hi, Ssabra. What's up? You sound upset."

Her heart leaped. "Jenny? Jenny, is that you?"

"Yeah, it's me."

"Why didn't you pick up?"

"Sorry about that. I'm watching a movie on television, so I was screening all of my calls. Why? Is something wrong?"

Ssabra started to blurt out about everything strange that was going on in her apartment, but she stopped herself. Jenny was one of her best friends, but even she wouldn't believe a story about an invisible person writing words on a steamy bathroom mirror. She might think Ssabra was pulling her leg, or maybe that she had had one glass of wine too many.

"Jenny, I think someone has been in my apartment." It was the only logical thing she could think of to say.

"Who? When?" Jenny asked. "Did you see anyone?"

"Not long ago. I was taking a shower, and some strange things started happening. I think maybe I had an intruder."

"How do you know? Is something missing?"

She shook her head, then realized Jenny couldn't see the gesture. "No. Nothing's missing. Not that I know of. I was in the shower, and the lights went off. At first I thought it was just a circuit breaker, but now I'm pretty sure someone flipped the switch. When I turned the lights back on, I found a word written on my bathroom mirror."

"Jeez, girl. This is serious. Did you call the police?"

"No. Not yet. I started to call them, but I wasn't sure what to say. I thought I would call you first. I don't think the intruder is still here; I think he left."

"But you're not sure, are you?" Jenny said, obviously concerned for her friend's welfare. "Listen, you can call the police later, but right now I want you to get out of that apartment. It's not safe staying there. I'm leaving right now. We'll meet at the all-night sandwich shop down the street from you. We can call the police from there."

Ssabra nodded, then said, "Okay. I'm leaving, but I have to change clothes first. I'm only wearing a bathrobe. I'll meet you at the sandwich shop. Please hurry, I'm really scared."

"I know you are, but everything's going to be all right. Just hurry up and get out of there. I want you to call my cell phone when you get to the sandwich shop. That way I'll know you're safe."

"Okay. I will," Ssabra said good-bye to her friend and hung up the phone. She crossed the bedroom and started snatching items of clothing from her dresser, slipping into a pair of khaki shorts, a knit blouse, and sandals. Once dressed, she dropped her cell phone into her purse and approached the bedroom door.

It took a great deal of courage for her to unlock the door, even more so for her to pull it open a few inches and peek into the living room. The living room was empty, at least she didn't see anyone. The bathroom door was still standing open, but she couldn't tell if anyone was in there. Nor did she want to find out.

Setting her sights on the front door, Ssabra left the bedroom and hurried across the living room. She had to circle several pieces of furniture, but she didn't take her gaze off the front door. For one thing, she was too terrified to look around, fearful of what she might see. She was halfway across the living room when she detected the unmistakable odor of pipe tobacco, further convincing her that someone had indeed been inside her apartment. The odor lay heavy on the air, as if the pipe smoker had just left the room. It was the same fragrance she had smelled earlier at the Huguenot Cemetery.

Ssabra made it to the front door and quickly worked the locks, pulling the door open and hurrying out of the apartment. She locked the door behind her and started down the stairs. Once outside the building she decided to leave her car sitting in the parking lot, and practically ran the block and a half distance to the sandwich shop.

Jenny lived on the other side of town, so it took almost half an hour before she arrived. Ssabra was already on her second cup of decaf, and still shaking, by the time her friend entered the all-night eating establishment.

"Jenny, over here," Ssabra called, waving to her friend as she entered the sandwich shop. It was an unnecessary gesture, because she was the tiny restaurant's only customer.

"Thank God you're okay." Jenny approached the booth, giving her a quick hug and kiss on the cheek.

"I was beginning to think that you weren't coming."

"You know me better than that," Jenny said, sliding into the seat across from her. "I said I would be here, didn't I?"

Ssabra nodded, feeling better now that her friend had arrived.

"Did you call the police?"

"Not yet." Ssabra paused as the waitress approached their booth with a pair of menus.

"Just coffee for me," Jenny said, ignoring the menus.

"How about you?" the waitress asked, turning her attention to Ssabra. "Would you like to order anything now?"

She glanced down at her half-empty coffee cup. "No. I'm fine. Thank you."

The waitress frowned, walking away to get Jenny's cup of coffee. She was probably annoyed that they weren't eating, thinking she wouldn't be getting a tip for just coffees.

"So, why didn't you call the police?" Jenny asked, waiting until the waitress was out of hearing range.

"I didn't know what to say to them."

"What do you mean? You tell them that some pervert broke into your apartment while you were taking a shower. That's what you tell them."

"But no one broke in. The door was still locked."

"Maybe they had a key."

Ssabra shook her head. "I had the chain on, and the deadbolt. I always put them on when I'm home alone. And you can't open either one of them from outside. No one could have gotten in after I set those locks."

The waitress brought another coffee. Jenny poured cream and sugar into the cup, thinking about what her friend had just said. "You said they can't open the deadbolt from the outside, but that also means you can't set it from the outside. Right?"

Ssabra nodded.

"Okay. Then maybe someone got into your apartment when you weren't there. Maybe they picked the lock and sneaked in, and were waiting for you to come home. Maybe they were hiding in a closet, or under the bed. They might even have been hiding in the cabinet under your kitchen sink. Jeez, girl. They could have been watching you for months, might even have been stalking you and you didn't even know it."

Ssabra thought about it for a moment. "If it was a stalker, then why didn't they do something when I was in the shower? I was naked and wet, and there was no one else around to help me. I was the perfect victim. If it was a sexual predator, I should have been raped, maybe even murdered."

Jenny shrugged. "It's hard to tell with that kind. Maybe something scared him off. Maybe he's only into watching women take showers, or just gets his jollies by sneaking into people's apartments." She took a sip of coffee. "I think you had better tell me everything that happened. Then we can decide if you need to go to the police."

She told Jenny about all the strange things that had happened at her apartment. She also told her about the weird encounter she had earlier at the Huguenot Cemetery.

"Osiyo," Jenny said aloud, pronouncing the word slowly. "That's what you heard someone say at the cemetery?"

"That's the word. It's the same thing that was written on my mirror. Do you know what it means?"

Jenny shook her head. "Never heard it before. It sounds more like letters than a word. Maybe it's an abbreviation of some kind. It might stand for Official State Idiot Police Organization."

"That's OSIPO. The word I heard and saw was 'osiyo'."

"Sorry." Jenny smiled. "I got a speeding ticket last week and cops have been on my mind."

"You're not helping," laughed Ssabra.

"Sure I am. At least your hands aren't shaking anymore."

Ssabra looked down, and saw that her hands no longer shook. She hadn't realized her shakes had stopped, nor was she aware they had been bad enough for her friend to notice.

"Okay," Jenny continued, trying to figure out what had happened at the apartment. "You said that you heard someone talking at the Huguenot earlier this evening. They spoke to you, but they only said one word. You also smelled pipe tobacco at the cemetery.

"And tonight, while you were taking a shower, someone turned off the lights in your bathroom. At least you think someone turned off the lights, but they might have turned off because the switch wasn't all the way up. When you got out of the shower you discovered that your apartment was freezing, and then someone wrote a word on your bathroom mirror. Is that it?"

Ssabra nodded. "That's it."

"Then I think I know what's going on."

"Tell me, then."

Jenny fumbled a pack of cigarettes out of her purse, double-checked to make sure that they were sitting in the smoking section, then lit the cigarette. "I think a man must have followed you home from the cemetery. That's where you heard the word 'osiyo' and first smelled the pipe tobacco. Right?"

Ssabra nodded again.

"Okay. So someone must have been hiding in the cemetery. Maybe he was sneaking around the place. Or maybe he was hiding there, hoping to scare one of the ghost tours when it came along. It was probably just a drunk. There's an Irish pub across the street, so maybe he had a few too many beers and decided to play a game. Only there weren't any more tour groups, there was just you. He thought he was going to scare you, but you didn't scare. Maybe this guy thought you were cute."

Jenny winked. "I mean, you probably do look kind of cute after a couple of six packs."

"Bite me," Ssabra retaliated.

Jenny laughed, amused at her own humor. "So he waits for you to go down the street, then follows you."

"But how did he follow me when I got into my car?" Ssabra asked, pointing out an obvious flaw in Jenny's theory. "Tell me that. If he followed me out of the cemetery, then he was on foot. My car was parked back by the tour office, a good six blocks away. If he followed me to my car, then he couldn't have followed me once I drove away."

"Not unless his car was parked near yours."

"And what are the odds of that?"

"It's a small town. Pretty good odds, I would say. There's a public parking lot just down the street. Maybe this guy had his car parked there, and decided to continue the chase. That late at night there isn't much traffic on the back streets, even on a Saturday night. It would have been easy for him to jump into his car and chase after you."

"That doesn't explain how he got into my apartment. I had the door double-locked."

"Did you set the chain and deadbolt as soon as you got home, or did you wait until you started your shower?"

Ssabra thought about it for a moment. "I'm not sure; I think I set them as soon as I got home."

"But you're not sure. Maybe you didn't set them right away, and maybe he picked the lock when you were undressing in the bedroom. Then maybe he hid in the closet, or in the kitchen while you stepped into the shower."

"That's a lot of maybes."

"Yes, it is," Jenny agreed. "But that would explain a few things."

"It wouldn't explain how letters formed on my bathroom mirror while I was standing there looking at it."

"I think I also have that figured out," Jenny said, obviously proud of herself. "Do you have a makeup mirror on you? If so, give it to me."

Ssabra dug into her purse, bringing out a round powder case with mirror. "Going to powder your nose?"

"No. Just watch." Jenny opened the case, then rubbed her fingertip across the mirror. She handed the compact back to Ssabra. "What do you see?"

"I see you smeared my mirror."

"Exactly. My fingertip left an oily streak across the glass."

"And this means what to me?"

"Maybe your intruder did the same thing to your bathroom mirror. While you were in the bedroom, getting ready to take a shower, he went into the bathroom and wrote on the mirror with his fingertips. He then hid while you climbed into the shower. Once you were in the shower he turned the air conditioner up on high. He also flipped off the lights. He might have left right after that, which is why you didn't see anyone.

"The room was cold, and the shower was hot, which caused condensation to form on the mirror. But the condensation didn't adhere to where he drew the letters with his fingertips, because of the oils from his skin. That's why it looked like letters were forming before your eyes."

Ssabra looked at her friend, then blinked. "What have you been doing, watching the Discovery Channel?"

Jenny laughed. "Actually, I'm a big fan of Mr. Wizard."

"So, what do we do now?" Ssabra asked.

"If you're not going to call the police, then I think we need to go back to your apartment to make sure no one is there."

"Forget it. No way. I'm not going back there. Not tonight. I'll sleep at a motel, or in my car."

"Relax. I didn't say you had to spend the night there. You can spend the night at my place. I said we should go check out your apartment, make sure that your intruder is really gone."

"What if he's not? It would be dangerous to go back there, even with the two of us."

"Not as dangerous as you think." Jenny set her

purse on the table and opened it, then tilted the purse so Ssabra could see the contents. Something shiny caught the light. It was a small pistol.

"What's that?" Ssabra asked, surprised.

"It's a .32 revolver. A gift from my father. He gave it to me when I moved out on my own."

Ssabra looked around nervously. "Jeez, girl. Do you have a license to carry that thing?"

Jenny closed her purse. "No. Not yet. I was going to get one, but I haven't gotten around to it yet. You have to take a course before you can get a gun permit, and I just haven't had the time."

"Aren't you afraid of the police catching you with that?"

"No. Not really. Most cops aren't going to search through your purse, not unless you've done something wrong. Besides, I know how to make a cop completely forget about the contents of my purse." Jenny unbuttoned the top two buttons of her blouse, showing off her cleavage. She smiled. "This works every time."

Ssabra laughed. "You really are a slut. Showing your boobs didn't keep you from getting a speeding ticket."

"That was a woman cop. I might have had a chance if she was a dyke, but she was married." Jenny buttoned up her blouse. "Let's get out of here. Maybe if we're lucky, we'll catch this creep still in your apartment. I've always wanted to shoot my gun."

Ssabra was horrified. "You mean you haven't even fired it yet?"

"I haven't had the chance. I was going to shoot it, but I've been really busy lately."

"How long have you been carrying that thing?"

"Almost ten years."

Ssabra couldn't believe her friend. "Do you even have bullets for it?"

"Of course I do." Jenny frowned. "Do you think I'm stupid?"

"No comment."

They paid their bill and left the restaurant. Jenny had her car in the parking lot, so Ssabra rode back to the apartment with her. Although she felt better having a friend with her, she was still nervous when they pulled into the complex. What if the intruder was still there, hiding somewhere in her apartment? Even though Jenny had a handgun, they could still be putting themselves in great danger by entering the apartment. Maybe she should have called the police.

Locking the car, they entered the building and walked up the stairs to the second floor. Ssabra started to take her keys out of her purse, but Jenny stopped her.

"What?"

Jenny put a finger to her lips, shushing her. "Shhhh . . . be quiet for a minute." She put her ear to Ssabra's front door, listening for any sounds of movement from the other side. After a few moments she stepped away from the door.

"I don't hear anything, so I think he's gone." She pulled the pistol from her purse, striking a pose that was almost comical. It reminded Ssabra of something from a television cop show. "Okay, open it. But let me go in first."

"I'm really starting to worry about you." Ssabra found her keys and stepped forward to open the door. Unlocking the door, she pushed it open and stepped back to allow Jenny to enter the apartment.

If she hadn't still been a little frightened, she would have laughed as she watched Jenny move from one room to the other, gun held outstretched in both hands before her, looking like a real bad imitation of an old *Charlie's Angels* episode.

The two of them searched the entire apartment, but didn't find an intruder. Nor did they find any evidence that one had been there earlier. Nothing had been taken or disturbed and there was no lingering odor of tobacco smoke. Ssabra turned the air conditioner back on and it seemed to be working normally again.

Jenny put the pistol back into her purse, and plopped down on the sofa. "Well, there's nobody here. If you had an intruder, he's long gone."

Ssabra double-checked the bathroom to make sure no one was hiding in the shower. She also looked at the mirror, but there weren't any words written on it. "I guess you're right," she said, stepping back out into the living room. "Maybe I just imagined the whole thing."

"Maybe," Jenny nodded. She lit up a cigarette and blew smoke at the ceiling. "If you ask me, I think you've given one too many ghost tours. I think you're starting to believe all that stuff you tell the tourists." She smiled. "Then again, you spend an awful lot of time at the cemeteries. Maybe one of the local spirits followed you home."

"You know I don't have much belief in the spirit world," she replied, shaking her head. "I've given hundreds of ghost tours, and I have yet to see a single spirit. Besides, ghosts don't usually write on bathroom mirrors."

"Maybe you have a literary ghost. A regular Edgar Allan Boo."

Ssabra laughed at the joke, then turned to look around the room. "Listen, if you don't mind, I'm going to accept your offer to stay the night at your house. I'm still pretty creeped out about everything, and I don't want to be here alone. Not tonight. I'll come back tomorrow, in the daylight, when things don't seem quite so scary."

"You're welcome to stay at my place as long as you want." Jenny smiled. "It will be nice to have a roommate, even if it's only temporary. Go ahead and grab your things. If you've got any wine, then grab that too. We'll have ourselves a little party."

"The wine's in the fridge. There should be an uno-pened bottle in the back. Help yourself. I'm going to get my things together." Ssabra left her friend in the living room, and went into the bedroom to pack her overnight bag with the items she would need to spend the night at Jenny's. She also grabbed her makeup case, and a change of clothing, just in case she didn't make it back to her apartment before going to work.

She looked around her bedroom to see if she had forgotten anything. Though there was no evidence that an intruder had been inside her apartment, something strange had happened. She felt violated; her peace of mind had been stolen, and that was something she might never get back. As she turned off the light and left the bedroom, Ssabra wondered if she would ever feel comfortable in her apartment again.

CHAPTER
8

Despite having his day off interrupted, Detective Jack Colvin got to work early the following morning. He was hoping to start his Sunday with a cup of coffee, and a few moments of peace and quiet, but he was handed a copy of a vandalism report as soon as he got to his desk. He started to hand the report back to the officer who had given it to him, citing that he was a homicide detective and did not investigate acts of vandalism, but then he noticed a name on the report that caught his attention. Nodding to the officer, Jack read through the report carefully.

The report had come in early that morning, filed by a city employee named Curtis Everette. According to the report, someone had again broken into the Tolomato Cemetery during the night. The city worker had found the chain cut and the gates standing wide open while making the rounds that morning.

Mr. Everette had signed his name to the bottom of
the report, after stating that nothing, other than the
gates, appeared to have been disturbed at the cemetery. He had also put two phone numbers on the
report, one for the office of the City of St. Augustine
Pubic Works Department, where he worked. The
other number was for his personal cell phone.

Jack looked at his watch and thought about calling
the office number, but figured that Mr. Everette
might still be out riding around in his truck. City
workers knew to stay away from the office during
the day, especially those who pulled weekend duty,
lest their boss find some additional work to keep
them busy.

Thinking that the recent act of vandalism at the
Tolomato Cemetery might somehow be connected
with his homicide investigation, he decided to call
the number listed for Curtis Everette's cell phone.
Dialing the number, he listened as the cell phone
rang four times. He thought he was going to get a
message service, and was surprised when someone
finally answered.

"Yeah, go ahead," a voice answered, the person
on the other end obviously fumbling with the cell
phone.

The detective smiled. He knew how difficult it
could be to talk on a cell phone while driving, especially when turning or driving in heavy traffic. It was
a wonder there weren't more accidents because of
the portable phones.

"Mr. Everette?" Jack said, speaking louder than he
normally would. Some cell phones were notorious
for having bad reception.

"Yeah, I'm Curtis Everette. Who's this? And how did you get this number?"

His smile grew wider. "You gave me your number. This is Detective Jack Colvin, St. Augustine Police Department. I'm calling about the report you filled out."

"Yes, sir, Detective." The voice on the phone changed, became a little less harsh and a tad more respectful. It was amazing how people often changed their tone of voice when they found out they were talking to the cops.

"You reported that you found the gates of the Tolomato Cemetery standing open this morning."

"Yes, sir, I did. Found them that way when I was making my rounds."

"Was the chain cut, or had someone picked the lock?"

"Neither one," Curtis replied. "The chain was broken."

"Broken?"

"Yes, sir. Broken. The metal was stretched, as if someone pried the links apart."

"I see." Jack jotted down a few notes on a yellow pad of paper. "Are the gates still open, or did you lock them back up?"

"I locked them. I got a new chain from the maintenance shed."

"What did you do with the old chain?"

"It's still in the back of my truck. Why?"

"Just asking. Would it be possible to see that chain?"

There was a pause. "I guess so, but I don't know what good it would do you. It's just a chain."

"It probably won't do any good at all," Jack replied. "But I have to follow up with the report you made. Paperwork and all that. Got to keep the boss happy."

There was a laugh. "I know what you mean."

"Would it be possible for me to meet you somewhere to take that broken chain off your hands?"

"When?"

"How about now?"

Again there was a pause. "Sure, it's possible. But I have to clear it with my supervisor first. I was on my way to a job. Where do you want to meet?"

"Tell you what, I'll make a phone call and clear it with your boss. Meet me at the Tolomato. I should be there in about fifteen minutes."

"You've got it, Detective. I'll see you in fifteen."

Jack said good-bye to Curtis Everette, then called the number for the City of St. Augustine Public Works Department. After a few minutes of being passed from one person to another, he was finally able to get the supervisor on the line. He explained that he would be pulling Mr. Curtis off his job for a few minutes to aid in a police investigation, promising he would send the man back to work as soon as possible. The supervisor told him to take his time, citing that they would send someone else to do the job.

Hanging up the phone, the detective grabbed his notebook and jacket and left the office. Since it was Sunday morning, traffic was still fairly light and it only took him ten minutes to reach the Tolomato Cemetery. Pulling into the parking lot adjacent to the Old Drugstore, which was separated from the cemetery by a metal fence, he spotted a white pickup waiting for him. The pickup sported the official seal of St. Augustine on its door; a thin, gray-haired black man was sitting in the cab reading a newspaper.

Seeing Jack's car pull into the lot, the city worker put down his newspaper and climbed out of the truck. Jack was in an unmarked patrol car, which was still easily identifiable as a police vehicle. He was also wearing a suit, standard clothing for undercover cops.

"Mr. Everette?" Jack asked, climbing out of his car. He already knew who it was, but was asking out of respect.

"Yes, sir. I'm Curtis Everette. You the detective I spoke to on the phone?"

He nodded. "I'm Detective Colvin." He shook hands with the man, then followed him to the back of the pickup.

Reaching into the bed, Curtis picked up a length of chain and handed it to the detective. "See what I mean? The chain's been broken, not cut." The chain had indeed been broken. Several of the links had been pulled out of shape, and one link was completely pulled apart. "Someone must have used a crowbar to stretch the metal like that. Maybe they hooked a winch to it, or used a truck."

Jack studied the chain for a few moments. He didn't worry about fingerprints, because the chain had already been handled by Curtis. It looked to be an exact copy of the one he had found yesterday, broken in two by pulling one of the links apart. "It took a lot of force to stretch this chain. Mind if I hang on to it?"

"No. Go right ahead. I don't need it for anything. It's no good anyway."

Opening the passenger door of his patrol car, Jack dropped the chain onto the seat. "I spoke to your supervisor; he said he would get another man on that job he assigned you. Since you have a few minutes to spare, let's say we take a look through the cemetery. You still got the keys to the front gate?"

Curtis nodded. "Yes, sir. I've got the keys right here. I'll be happy to look the place over with you. No need to hurry, because I'm really not all that anxious to get back to work. If you know what I mean."

"I understand perfectly." Jack smiled. "I'm not much of a morning person myself."

They left the vehicles where they sat, and walked across the parking lot toward Cordova Street. As they crossed the lot, they passed a green Dumpster sitting next to the fence that separated the parking lot from the Tolomato Cemetery. Passing the Dumpster, Jack detected a bad odor coming from inside the metal container and wondered how often it was emptied.

The metal gates of the Tolomato Cemetery were closed, held secure by a new length of chain. It was the second time in two days that the chain had been replaced. Approaching the gates, he noticed that the two center posts were now slightly bent. He suspected the previous chain had been pried off the gates, which would explain the condition of the posts.

The detective couldn't help feeling a bit of déjà vu as he entered the Tolomato. Less than twenty-four hours had passed since his last visit to the graveyard.

Funny, but he no longer had a desire to sketch the cemetery. As a matter of fact, he no longer had a desire to sketch any cemetery. Finding human remains and working overtime took all the fun out of drawing.

Entering the cemetery, he turned right and followed the fence line to the back of the grounds. Turning left, he wandered between the headstones until he reached the mausoleum. He stopped and checked the door of the stone mausoleum, making sure that it was secure.

From the mausoleum he continued south to the corner of the fence line, then walked back toward the front of the graveyard. Finding nothing out of the ordinary along the fence, he wandered slowly back through the cemetery toward the front.

Jack had an uneasy feeling that he was going to find something upsetting in the cemetery, but this time he came up empty-handed. There were no human remains, ornate silver rings, or pieces of tattered clothing. He let out a sigh of relief, thankful not to have another incident on his hands. So, why had someone broken into the cemetery during the night? Had the perpetrator returned to the scene of the crime, a murderer checking to see if the remains of his victim had already been discovered? Perhaps it was someone merely curious, wondering why so many police officers had been in the Tolomato the day before. It might even have been a local reporter in search of a story to write.

"Find anything?" Curtis called out. He was standing by the front gates, waiting for the detective to finish his search.

Jack shook his head. "No. Nothing. Whoever broke in here last night didn't do any damage. Nothing was taken. Nothing destroyed."

"Glad to hear that," Curtis said. "But didn't something happen in here the other night? I think there was even a write-up in the paper about it, something about a body being found."

The detective stepped out into the street and lit up a cigarette. "We didn't find a body; just a few bones, teeth, and some clothing. Someone might have taken the remains from another cemetery, but we're treating it as a homicide until we know otherwise."

"I'll be damned. You never know what you're going to find around here." Curtis glanced at his watch. "You finished here, or do you need to look around some more?"

"No. I'm done. Go ahead and lock it back up."

"Okay then, I'll put the new chain back on the gates. Thanks for giving me a break this morning; I guess I had better get back to work."

Curtis closed the double gates and wrapped the new chain around the two center posts. Fastening the chain in place with a heavy duty padlock, he said good-bye and walked back to his pickup truck. Jack stood in front of the cemetery for a few more minutes, finishing his cigarette, waving as Mr. Everette drove past in his truck.

"I guess I had better get back to the office. Nothing more here to be seen." He dropped the cigarette butt on the street, crushing out the fire beneath the toe of his shoe. Walking back along Cordova Street, he circled around the Old Drugstore to the parking lot where he had left his car.

As he walked across the parking lot, he again noticed a rancid odor coming from the green Dumpster that sat next to the fence.

"Jesus," he said, coughing. "What in the hell did someone put in there?" He had searched through the Dumpster the day before, looking for clues to the homicide, and the only thing it contained were empty cardboard boxes. Apparently, someone had come along after him and tossed something foul into the container.

He started past the Dumpster, but stopped and turned back around. The stench coming from the metal container reminded him of rancid bacon or grease, an odor that would be almost expected if the Dumpster was being used by a restaurant. Discarded food scraps could stink to high heaven, especially on a hot summer day. But there were no restaurants in the area, just the Old Drugstore, a few homes, and the cemetery.

Curious, Detective Colvin retraced his steps back to the Dumpster. He opened the lid and peeked inside, looking for the source of the offensive odor. The smell was even worse with the lid open.

"Damn, that stinks."

At first he didn't see anything, just empty cardboard boxes, but then he spotted a large strip of greasy brown material. He thought it was a piece of plastic, but that was until he noticed the tiny hairs growing out of it. There was also a dark stain on one end that, when stretched tight, took on the shape of a turtle.

Jack dropped the material and stepped back, holding his breath to keep from gagging. He removed a white handkerchief from his jacket pocket and wiped his hands. What he had mistaken for a piece of greasy plastic was actually a long strip of human skin, complete with tiny hairs and a turtle tattoo.

"Oh, bloody hell. Not again."

Looking around, he spotted a coat hanger lying on the ground a few feet from the Dumpster. Picking up the hanger, he bent the wire back and forth until it broke. He then straightened out the wire, forming a hooked rod he could use to poke around in the Dumpster.

He used the wire to pick up the piece of skin for closer examination, making sure to hold his breath as he lifted it from the Dumpster. He discovered more pieces of skin hidden beneath several empty cardboard boxes. Almost a dozen pieces altogether, all of them much smaller than the first he had found.

Tossing the empty boxes out of the way, he found another large piece of skin in the bottom of the Dumpster: a jagged oval, about nine inches long and five inches across, complete with a man's lips, a nose, eye-holes, and part of a beard.

"Sweet Mother of God." He dropped the coat hanger as if burned, stepping back from the Dumpster. A human face was staring up at him from the bottom of the container, a man's face that had been literally peeled off of some poor bastard's skull.

And though he looked away, he could not shake the hideous vision of that face from his mind. Nor could he stop the bile that burned its way up from his stomach to his throat. The detective had seen a lot of grim sights in his line of work, but nothing compared to what lay in the bottom of the small green Dumpster. Grabbing his stomach he leaned over and heaved, throwing up a breakfast of scrambled eggs, toast, and those little sausage links he liked so much.

Wiping the back of his hand across his mouth, Jack straightened up and turned around. He felt better now that he had thrown up, but he made no move toward the Dumpster. He had seen enough, and he had no desire to take another peek inside the metal container. Nor did he want to smell any of the stench that hovered above the trash container, the reek of rotting human flesh and death.

He had another murder on his hands, another brutal homicide with skin and no body. Two murders in two days, both of them very similar. But who were the victims, and where in the hell was the rest of them?

He stared at the Dumpster for a moment, then turned his attention toward the cemetery on the other side of the fence. He was pretty sure the Tolomato Cemetery was in some way connected to the homicides, but he wasn't sure how. So far, the ancient graveyard was refusing to give up its secrets.

"What am I not seeing here?" he asked himself. "What clues am I missing?"

CHAPTER
9

The sun was already shining brightly when Ssabra returned to Cypress Pointe, which made the events of the previous evening seem distant and far less frightening. It was hard to think about unseen intruders when the mockingbirds were singing in the treetops, and there was the smell of the ocean in the air. Invisible intruders and eerie happenings belonged to the night, and to the world of darkness, and had little substance on a beautiful September morning in northeast Florida.

Still, a tingle of apprehension danced down her spine as she climbed out of Jenny's car, saying good-bye to her friend and thanking her for all that she had done. Jenny offered to take a look through the apartment one more time, just to be on the safe side, but Ssabra declined. She didn't want her friend to be late for work, nor did she want her to start waving around a pistol again.

Climbing the twenty-one stairs to the second floor,

she slipped a key into the lock and opened the door. Even though it was already daylight out, the tiny apartment was still draped in heavy layers of shadows. It was also much cooler than the outside temperature, but not nearly as cold as it had been the night before. Apparently, the air conditioner was still working normally.

Standing in the doorway, she tried to sense if there might be someone in the apartment waiting for her. She listened for sounds of movement, breathing, or something else that might warn her that she was walking into a trap. But the apartment was quiet, the only sound to be heard was the soft hum of the refrigerator. Nor did she detect any smells that were out of place: no lingering trace of tobacco smoke, cologne, or sweat.

Concluding that everything seemed to be back to normal, Ssabra entered the apartment and closed the door behind her. She flipped on the lights and opened the curtains over the living room windows, doing a quick walk around to make sure no one was hiding behind the furniture.

From the living room she went into the kitchen, opening the cabinets to check under the sink, and then into the bathroom to look in the shower and behind the door. She retraced her steps through the apartment to the bedroom, searching through the closet and under the bed, breathing a sigh of relief to find that she really was alone. Nor could she find any evidence that anyone else, other than Jenny, had been inside the apartment.

She walked back into the bathroom and flipped on

the lights, staring at the mirrored door of her medicine cabinet. Except for a few tiny spots of dried soap, the mirror was completely clean. No lettering, words, or anything else out of the ordinary. What she had seen the previous evening was probably due to condensation and nothing more. Maybe her mind had played a trick on her, and she only thought she had seen a word written on the glass.

Stepping to the side, she examined the mirror from a different angle. Perhaps Jenny's theory had been right. Maybe someone had traced the letters with a fingertip, the oils of their skin causing a word to form once the glass had steamed over.

That would mean someone had indeed been in her apartment yesterday, or sometime last night. But why would they sneak into the apartment just to scrawl graffiti on a bathroom mirror? Would a stalker do something like that? Or a pervert? Surely a thief wouldn't be that stupid, since touching the glass would leave behind identifiable fingerprints.

She stepped closer to the mirror, trying to see if there were any fingerprints. She didn't see any prints, and there weren't any marks to indicate that an oily finger had been dragged down the glass. The mirror was the same all over, clean except for the tiny soap spots.

"Weird." She turned away from the mirror and left the bathroom. The more she thought about it the less convinced she was that anything strange had happened. Her imagination had probably just been working overtime. One thing for sure: Ssabra was extremely thankful she had not telephoned the police. They would have thought her an idiot for calling them, because there was no evidence to suggest that an intruder had been inside the apartment.

Stowing her overnight case in the bedroom closet, she slipped into a clean change of clothes. She then donned her makeup in the bathroom, and heated up a pot of water for instant coffee. She had a tour group that morning, and needed to be awake and looking her absolute best. Pouring a touch of hazelnut creamer into the cup, she took her coffee into the living room.

Setting the cup down on the coffee table, she took a seat on the sofa and grabbed the remote. She turned on the local news, hoping to catch the weather report before heading off to work. The weather in Florida could change at a moment's notice, so it always paid to be prepared. The dress she wore for the ghost tours was expensive, and she didn't want it to get ruined by an unexpected shower.

She set the remote on the sofa beside her and started to reach for her coffee, when the cup suddenly slid across the table away from her.

Ssabra Onih let out a scream and jumped up off the sofa, watching in shocked surprise as the full cup of coffee slid magically from one end of the coffee table to the other. It stopped near the edge, in danger of falling to the carpeted floor, and then it slid back toward her, stopping where it had originally been placed.

"No way," she said aloud. "That didn't just happen. It couldn't have happened. I didn't see my cup of coffee slide across the table."

As if in answer to her comments, the cup again

slid across the coffee table, causing her to let out a cry and run to the other side of the room. The cup again stopped near the edge of the table, and then returned to its original spot.

"It's moisture," she said, trying to find a logical explanation for what she had just seen. "There must be condensation on the table. That's why the cup slid."

But the table was dry. So was the cup. And even condensation would not cause the cup to slide back and forth in two different directions. Somebody, or something, had moved it.

"First the bathroom mirror, and now this."

She thought about what Jenny had told her in jest at the sandwich shop, her arms breaking out in goosebumps. *Then again, you spend an awful lot of time at the cemeteries. Maybe one of the local spirits followed you home.*

No way. It couldn't be. Ssabra didn't believe in ghosts. Not really. She had wanted to believe in ghosts when her fiancé was killed in an automobile accident, had hoped and prayed that Alan would come back from the grave to visit her. But his spectral image had not returned to say his final goodbye, or give her one last kiss before departing on his way to the spirit world. Since then she had dismissed all reports and stories about ghosts as nothing more than make-believe.

Even though she was half-Cherokee, and Native American culture was quite open to the beliefs of spirits, she had never had an encounter with the un-explained. Not that she followed her cultural heritage all that closely. She knew very little about the Indian side of her family, her full-blooded father having abandoned her when she was just an infant. She inherited his looks: straight black hair, dark complexion, dark eyes, but none of his knowledge.

But now, unless her eyes were playing tricks on her, and unless there was some scientific explanation for why the cup was moving under its own power, it would appear that she was indeed having an experience with the unexplained. She was having her very own supernatural encounter in the middle of her living room, an encounter with forces that could not be seen. Spiritual forces.

She nervously looked around the room. Her apartment had grown alien to her, as if she were seeing it in a dream. She would have run for the front door, but was terrified that, like in a dream, the white carpeting would suddenly become liquid marshmallow, slowing her attempted flight from the room. Not that she could find the strength to run for the door, because her legs were shaking so bad it was all she could do to just stand up.

Her attention riveted on the coffee table, Ssabra held her breath as she waited for the cup to move again. A minute passed, maybe two, but the cup remained stationary, sitting in the same spot she had originally set it. Had she really seen it move, or was it just her imagination? Maybe she was still afraid from last night, and her eyes had only played a trick on her. Maybe the cup had not moved at all.

"Bullshit. I know what I saw. I am not crazy."

Not knowing what else to do, Ssabra decided to try something she had seen numerous times in movies and television shows. It was rather cliché, but it was the only thing she could think of doing. Keeping her eye on the coffee cup, she asked in a loud, clear voice, "If there are any ghosts or spirits here in this apartment, will you please give me a sign?"

A moment of silence passed. She started to repeat the question, but was interrupted by a man's voice.

Ssabra jumped back and looked around. The voice had come from right next to her, but there was no one else in the room. She only heard one word, but it was enough to cause the blood to drain from her face.

"Osiyo."

It was the same word she had heard at the Huguenot Cemetery the night before, the same word that had magically formed on her bathroom mirror. Jenny was right; someone, or something, had followed her home from the cemetery. She had a spiritual intruder in her apartment, one that was fond of playing games and scaring the daylights out of people.

She looked around the room, terrified she might see something to go along with the voice: a ghostly specter with rotting skin and empty eyes, a corpse freshly risen from the grave, or perhaps an animated skeleton to dance around her tiny apartment. The voice was terrifying enough, and she would surely lose her mind if a dead man suddenly appeared to go along with it.

"Enough of this," she said, finally finding the strength to move. "I'm out of here."

Ssabra hurried across the room, picking up speed as she went. She ran for the front door, pausing only long enough to grab her purse and keys off the kitchen counter. She had just reached the door when she remembered that she had left her historical dress lying on the bed.

"Dammit," she stopped and turned back around. The bedroom looked an awfully long way away, but she had to go back. She needed the dress for work. It was either take the dress with her now, or come back for it later in the afternoon. The apartment would be dark then, the sun on the backside of the building. Dark and spooky, and very much haunted.

Taking a deep breath, she decided to dash back into her bedroom to grab the dress. Moving at almost a dead run, she looked neither left nor right as she crossed the living room, afraid of what else she might see. Grabbing the dress off the bed, she hurried back toward the front door. She was halfway across the living room when she again heard the voice.

"Osiyo."

Turning in the direction of the sound, Ssabra saw the coffee cup was once again moving under its own power, sliding from one end of the table to the other.

Though she didn't slow her pace, she shouted as she ran past the table, "Stop that! You're going to spill coffee on my carpet!"

She didn't look back over her shoulder to see if the cup had stopped moving. Nor was she really worried about a little spilled coffee. That was the least of her troubles. Jerking open the front door, she exited the apartment as fast as she could, slamming the door behind her.

Ssabra didn't linger in the hallway, but hurried down the stairs to ground level. Nor did she take her time getting into her car. Only when the engine was started, and she was driving out of the parking lot, did she start to feel safer. Maybe she would be a little less frightened at work, her mind occupied with giving tours to senior citizens and school kids. But work only lasted so long, and sooner or later she would have to return to her apartment. Sooner or later she would have to deal with a most unwelcome houseguest.

CHAPTER
10

It definitely looked like Detective Colvin had another homicide on his hands. The Crime Scene Investigation Unit had gone through the Dumpster,
located in a parking lot bordering the north side of
the Tolomato Cemetery, carefully removing pieces of
what were obviously human skin. There was no
doubt they were human, not when one of the pieces
was the face of a man, complete with lips, nose, partial beard, and eye-holes.

All together they had removed over a dozen pieces
of skin, ranging in size from a few centimeters in
diameter to almost a foot in length. In addition to
the skin, several pieces of bone had been discovered
in the bottom of the Dumpster. Bones had also been
found scattered on the ground along the fence line,
a few feet to the left of the container: fragments of a
rib, half a vertebra, a sliver of cranium. It was a jig-
saw puzzle of the macabre; not enough parts to put

the body back together, but enough to help with a possible identification.

One of the most identifying pieces of evidence was the turtle tattoo, found on a piece of skin that had come from the left side of the victim's chest: it was definitely his chest, because part of a nipple was still attached to the skin. The turtle tattoo was a tribal design, completely black in color, and could prove useful in providing a name to go along with the remains. Jack would check the missing persons reports back at the office to see if anyone disappearing in the last year or two sported similar body art. He would also send out a bulletin to other police agencies in the state, just in case they were searching for someone with such a tattoo.

The CSI officers had taken close-up photographs of the turtle tattoo. Once the photos were developed, he would have one of his men take copies around to the local tattoo shops to see if any of the artists recognized the design. It was an unusual piece of art, and he didn't think that too many people were fond enough of turtles to get one permanently drawn on their chest. The tattoo shops usually kept records of who their customers were, and often made them sign releases before getting any artwork. Some of the shops even kept photos of the designs, especially if it was something unique.

According to the medical examiner, the remains found in the Dumpster had once belonged to an adult Caucasian male, between five feet ten inches tall and six feet, with sandy brown hair and a full beard. Once he got the remains back to the labora-

tory, the ME would be able to obtain DNA samples
from the victim's skin and hair. The information the
DNA samples contained could then be run through
the Combined DNA Index System (CODIS), a database sponsored by the Federal Bureau of Investigation.

Each state maintained its own database, and the
entire system was linked together in a network. That
allowed local police departments, and law enforcement agencies, to conduct DNA searches across the
entire country. Unfortunately, the only DNA samples
listed in the database were those belonging to felons
who had been sentenced to state prisons. Civilians
were not in the system, which meant they would not
be able to come up with a match for the second victim unless he had been convicted of a felony in recent years.

Since the medical examiner's office was not normally open on the weekend, tests had not yet been
run on the remains found at the Tolomato Cemetery
the previous day. The office would open at nine on
Monday morning, and tests would be run on both
victims at the same time. There was a possibility that
the remains found on the two different days had actually come from the same person. Jack had suspected the remains found inside the Tolomato were
from a woman, but only because of the tattered clothing that had also been found. But the perpetrator
might actually have planted the clothing in an effort
to throw off the police.

No clothing had yet been found in connection with
the second crime scene, even though Jack had sent
several police officers to search a two-block area

around the scene. Nor had they discovered any jewelry, leather bags, smudge sticks, or magic rocks.

In addition to the DNA testing, the Crime Scene Investigation officers had tried to obtain a few latent prints from the largest piece of skin, using the Magna Brush Powder Technique, but hadn't had much luck in the process. It was extremely difficult to develop latent prints on human skin, because the fingerprints usually only lasted for an hour or two. To make matters even more difficult, the skin they were testing had been contaminated by dirt and other foreign debris when it was tossed into the Dumpster.

The CSI officers had much better results lifting prints off the metal surfaces of the trash container. Unfortunately, the bright green Dumpster had been used by dozens of people over the past few days, and its smooth surfaces were covered with hundreds of prints, many of them overlapping one another. If the perpetrator had left fingerprints on the Dumpster, then it would be nearly impossible to pick his out of all the others. Still, the crime lab was going to process the prints that had been lifted, hoping to obtain a few leads in the case. The investigating officers were also going to take elimination fingerprints of everyone who worked at the Old Drugstore, in an effort to rule out as many useless prints as possible.

Deciding that a break was needed, Detective Colvin left the crime scene in the capable hands of the medical examiner and CSI officers, and slowly walked across the parking lot to his patrol car. His car was the only vehicle sitting in the lot, because it had already been parked there when he sealed off the area with barrier tape. He had not even allowed the medical examiner, or the CSI officers, to drive their vehicles onto the lot, fearful of valuable evidence being destroyed in the process.

Directly in front of his vehicle was an ever-growing pile of garbage, for the spot had been designated as the official trash pile. A certain amount of waste material accumulated during the investigation of a crime scene, including empty film canisters, paper bags, coffee cups, packing material, and discarded blood testing kits. The trash pile was always located as far away from the actual crime scene as possible to prevent any contamination of the area. Since they didn't have an actual trash can handy, Jack had spread a newspaper on the parking lot to mark the location of the trash pile.

In addition to serving as a spot to discard waste materials, the trash pile was also used as a place for investigating officers to take a break away from the crime scene. Judging by the number of cigarette butts in front of his car, and by the empty coffee cups and soda cans, several of the officers had already put the trash pile to good use.

Jack pulled a pack of Winstons out of his jacket pocket and shook out a cigarette, lighting it with a butane lighter. He was starting to get a headache, and was hoping a little nicotine would stop the pain before it got any worse. He wished he had a coffee to go along with the smoke, black and extra strong, but he had not brought along a thermos, and there were no convenience stores in the area. He actually had a portable coffeepot back at the office that he often set up at crime scenes, creating a place for visiting officers to gather around and to keep them out of the way. But he hadn't had the opportunity to go back to his office after discovering the remains in the Dumpster.

Nor had he been able to contact his partner, Detective Moats, to inform him that another set of human remains had been found. It was Bill's day off, and he was obviously smart enough not to answer his cell phone when he wasn't working. Jack had tried calling the other detective three times, but all he had gotten for his trouble was an answering service. He had left two different messages, and was hoping Bill would get in touch before very much longer, because he really needed the help.

"Wild Bill, where are you when I need you?" The answer to that question was easy. Bill owned a twenty-five-foot fishing boat and spent most of his free time out on the water, hunting for the big ones along the Intercoastal Waterway. That's where he always was on his days off, beyond the reach of friends, family, and coworker, safe from interruptions that might threaten to hamper his leisure activities. Jack had gone along with Bill on numerous fishing trips, and knew that his fellow detective always left early in the morning, and rarely returned before sunset. Sometimes, when the fish were biting, he would stay out on the water all night, coming to work the next day with bloodshot eyes and smelling a little bit like bait.

With any luck, Bill would check his messages and give Jack a return call. Or better yet, he would cut his fishing trip short and show up at the crime scene.

Jack had great respect for the senior detective, and really appreciated his keen insight and logical way of looking at things.

In the meantime, Jack would just have to go it on his own. Once the CSI officers had finished with the crime scene, and the medical examiner had removed the remains of the second victim, he would be free to start investigating clues, as well as tracking down a few leads.

Jack inhaled the cigarette, and released the smoke slowly out of his nose.

The only problem was he really didn't have any clues or leads to go on. He knew that one, or maybe two, people had been murdered, their bodies apparently cut up and mutilated. Where the homicides had actually transpired, the identity of the victims and why they had been killed, as well as who the killer was and the motive behind his or her action, remained a mystery.

The two homicide cases were still in the early stages, and Detective Colvin knew from experience that clues and leads would fall into place as the investigation went along. Since there were no bodies in either case, the work done in the laboratory would be of vital importance. DNA samples might provide the identity of one, or both, of the victims. The turtle tattoo found on the remains of the second victim, as well as the ornate silver ring found inside the Tolomato the previous day, might also produce valuable leads.

Knowing things would probably fall into place as the case went along did not make him feel any better. He wanted answers now, and he didn't like having to wait while the boys in the lab did most of the investigative work. He wanted to interview witnesses, but sadly there didn't seem to be any. And he wanted to slap around a perpetrator, but there were no suspects in the case. Not yet, anyway.

Jack also felt like he was overlooking something, as if someone had laid the big picture out in front of him but he was too stupid to see it. He knew the Tolomato Cemetery played an important part in the two homicides, but he just couldn't figure out the connection. There was something special about the ancient cemetery, at least there was something special about it to the perp. Figure out the mystery of the Tolomato and he might possibly be able to solve the case.

The detective finished his cigarette and dropped the butt on the parking lot, crushing it beneath the toe of his shoe. He needed to finish up his work at the crime scene, but made no effort to leave the spot where he was standing. Instead, he remained next to the trash pile, his attention focused on the ancient graveyard on the other side of the fence.

The Tolomato Cemetery lay cloaked in heavy layers of shadows, looking no different than it did any other day. It didn't look any different to Jack Colvin, but it definitely felt different. The atmosphere around the graveyard was one of silent expectation, as if the ancient burial ground was holding its breath, waiting to see what would happen next. It was a nervous feeling, and it caused a slight tingle to walk down his spine.

Speak to me, Tolomato. What horrors have you recently seen? What secrets can you share?

CHAPTER
11

Ssabra arrived at First City Tours a few minutes early, which gave her time to call Jenny at work. It was almost nine a.m., so she was hoping the restaurant's breakfast rush would be just about over and her friend would be able to talk. Dialing the number, she asked the hostess to speak to Jenny Sanders.

"Jenny?" The hostess fumbled with the phone, obviously waiting on a customer at the same time. "That's three-fifty back to you. Thank you and have a nice day. Yeah, Jenny's here. Let me see if she's free. Hold on a minute."

She was placed on hold for a few moments, then someone answered the phone.

"Hello. Jenny speaking. Can I help you?"

Ssabra cleared her throat. "Hi, Jenny. It's me. Ssabra."

"Hi, honey," Jenny answered, her voice becoming more pleasant. "How you doing? No problems back at the apartment?"

"No. Not really," she answered. "But there is something I need to talk to you about. Do you have a few minutes, or is this a bad time?"

There was a pause. "No. No. It's okay. I can talk. We just finished up with the breakfast crowd. I was planning on taking a few minutes anyway. What do you need?"

She hesitated, trying to come up with the right words. "Remember what you said to me last night?"

"Honey, I said a lot of things to you last night, especially after the wine at my place. Oh, God, I didn't try to make a pass at you, did I?"

"Quit being silly, you know perfectly well that you didn't try to make a pass at me. You're not gay, and you never have been."

"Whew, that's a relief. You didn't try to make a pass at me, did you?"

"No, I didn't. And will you please be serious for a moment?"

"I am being serious. You know how I get after two glasses of vino. I was drunk and vulnerable, and you might have tried to take advantage of me."

"I'm not gay either," Ssabra said, trying not to laugh.

"Really? You're not gay? You could have fooled me. I've never seen you with a man."

"What are you talking about? I had a man in my apartment last night. Remember?"

"Yeah, I remember. And what did you do? You ran away from him."

She laughed. "Stop it. Let's get serious. I need your help. Remember what you said to me last night, about how you thought a ghost might have followed me home from one of the cemeteries?"

"I said that? I must have really been drunk."

"Yes, you said it. You said it at the sandwich shop, and you weren't drunk. You were sober."

"That must have been the problem," Jenny laughed. "Yeah, I remember saying it. Why?"

She again cleared her throat. "Because I think I might have a ghost."

There was a moment of silence on the phone. "You're kidding me. A ghost?"

Ssabra nodded, then remembered that she was speaking on the phone. "I'm not kidding. Remember what I told you last night, about the lights in the bathroom turning off, and the word 'osiyo' appearing on my mirror? And how cold it got in my apartment, and the smell of tobacco?"

"Yes, but you said it was an intruder."

"I thought it was," she replied. "But now I'm not so sure."

"What do you mean?"

She told her friend about how the coffee cup had moved across the table, not once but three times. She also explained how everything seemed to have started after visiting the Huguenot Cemetery, as if something had followed her home from the graveyard.

"Are you sure your coffee table wasn't just wet?" Jenny asked.

"Positive. I checked it. Dry as a bone."

Jenny thought about it for a moment. "I don't know. It sounds pretty far-fetched to me, but a lot of people in this town believe in ghosts. Shoot, half my regular customers claim to have seen them, and I'm talking about normal, everyday people. Not kooks. If ghosts do exist, then I can't think of a better place to find them than in St. Augustine.

"Maybe this ghost of yours is some kind of spirit guide. You're half Indian, so one of your tribal ancestors might have stopped by to pay you a visit. Maybe he wants to teach you the old ways: how to use a bow and arrow, bead moccasins, and skin a buffalo."

"Don't start that," Ssabra warned. "You know how little I know about my heritage."

"Exactly. That's why this ghost is paying you a visit. He wants to teach you the ways of your people."

She laughed. "You're lucky that we're not speaking in person, otherwise I might be tempted to choke you."

"See there," Jenny laughed. "You've got an Indian temper. You'll probably want to take my scalp after you choke me."

"Take your scalp. Now see here, the one thing I know about history is that the French invented scalping. Not the Indians. But getting back to what I was saying about having a ghost in my apartment—"

Ssabra heard a click on the line, and realized someone had been listening in on the conversation. There was another phone in the other room. A few seconds later the voice of Claire Jones came on the line.

"Ghost? What ghost?" Claire asked, joining the conversation.

"It's nothing," she answered, angry that someone had been listening in on a private conversation. Claire was a likable person, but she did have her bad habits, the worst of which was sticking her nose where it didn't belong.

"Ssabra has herself a ghost," Jenny blurted out.

"A ghost? Really?" Claire asked, giggling with excitement. "Wow. That's great. Tell me about it."

"It's nothing. Really," Ssabra repeated, wishing she had never brought the subject up.

"The ghost is in her apartment," Jenny continued. "Ssabra thinks it followed her home from the Huguenot last night. It turned off the lights in her bathroom, and wrote on her mirror. Scared her so bad she called me to come over. And this morning it moved a cup of coffee across her table."

"No kidding? Wow. That's fantastic," Claire said, nearly beside herself. "But why didn't you call me last night? You know how I love scary things."

"I did try to call you," Ssabra lied, "but your line was busy. You were probably surfing the Internet again."

Claire seemed satisfied with the answer. "Probably."

Seeing an opportunity to make good her escape, Jenny said, "Listen, I hate to cut this short, but I still have a few customers. Ssabra, you call me later on, when I get home. I want to hear more about your ghost. Got to go. Bye."

Ssabra said good-bye to her friend, and heard a click as Jenny hung up. She heard a second click and knew that Claire had also hung up the phone, which meant she was on her way into the room. "Oh, God."

Claire came bustling through the doorway, a big smile on her face. "If you have a ghost, then you must talk with my aunt. She's a psychic, you know. One of the best. If you have a ghost, she'll be able to tell you all about it."

"Your aunt is a psychic?" Ssabra asked, surprised. "I didn't know that."

"I thought I told you." Claire nodded. "Maybe I didn't. I've been so forgetful lately. She's one of the best, at least that's what everyone tells me. She's done a lot of research into ghosts and haunted houses. She was even on the television show *Sightings* once or twice."

Ssabra thought about it. If Claire's aunt was a real psychic, then she might be able to explain the strange things that had been going on in her apartment. "That's great, Claire. But where does your aunt live?"

"She lives right here in town. If you want, I can call her. Maybe she'll be able to come over to your apartment tonight, after you get off work."

"That would be great." For once she was actually glad to have Claire's help with something. Maybe her aunt could shed some light on all the weird happenings. "Please, give your aunt a call. If she's not doing anything, I would love to have her come over tonight."

Claire hurried off to make a phone call, leaving Ssabra standing alone in the back room. She didn't really put much faith in psychics, but up until that morning she didn't really believe in ghosts either.

Intruders. Ghosts. Psychics. What next? Vampires?

CHAPTER
12

The three-story red building that stood at 46 Avenida Menendez, overlooking the bay, was yet another of the many historical structures of old St. Augustine. Built around 1745, it had originally been the private home of Francisco de Porras. Francisco and his lovely wife, Juana, and their nine children, had lived in the house until 1763, when Spain relinquished Florida to the British.

The house stood empty and unloved during the twenty years that the British occupied St. Augustine, falling into a sad state of disrepair. The city was returned to Spanish control in 1784, but Francisco and Juana never returned from Cuba to reclaim the house they loved. Only their youngest daughter, Catalina, returned, petitioning the Spanish governor to gain back her childhood home. But her happiness in the house only lasted a short time, because Catalina died six years later.

The house was later destroyed in the great fire that

swept through St. Augustine in 1887, but was rebuilt exactly like the original. Various families lived in the house up until 1976, when the home was turned into a restaurant. It had been a restaurant ever since, although it changed ownerships, and names, several times.

The building at 46 Avenida Menendez was now known as Harry's Seafood and Grill. Before that it was called Catalina's Garden, The Chart House, and the Puerta Verde Restaurant. It was a popular place with the tourists and locals, not only for the good food and the historic atmosphere, but for the magnificent view of the bay and the Bridge of Lions offered from the restaurant's front windows.

Cindy Hawkins had seen the view from the front windows enough times that it didn't really distract her anymore. Although she sometimes liked to slip up to the office on the third floor to smoke a cigarette and watch the boats sail in and out of the harbor. She only did this when she wasn't busy, and had a few minutes to spare, which didn't come very often. Harry's Seafood and Grill was usually packed, especially during the evening.

Not that she minded the restaurant staying busy. As a waitress, she earned most of her income on tips. On a good night she could make as much as many people made in a week. Of course she never reported the full amount to the IRS. What the government didn't know wouldn't hurt it, nor would it hurt her.

She had been working at Harry's for over a year, and it was one of the best jobs she'd ever had. Her fellow employees were great to work with, and her bosses weren't that bad. They didn't even get upset when she occasionally came to work late, or asked to get off early to take in a show. She also liked the restaurant itself, everything except for the stairway that led up to the second floor.

The stairway was narrow, and had been built for single family use. It was nearly impossible to pass someone on the steps, and she often had to wait for a customer to clear the way even when she was in a hurry. But the stairway added charm to the old building, as did the fireplace in the downstairs dining room.

Along with the original furnishings, there were a few well-told legends that added to the atmosphere of the restaurant. Like many of the old buildings in St. Augustine, the house that was now Harry's was reputed to be haunted. Cindy had never seen a ghost herself, but there were those who claimed the spirit of a young woman inhabited the building. Some called the spirit Brigitte, but most believed it was the ghost of Catalina de Porras.

Most of Harry's customers came for the excellent Cajun food, but some arrived with hopes of seeing the ghost. Cindy could usually tell who the ghost hunters were, for they often carried cameras and took quite a few photos of the interior. And at some time during their visit, they would make their way up the narrow staircase to the second floor. Supposedly, many of the sightings of Catalina took place upstairs, near the women's bathroom.

Several people also claimed to have seen the spirit of a man in the downstairs dining room, standing by the fireplace or gazing out the front windows. One woman supposedly mistook the spirit for a waiter and tried to order a drink. She was horrified when he disappeared before her eyes, and left the restaurant without paying her bill. Then again, maybe that was just an excuse to get out of paying.

Cindy had not seen either one of the spirits, but she didn't discount the stories. There was an ambience within Harry's that was hard to describe, as if an unseen presence watched over everyone. It was a good feeling, not scary at all, like someone was protecting them, keeping them safe. The sensation made her happy, and she often found herself whispering a greeting to the spirits when she came in to work.

She wasn't the only one who noticed the atmosphere of comfort and warmth that seemed to hang over the old building. Some of the other employees also noticed, and spoke about it on their breaks. They also told stories about the strange encounters they had over the years, glimpses of movement out the corners of their eyes when no one else was around, doors opening and closing, footsteps coming up the stairs, laughter, and the momentary sighting of a woman dressed in a long white dress. Even the manager had such experiences, though he was less inclined to talk about them than some of the other employees.

One thing for sure, whether or not the restaurant had any real spirits, the ghost stories were good for business. Not only did the stories draw in customers, but the ghost hunters always tipped generously. It was as if they were leaving a little something extra for the spirits. Not that Cindy was going to share her earnings with anyone, dead or otherwise.

The waitress wasn't thinking about spirits as she

hurried across the second floor dining room to the kitchen. Instead, she was thinking about the salads she had ordered for table number four, and wondering what was taking them so long. Glancing up at the large round mirror hanging above the waiter's station, she rounded the corner toward the kitchen. The mirror was placed strategically at the junction of a blind corner, and was used to prevent servers from crashing into each other. It came in handy, especially on a busy night.

Entering the kitchen, she found her salads on the counter, ready for delivery to the table. Cindy quickly arranged the salads on a round serving tray, then hurried back to her hungry customers. Making sure nothing else was needed, the waitress hastened to check on her other tables.

She was on her way back to the kitchen when she nearly collided with a man coming up the stairs. He was tall and bearded, dressed in a black shirt, jeans, a denim jacket, and boots. Probably a biker on a sacred pilgrimage to Daytona, stopping off in the old city long enough to eat.

"I'm sorry. Excuse me." Cindy stepped aside to let the man go ahead of her, but he made no move to go past. He just stood at the top of the stairs, staring at her.

Cindy felt her skin break out in goosebumps. She started to ask the man if he needed any help, but he broke eye contact and moved past her, making his way toward the rest rooms. She watched as he crossed the room, letting out a sigh of relief. "What a creep. We do get some strange ones in here."

Dismissing the man as being slightly eccentric, or

perhaps drunk, she entered the kitchen to check on
the appetizers for table five, then stopped by the wait
station to enter an order into the computer. As Cindy
punched in the numbers, one of the other waiters,
Tom Crawford, joined her at the station.

"How's it going?" Tom asked, favoring her with
a smile.

"Not too bad," she replied, returning the smile.
Tom had a bit of a crush on her, but he was much
too shy to ask her out. "I'm keeping busy. No real
headaches, except for the old lady at number four.
How are you doing tonight?"

"About the same. I've got rest room duty tonight,
so I had to make sure there were plenty of paper
towels for the drunks."

Cindy punched the last number into the computer,
then stepped aside so Tom could use the machine.
"Were you just in the men's room?"

He nodded. "I just came out of there. Why?"

"Did you see the guy that just went in? What a
strange one. There's something about him that gave
me the chills."

"What guy?"

"The man with the beard, and the Levi jacket. He
just went to the men's room. You must have seen
him."

Tom entered his order, stepping away from the
computer. "I just came out of the men's room, but
there was no one else in there. Just me."

"Maybe you passed him on the way out."

He shook his head. "Didn't see anyone, especially
a man with a beard."

She turned and looked around the room. "That's

odd. I could have sworn he was on his way to the rest room. He's not sitting at one of the tables. He's not at the bar either."

"Maybe he went downstairs," Tom suggested.

Cindy shook her head. "I would have seen him if he did. He would have walked past me." She turned to Tom. "You don't suppose he's in the women's rest room. Do you? Maybe he's another ghost hunter, looking for Catalina."

"That's possible," he agreed. "Think you should check it out?"

"No way. Not without backup."

"I can't go into the women's room. There might be a customer in there. They would freak if I went walking in there. How about if you go in, while I wait outside by the door?"

"Thanks," she smiled. "I really appreciate it. Let's go check out the ladies' room."

Not wanting to waste more time than was necessary, they made their way to the rest rooms. Cindy opened the door to the women's room slowly, a little fearful that she might find a man standing inside. But the rest room was empty, even the two stalls were unoccupied. She stepped back outside; Tom was still guarding the door.

"He's not in here," she said. "The place is empty."

"Let me check the men's room. Maybe he went in after I came out." Tom entered the men's room, but found it empty and returned a few moments later. "No one in there either."

"That's odd." She looked around the room. "He must have gone back downstairs when I wasn't looking. Oh, well, I'm not going to worry about him. I've got food to deliver. Thanks, Tom."

Putting the bearded man out of her mind, she went back to work. The restaurant was filling up quickly, and she kept busy with hungry customers. About an hour later she was standing alone at the wait station, when she happened to glance up at the mirror. Standing behind her was a man, but his image in the mirror was dark and cloudy, appearing to shimmer and ripple as if made out of smoke. And instead of arms, the man in the mirror had long black tentacles.

Cindy almost screamed. She spun around expecting to find a shimmering monster with tentacles for arms, and instead found herself standing nearly nose to nose with the bearded man she had seen earlier. The man didn't say a word. He only stared at her for a moment or two, then turned and slowly descended the stairs to the first floor.

She watched the man go down the stairs, but her heart continued to jackhammer long after he was gone.

CHAPTER
13

Claire Jones and her psychic aunt showed up at the apartment a little after eleven p.m. Ssabra had only been home for a few minutes when the doorbell rang, her evening ghost tour having lasted a little longer than usual. Hearing the bell ring, she finished changing clothes and hurried out of the bedroom to open the door.

"Sorry to make you wait," she said, slightly out of breath. "I just got home and was changing clothes."

"Hi, Ssabra," Claire said, stepping across the threshold to give a quick hug. "This is my aunt, Barbara Jaeger. She's the psychic I was telling you about."

Barbara was a large woman, but she was not fat. She was tall and stout, with curly black hair and pale skin. She was wearing a long dress of purple and black that looked almost medieval, like something out of a renaissance fair, accented with silver earrings and a matching necklace. The dress revealed more cleavage than it should have, drawing attention to the tiny purple and green salamander tattooed on her left breast.

"Hi, Barbara. I'm Ssabra. I'm so glad you—"

Barbara placed an index finger against Ssabra's lips, cutting her off midsentence. "Shhhh . . . Not another word. Don't tell me anything. We'll talk later. Just let me come in and walk around, see what kind of vibrations I can pick up. I don't want any descriptions of your encounters to taint my psychic impressions."

She removed her finger from Ssabra's lips and stepped past her. Slightly dumbfounded, Ssabra turned and watched as Barbara entered the room. Quickly regaining her composure, she closed and locked the door.

The psychic was carrying a large purse that matched her dress, which she set down on the kitchen counter. Opening the purse, she removed several small scented candles, a handful of dark blue incense sticks, and what looked to be an herbal smudge stick. She set the items on the counter, and then crossed the room to the sink. Waving her right hand back and forth over the faucet a few times, she reached down and turned on the water.

"Running water attracts spirits, draws them out of the woodwork. We'll leave this on while I'm here." Barbara turned around and looked at Ssabra, offering her a slight smile. "I learned that bit of wisdom when I was in the Orient. Asian people consider spirits to be good luck, and they want to keep them around. That's why you always see an aquarium, or a waterfall, in Chinese restaurants. It draws the spirits, and brings good luck to the business."

She walked back to the counter and picked up the incense sticks. "Do you have any ashtrays?"

"I have one in the living room," Ssabra replied.

"Just one?" Barbara shook her head. "Not nearly enough. We'll need more than that. How about saucers, or plates? Do you have any of those?"

"I have some in the cabinet. Not many."

Barbara rubbed her hands together. "Good. Get what you have. We need to place the candles and incense around the room."

Ssabra crossed the kitchen and opened her cabinets, searching for plates and saucers they could use. Claire also started looking through the cabinets, although she confined her search to the places where food was kept.

"MMMMM. . . . cinnamon Pop Tarts. My favorite." She grabbed a package of foil-wrapped Pop Tarts out of the box. "Do you mind if I have one?"

Ssabra started to reply, but Barbara interrupted her, "Claire, put that back. No eating when I'm working."

Claire frowned, disappointed, but she put the Pop Tarts back into the cabinet. Ssabra finished collecting the plates and saucers, setting them in front of Barbara.

"Good. Good." The psychic nodded. She spread the plates and saucers out, setting a candle, or a stick of incense, on each of them. She then took each item and placed it in a specific spot in the apartment: one candle and one stick of incense in the bedroom, the same in the bathroom, two of each in the kitchen, with the rest scattered around the living room. She lit each item as she set it down, saying a short prayer, and asking any and all spirits residing inside the tiny apartment to make their presence known.

Returning to the kitchen, Barbara picked up the herbal smudge stick. The smudge stick was a combination of dried cedar and desert sage, held together with a wrapping of red string. Removing the string from one end of the bundle, she lit the stick and then blew out the flame so it would smoke, waving it back and forth in front of her.

"Sage and cedar cleanses the air, takes all the negativity out of it. It also helps you stay in balance. American Indians use it in all their important ceremonies."

Ssabra wondered if the psychic was trying to impress her with a knowledge of Native cultures. Claire had probably told her that Ssabra was half Cherokee. Maybe it was something she did to get more money out of paying customers.

She didn't know if sage and cedar could really cleanse the air of any negativity, but it was definitely stinking up her kitchen. Ssabra held her breath, resisting the urge to cough, greatly relieved when Barbara finally took the smudge stick out from under her nose.

After cleansing the three of them, Barbara took the smudge stick and slowly walked through the apartment, getting rid of any evil elements that might be hanging around. At least that's what she said she was doing. Ssabra didn't think she had any evil elements in her apartment. Then again, up until the previous day, she didn't think she had any ghosts either.

Barbara returned to the kitchen and set the smudge stick on the last empty saucer. "Now that I've gotten rid of the negativity in here, let's see who your visitor might be. Follow me."

The psychic turned and walked back into the living room. She moved slowly, her arms out by her sides, palms facing down. It looked like she was moving through a field of tall wheat, feeling the tops of each plant. As she proceeded through the room, circling the furniture, she made comments to herself. "Ah yes, I feel something here. Definitely a presence of some kind. Someone has been in here, but I'm not sure who. Not yet.

"Ssabra, come here and feel this. Here's a cold spot. A spirit was just here."

She walked to the spot where Barbara was pointing, just left of the television, but didn't feel anything. No cold spot. No tingling on the back of her neck. Nothing. "I don't feel it."

"You're not trying." Barbara took Ssabra's wrist and held her hand over a certain spot on the floor. "Here. How about now?"

"Nothing."

"You're still not trying," Barbara frowned. "What about you, Claire?"

Claire hurried to the spot, nearly knocking Ssabra out of the way. "Yes, I feel it. It's cold. Very cold. Almost freezing."

Barbara favored her niece with a smile. "There. See? I told you. Just like I said, it's a cold spot. Your friend must not be very gifted. Psychic abilities do run in our family."

Ssabra bit her tongue to keep from saying anything. Claire absolutely beamed over the compliment
she had been given.

Moving away from the television set, Barbara continued with her psychic detective work. She circled
around the living room, touching various items of
furniture and feeling along the wall. Twice she
stopped and stood perfectly still, her eyes closed and
her head tilted to one side, as if listening to something only she could hear, perhaps hearing a voice
calling to her from the great beyond.

She entered the bedroom, but didn't stay in there
long, declaring that there had been no visitors in the
bedroom. Ssabra almost laughed. She could have told
the psychic there had been no visitors in her bedroom, or in her bed, for a long time. She had been
without a man in her life since Alan had been killed.
At first she had been alone by choice, mourning the
loss of the man she loved. But even after the wounds
had started to heal, she still found herself alone. It
had been years since she dated, and she was a little
afraid to put herself back into the game. Nope. No
visitors in the bedroom, spiritual or otherwise.

Barbara left the bedroom and proceeded to the
bathroom. She spent a few minutes inside the tiny
room, turning on the water in the sink and tub, and
feeling along the wall. She was just about to leave,
when she suddenly turned and faced the bathroom
mirror.

"Here. I feel it. There's a very strong presence in
this room."

Ssabra felt the breath catch in her throat.

"Right here. Where I'm standing. There's something about this mirror. I see letters. A word. Something is written on the mirror."

Ssabra's heart began to race. She stepped forward to get a better look, thinking the strange word had once again appeared on the mirror, but the glass was blank. The psychic was obviously seeing something that was invisible to the mundane.

"Yes. Yes. I see it," the psychic continued. "A word. No. No. Not a word. A name. A spirit is trying to communicate with us. It's giving us a name. Wait a minute. It's getting clearer. Yes. There it is. Elizabeth. The spirit's name is Elizabeth."

Elizabeth? That wasn't the word that had appeared on her bathroom mirror. The word she had seen was "osiyo," not Elizabeth. A thought suddenly popped into her head; she turned to look at Claire.

Claire had been eavesdropping on her phone conversation with Jenny that morning. And Jenny had even told Claire about the possible ghost, saying a word had appeared on the bathroom mirror. But she hadn't said what word. Claire must have passed the information on to her aunt.

Now Claire's aunt was using what her niece had told her to put on a show. Claire hadn't told her what the word was that had magically appeared on the glass, so Barbara was making up her own word. A name. A woman's name.

"It's all coming through to me now," Barbara continued, never missing a beat. "The name I see here is Elizabeth. It was left here by the spirit. She's reaching out to us, trying to let us know who she is."

Barbara stepped out of the bathroom and looked

around the living room. "Elizabeth, are you here? Are you here with us? Don't be afraid. Come out and show yourself. We won't hurt you."

The name Elizabeth had not appeared on the bathroom mirror, and Ssabra didn't think it was the spirit of a woman they should be looking for. "Look, I don't think—"

"Shhhhh . . . be quiet," Barbara warned, silencing her. "I see something. Over there, by the television. Something is forming."

"What is it?" Claire whispered.

"It's a figure," answered the psychic, speaking in a whisper. "I see a little girl. She's standing next to the television, in the same place where I felt the cold spot. She's very young, no more than six or seven years old, with long blond hair. She's dressed all in white, and she's holding a bouquet of flowers."

"Where? I don't see her." Claire was obviously disappointed that she couldn't see the little girl.

"She's still there, next to the television. She's becoming more clear to me now. A lovely girl. Very pretty. There's a radiance about her that hurts my eyes. She's looking at us, and she's smiling."

"Are you Elizabeth?" Barbara asked. She stood silent for a moment, then said, "The little girl is nodding. Her name is Elizabeth; she's the one who wrote on the bathroom mirror."

Ssabra didn't see anyone standing next to the television, and she had a sneaking suspicion that no one was really there, spirit or otherwise. She was beginning to suspect that Barbara Jaeger was making everything up, creating a ghostly story as she went along. Then again, maybe the self-proclaimed psychic actually believed she saw a little girl standing next to the television, even if what she saw might only be smoke from the burning incense and smudge stick.

"Elizabeth, why are you here?" Barbara asked. She stood perfectly still, her head cocked to one side.

"Can you hear her?" Claire whispered.

Barbara nodded. "Yes, but her voice is very faint. Elizabeth says she died of the fever in 1821, and her body is buried in a mass grave at the Huguenot Cemetery. That's where she met Ssabra. She saw Ssabra giving a ghost tour and decided to follow her home. Elizabeth says she likes the pretty lady, and wants to live with her. She promises she won't cause any trouble. If that's okay?"

Ssabra was staring at the spot next to the television, so it took a few moments to realize the others were looking at her, apparently waiting for an answer.

"Is it okay if Elizabeth stays here with you?" Barbara asked, repeating the question. "She promises not to cause you any trouble."

"Here? With me? I don't know. I guess. I mean, it's a free country. Ghosts can live where they want. But why would she want to live with me? What about her parents? Why doesn't she live with them?" Ssabra couldn't believe she had just given permission for a ghost to move in with her.

"Elizabeth says she can't find her parents," Barbara answered, apparently speaking for the ghost. "And yes, it's a free country, but the good spirits always ask permission before moving in. By the way, they don't like it when you call them ghosts. They prefer being called spirits."

"Spirits. Right. I'll remember that."

Barbara turned her attention back to the spot across the room. "Elizabeth, Ssabra said you can stay here with her. Would that make you happy?"

The psychic turned to look at the other two women. "Elizabeth is smiling. She's very happy with the decision."

"That's great. I'm thrilled," Ssabra mumbled under her breath.

"That's super," Claire said, bubbling with enthusiasm. "You have your own ghost. Wait until I tell everyone at work. Hey, maybe they will put your apartment on the ghost tour. Wouldn't that be great? You'll be a local celebrity."

Ssabra turned to face Claire, a frown forming. "Claire, there's really no need to tell everyone about this. My apartment is too far away from the old section of the city to be put on the ghost tour. And I don't want tourists and ghost hunters hanging around my front door."

"Oops, she's gone," Barbara said, interrupting the disagreement. "Elizabeth just faded out, but I'm sure she'll be back soon. She likes it here."

"Wonderful," Ssabra said, somewhat sarcastically. "But I don't have a spare bedroom, so Elizabeth will have to sleep on the couch."

Ssabra didn't really believe she had the ghost of a little girl as a house guest. Instead, she thought the whole "Elizabeth" thing was part of a show being put on by the psychic, perhaps as a way to enhance her reputation. She had gotten the name wrong on the mirror, and the cold spot she had felt in the living room was not where anything strange had happened.

Deciding it was time to clear out a few people, Ssabra said, "Barbara, I want to thank you and Claire for coming over. I really do appreciate the help. Now that I know my ghost, I mean spirit, is friendly, I feel a whole lot better. I know you both probably have very busy schedules, so I don't want to keep you any longer."

"We were planning on going out for drinks after we got done," Claire said. "You want to come along with us? We could talk about some of the other cases my aunt has worked on."

Ssabra shook her head. "No. No. That's okay. Thank you for the invitation, but I think I'll pass. I didn't get much sleep the last few nights, what with the haunting and all that, so I think I'll just stay home and turn in early. You guys go ahead, have yourselves a wonderful time."

"Okay, if you're sure," Claire responded.

"I'm sure."

The three women chatted for a few more minutes, then Barbara started gathering up her things. She extinguished the incense and the smudge stick, putting them back into her bag, but she left the candles where they were, a gift for Elizabeth. Ssabra again thanked the women for everything, seeing them to the door. Locking the door behind them, she turned back around to face the room.

Ssabra Onih was now more confused than ever. She still didn't have an explanation for the strange things happening in her apartment. Barbara said the events were caused by the spirit of a little girl, but the psychic was wrong about the word that had appeared on the bathroom mirror. And it was a man's voice she had heard at the Huguenot Cemetery, not that of a little girl.

Walking back through the apartment, she extinguished all the candles. If Elizabeth did exist, then she would just have to get her own candles to play with. She also gathered up the plates and saucers, cleaning off the melted wax and ashes. Turning off the water in the kitchen sink, she suddenly remembered the water in the bathroom was still running.

She hurried to turn off the water in the sink and tub, checking to see if any more words had been written on the mirror. The glass was clean, no more strange words or names. Finished with the tasks at hand, she walked back into the living room and took a seat on the sofa. She had just put her feet on the coffee table when she heard a man's voice.

"Osiyo."

Ssabra nearly jumped out of her skin, and came damn close to wetting herself. She jumped up and looked around the room, but there was no one there. But she hadn't imagined the voice; she heard it clearly. Doing a slow turn to look around the room, she asked out loud, "Who said that?"

She didn't expect an answer, and nearly had a heart attack when one came.

"I said it."

CHAPTER
14

The clock on the wall above the bar finally struck midnight, a few minutes after the last two customers of the evening walked out the front door of Harry's Seafood and Grill. Naturally, those customers had sat at one of Cindy's tables, preventing the young waitress from getting off work a little early. She didn't mind staying late, especially on good nights, but the customers, and the tips, had trickled to a slow stop hours earlier. The few people who had stayed late were only interested in coffee and conversation, and had only left a few lousy coins for the service they received.

"Tough night?" Frank asked, as she sat down wearily on one of the stools at the upstairs bar. Frank was one of three assistant managers, and usually worked the night shift. He was tall, dark-haired, and good-looking. He was also married. It seemed the good ones were always taken.

"No tougher than any other night," Cindy answered. She spread out her receipts on the bar, sorting them by credit card, cash, and discount coupon. "Is there anyone left in here, or are we closed?"

Frank looked around. There was no one left upstairs, and he guessed that the downstairs was also empty. "I think we're closed."

"Good. Then you don't mind if I light up?"

"No. Go ahead."

She started to pull a pack of cigarettes out of her apron pocket, but Frank grabbed a pack off the back counter and handed it to her, along with a lighter. "Thank you." Cindy took one of the cigarettes, lit it, then slid the pack back across the bar. Adding up her receipts, she double-checked to make sure the individual totals matched her final tally. Happy to see that she had made no mistakes in her math, she laid out the receipts for Frank to take a look at.

He leaned over the bar, checking the register totals with the individual receipts. He added up what tips had been placed on credit cards, giving her cash from the register for that amount. "There. You're all set. Anything else I can do for you?"

"How about making me a free drink? I've had a rough night."

"You've got it. What would you like?"

"I'd love a margarita. Make it strong, with extra salt."

"A margarita, huh? Sounds like you're planning on going out tonight."

"I don't have to work tomorrow, so I'm going to go party. I want to get drunk and listen to music."

"You're not driving, are you?" he asked, a little concerned.

She shook her head. "No, Daddy. I'm not driving.

I'm going to hit the local bars, a few streets over. I'll leave my car here, and probably take a cab home. Or have a friend drive me."

"Good girl." Frank grabbed a bottle of tequila, and the triple sec, mixing up a strong margarita with extra salt on the rim of the glass. Setting the drink on the bar, he left to attend to business downstairs.

Cindy was quietly sipping her margarita, when the waitress realized she was completely alone. Harry's Seafood and Grill could be quite spooky at night, especially the second floor. She had all but forgotten the weird image she saw in the mirror earlier in the evening, but now it came back to her. It had probably been nothing more than a trick of the lighting, but it scared the hell out of her. And then there was the creepy-looking guy with the beard who had stared at her.

Growing more nervous by the minute, she looked around at the empty room. Several of her fellow employees claimed to have had ghostly encounters on the second floor of the restaurant. Meeting a ghost was the last thing in the world she wanted to experience, especially when she was by herself. Finishing her drink, she hurried downstairs to be with the others.

Most of the employees had already gone home for the night, but there was still a handful of people in the kitchen, mopping up and making sure that everything perishable was put away. There were also a couple of the front staff sitting at the downstairs bar, waiting to check out. Frank was behind the bar, and it was obvious he was still in a good mood because he had served drinks to the other employees.

Frank smiled when he saw Cindy approaching the bar. "Did you get lonely upstairs by yourself?"

"You could say that."

"Did you see any ghosts?"

"No, and I don't plan on seeing any tonight either. That's why I came down here."

The others laughed. They all knew the stories associated with the restaurant, and probably none of them would have felt very comfortable about being upstairs alone after closing time.

"How was your drink?"

"Excellent," she replied. "But I want another one. I'll pay. Put it in a go cup."

Frank made her another margarita, doubling up on the tequila, and putting it in a plastic cup so she could take it with her. The cops didn't usually hassle people if they were walking with a drink in their hands, as long as it was in a plastic cup so they couldn't tell what it was.

"Thanks, darling." She paid for the drink, leaving a tip on the bar. Grabbing her purse out of her locker in the back room, she said good-bye to the other employees and headed for the side door. The patio area was empty and quiet now that all of the customers had gone home, but the torches still burned, casting a dancing glow over the empty tables.

She took a deep breath as she stepped outside, savoring the fresh air blowing in off the bay. As she inhaled, Cindy realized she was already starting to feel the effects of the first margarita. Taking a sip of her second drink, she walked through the outside dining area to the cobblestone street behind the restaurant. It was getting late and the street was deserted. Even the public parking lot behind the restaurant was already empty.

Turning left, she proceeded down the narrow street, being cautious of the potholes and loose bricks. She didn't want to trip and fall, nor did she want to spill her drink. The margarita was quite tasty, and she wanted to enjoy every drop. Nobody made drinks the way Frank did, at least nobody made them quite as strong.

Cindy Hawkins had only gone a few blocks when she noticed someone was following her. Well, maybe not following, but there was a man coming down the street behind her. The street was dark and she couldn't tell who it was; it was probably just a tourist enjoying the atmosphere of the historic district at night. Parking was also a problem in the old section, so the man might be walking back to his car after having dined at one of the local restaurants.

Next time eat at Harry's. You won't have to walk so far.

Turning right at the corner, she cut down a side street even darker than the one just traveled. It was darker, but it was also a shortcut to where she wanted to go. She was halfway down the street, when she glanced over her shoulder and noticed someone enter the alley behind her. It was the same man she had seen before, and she couldn't help but wonder if he really was pursuing her.

That's ridiculous.

She smiled and took another sip of margarita. The man just happened to be walking in the same direction. He might even be going to the same bar. If he was stalking her, then he wouldn't be so bold about it. He would be sneaking around in the shadows, not walking out in the open where he could be seen.

To prove to herself that she wasn't really being followed, Cindy decided to stop walking and act as if she was looking for something in her purse. She stood there for a moment or two, expecting the man who trailed behind her to walk on past. But when she didn't hear footsteps, she looked up to see where he had gone. The waitress felt a flutter of nervousness pass through her stomach as she spotted him back down the street. Apparently, he had stopped when she did, and was now standing there watching her.

What the hell. Someone is playing games with me.

But maybe the situation was perfectly innocent. Maybe he had a reason to stop when she did. Perhaps he was tying his shoelace, or lighting a cigarette. He might even be the shy type and didn't want to walk past her.

Or he might be the protective type. Maybe he had seen a young woman walking down a dark alley, and decided to keep an eye on her. He might be an off duty cop, or a security officer.

Another thought crossed her mind. Maybe it was one of her fellow employees that now followed her. It might even be Frank. The assistant manager had served her two very strong drinks, so maybe he was making sure she got safely to her destination. He was the type of guy to do something like that: watch over her to keep her safe, but stay back so as not to be seen or take any credit.

"Yoo-hoo, Frankie. Is that you?" Cindy giggled. If it was Frank, then he should be rewarded for his gallantry.

"I'll give you a reward." She laughed harder, spilling margarita across the back of her hand. She licked the liquid off her skin. "Don't spill your drink. It's alcohol abuse."

Maybe Frank wanted to party with her, but he didn't have the nerve to ask. He was probably afraid she would reject him because he was married, or run tell his wife. Perhaps the assistant manager was looking to add a little spice to his life.

Is that it, Frank? Are you looking for a little spice?

Cindy thought it over for a moment. She didn't have a problem with having sex with married men. As a matter of fact, she actually preferred married men to the single guys. They were usually more experienced in bed, and much more willing to please. They weren't in it just for themselves, and actually cared whether or not their partner had an orgasm. Married men were also less likely to be carrying around diseases.

The tequila was causing her vision to blur around the edges, making it difficult to see. It might be Frank standing there in the darkness, or it might be one of the other employees. Maybe the assistant manager had sent one of the waiters after Cindy to keep an eye on her.

"Well, in that case, there's no reason to be shy." She finished the last of her drink in one gulp and tossed the empty plastic cup to the sidewalk. Convinced the man was someone she knew, she started walking toward him.

The young woman was only a few feet away when she realized that he wasn't one of her coworkers. Nor was he one of her regular customers.

She stopped and looked around nervously. Cindy was alone in the alley, just her and a man whose features she could not make out in the darkness. She could only see his eyes, unnaturally shiny in the night.

"Hello? Can I help you?" Her tongue felt too thick and the words came out slurred. "Are you following me?"

He didn't answer, but maybe he didn't speak English. St. Augustine drew tourists from all over the world; there were also a lot of Hispanic people living in Florida.

"*Qué pasa?*" she asked, speaking one of the few Spanish phrases she knew. The man still didn't reply. He just stood there, his image blurring in and out; his features clear one second and fuzzy the next.

Suddenly, Cindy realized that what she was seeing was not the result of too much tequila. He really was shifting in and out of focus. One second his image was crystal clear, the next it was nothing more than a mass of blurry movements. It was as if his body was constantly reshaping itself around the edges.

"What the hell?" She took a step back, fear blowing spider kisses up and down her spine.

The flesh on his face began to quiver and roll, as if dozens of cockroaches scurried beneath the surface of his skin. His arms grew longer, fingers and hands disappearing, changing into black tentacles. More tentacles sprouted from his body: perhaps a dozen, maybe more.

The warm buzz of alcohol left her in a flash, leaving behind the icy numbness of terror. She recognized the person standing before her. It was the bearded customer she had seen earlier in the restaurant; the man with the icy stare, whose image in the mirror was obscene and inhuman. But it wasn't just his reflection that wasn't human, it was the man himself.

"Oh, my God."

Cindy staggered back and turned to run, but several tentacles quickly reached out and grabbed her. She tried to scream, but one of the tentacles wrapped around her throat and cut off her air. She could only stare in wide-eyed terror as the bearded man made the final transformation into his true form, revealing a shape that was beyond madness.

Again, she tried to scream, but only a soft hissing of air escaped her throat. Nor could she break free of the tentacles holding her, her struggles growing weaker by the second. Her arms and legs felt like lead, her punches and kicks having little effect on the monster.

Her struggles finally stopped, and she could only watch in helpless terror as the body of the thing began to quiver and quake in apparent excitement, could only stare as a glistening wet appendage appeared from its lower torso, growing in length, stretching out toward her.

A shudder of revulsion passed through her body. There was no mistaking that the appendage was a penis, and the sight of it sickened the young woman. She tried to pull back, but all of her strength had been drained from the struggle. Nor could she stop the tentacles from tearing off her clothing, shredding the material of her blouse and pants like tissue paper.

The night air was chilly upon her bare legs, but the goosebumps breaking out on her skin were from fear and not the cold.

One of the thin black tentacles slipped inside her panties like a wet eel, and there was a soft tearing sound as the silky material was pulled from her body. The tentacle was now free to explore and probe, searching out her various orifices. Other tentacles joined the first, coiling around her lower back and buttocks, drawing her closer to the monster.

Her thighs were encircled, and her legs pulled apart, the monster using its tentacles to position her vagina for a quick and very painful insertion.

Cindy screamed a silent cry as the monster entered her, tearing delicate flesh and causing blood to flow wet and warm down her legs. She struggled like a fish on a hook to get free as wave after wave of pain surged through her body. She prayed for release from the searing pain, and for death to come on silent wings to end the nightmare, but her prayers fell on deaf ears. She remained fully conscious as the monster thrust against her, each passing second an eternity of agony.

The monster's thrusts began to slow, and finally came to a stop. Its penis remained deep inside of her for a few more seconds, then withdrew.

A few moments of dead silence ticked past, then the creature made an angry hissing noise. Cindy felt the tentacles tighten around her body, and knew something even more terrible was about to happen to her. She watched as the monster's hideous beaked mouth opened wide, and felt pain beyond description as dozens of tentacles stripped the flesh from her bones to feed that mouth. She closed her eyes, but it did not stop the pain. Nothing could stop the pain.

CHAPTER
15

It had to be a trick, someone must be playing some kind of sick joke on her. That could be the only logical explanation for the voice she heard. A prank. If it wasn't a joke then the invisible man had just stopped by her apartment for a little visit, because the voice Ssabra heard belonged to a man who could not be seen.

There was another possibility, but she really didn't want to think about it. If it wasn't a trick, and if the invisible man hadn't stopped by for tea, then the voice might mean that she had finally gone crazy and was now a few cards short of a full deck.

Placing her hands on her head, she checked to see if there was any noticeable change in the size and shape of her cranium. She didn't feel any swelling, so she could probably rule out a tumor, or an aneurysm, and she had never taken hallucinogenic drugs, nor was she a manic-depressive. If she had gone insane, then it wasn't from a severe medical condition, or from anything she had done to herself during her younger years.

Thinking that perhaps she was losing her mind, she resisted the urge to flee from her apartment. No point in running from insanity. Sooner or later, it would find you no matter where you hid. Better to face the problem now; she could always run later, provided the men in the funny white coats hadn't already taken her away.

At first, the voice seemed to be coming from several different directions at once. When Ssabra got over her initial shock, however, she realized that she was actually hearing the voice inside her head. It was very faint at first, but the more she listened the louder it became, finally sounding as if someone were standing next to her.

"Where are you?" she asked, finding enough courage to voice a question.

"I am here," responded the voice. It was definitely a man who spoke.

"Here? In the room with me?" She looked around nervously, still not quite sure what to make of the situation. Her instinct told her to get the hell out of there, but it was her home and she was not about to give it up without a fight.

"Yes. I am here."

Ssabra was doubtful that there was really someone in the room with her, despite what she heard. "Can you see me?"

"Yes."

"Then what am I wearing?" The blinds had all

been drawn, so she knew none of her neighbors could see into the apartment. Even the fat man in the neighboring building could not see her.

"You are wearing white shorts, a red top, and shoes. You have very nice legs."

She looked around, suspecting there was a hidden camera, and maybe a tiny speaker, somewhere in her apartment, but she didn't see anything out of the ordinary. If there were such devices, the installer had done a good job of hiding them.

Then again, a hidden speaker would not explain why she seemed to be hearing the voice inside her head. To create that kind of effect there would have to be a dozen different speakers, each of them broadcasting in stereo sound. Or someone would actually have had to implant a tiny speaker in her head, but that sort of thing only happened in science fiction movies.

"Are you a ghost?" she asked, finally getting around to the question she was most afraid to ask.

"You could say that."

She let out her breath, feeling her hands start to shake. "I'm sorry. You probably prefer being called a spirit."

"Why should I care what you call me? I am dead."

"Are you the spirit of a little girl?"

"Do I sound like the spirit of a little girl?" answered the voice, chuckling. "I was a man."

"But Barbara said you were a little girl."

"Who is Barbara?"

"Barbara Jaeger. She was here a little while ago. She's supposed to be psychic."

"Ah, the big woman. She who likes to burn candles." Again the voice laughed. "I would not listen to much that woman has to say. She claims to be a person of medicine, but she is nothing but a fool. So is the young one who came with her."

"Claire?"

"Yes. That one too. She has spiders in her head."

Ssabra laughed. It was a perfect description for Claire. "I'm sorry if I offended you. Barbara said that you were the spirit of a little girl named Elizabeth."

"I know Elizabeth, and I am not her."

"You mean there really is a ghost named Elizabeth?"

"Yes. But not here."

She glanced around the room, hoping to see the person who was talking to her. She still wasn't convinced that she was communicating with the dead, but she was willing to go along with the game for now.

"If you're not Elizabeth, then who are you?"

"My name is Tolomato."

"Tolomato?" she asked, surprised. "Like the cemetery?"

"Yes."

"You were a Seminole chief?"

There was a hiss of anger. "I am not Seminole. I am Guale."

"But the sign in the Old Drugstore says—"

"The sign is wrong."

"This is just too weird." Ssabra began to pace the room out of nervousness. "If you really are Tolomato, then you've been dead for a long time."

"Do you think I do not know that? I am the one who is dead."

"No. No. That's not what I meant," she stuttered. "Hell, I don't know what I mean. I guess I'm just a little upset, and not thinking too clearly. It's not every day that I have a conversation with a dead person."

"You will get used to it."

She stopped pacing. "What do you mean by that?"

"We will have many conversations together."

"We will? Wait a minute. We can't. What will my neighbors think? Can anyone else hear you?"

"Only you."

"Why's that?"

"That is how it is."

"But why me? Why not go talk to someone else? Why not talk to Claire? She would love having a ghost in her house."

"You would have me talk with an idiot?"

"She's not that bad."

Tolomato laughed. "I would rather talk to a rock."

"But why me? Why are you talking to me?"

"Because you are Indian."

"I'm only half Cherokee," Ssabra protested. "I don't even know how to speak the language."

Tolomato sighed. "Yes. I know. I tried to talk to you in your native tongue, but you did not understand."

"You tried to talk to me in Cherokee?"

"Several times. 'Osiyo' is the Cherokee word for hello."

"Osiyo means hello? Really? That's what you were trying to say to me. Hello? Then you're the one who wrote on my bathroom mirror, and it was you I heard at the Huguenot Cemetery."

"Yes. Yes. That was me. I have been trying for days to communicate with you, but you have ignored everything I did. Before you ask, I also moved the cup across your table."

"Wow." She smiled. "And here I thought I was going crazy."

"You are not crazy, but you are beginning to make me that way."

"Sorry," she said, a little sheepishly. "I didn't mean to make you crazy. I just never believed in ghosts."

"There are probably ghosts who do not believe in you."

Ssabra's nerves were starting to settle down a bit. The more she listened to the voice, the more convinced she became that what she was experiencing was really happening. She no longer looked for hidden microphones, speakers, or cameras. She was actually starting to accept the possibility that she was standing in the middle of her living room, having a quiet conversation with a ghost. No longer frightened, she took a seat on the sofa and lit up a cigarette.

"Ah, tobacco," he said. "You are wise for someone so young. We should smoke when we talk of important things."

She took a puff, then set the cigarette in the ashtray. "That's right. I smelled tobacco when I first heard your voice. And I smelled it again, here in the apartment. That was you, wasn't it? But how did you get tobacco? Do they have such things on the other side?"

"You would be surprised to know of the things we have in the spirit world."

"Really? Can you tell me? What's it like over there?"

"My world is very much like yours, but we will talk of such things later. First, I must tell you why I am here, and why I have chosen you."

"Chosen?"

"To be the person who hears my voice."

"Why did you pick me?" Ssabra asked. "Why are you here?"

Tolomato explained. "A few days ago three women of magic came to this city in search of power and guidance. These women were like children playing with fire; they opened a doorway to the other side, allowing something dark and dangerous to come into this world. I too heard their call, and followed the dark one through to this side."

The voice in her head was starting to scare her. Getting up, Ssabra crossed the room and put a pot of water on the stove. She could still hear the Indian chief, but she didn't want to sit still and listen. She felt the need to be doing something with her hands.

"What came through?" she asked, stepping back from the stove.

"One of the old ones."

"Old ones?"

"A creature that lived in this land long before me. A thing of darkness with the power to change its shape, and wear the skins of others. A dark god called a Shiru."

"A Shiru." Ssabra said the word aloud, rolling the syllables on her tongue. She had never heard the name before. It sounded Japanese. "I've never heard of it."

He sighed and continued. "It has been a long time since the Shirus last lived in this land. A very long time. They were once considered gods by the native people. Knowing that the old ways were disappearing, the Shirus bred with humans so their bloodlines would be carried on to future generations. But the chiefs and medicine men told their people to fear anything that was not of the light, and the Shirus were cast down, driven from the villages to die of starvation. The offspring of the Shirus were put to death under the knife, or thrown into the cleansing flames of fire.

"The Shirus were hunted down and killed, crossing over to the eternal darkness of the spirit world. But one Shiru has returned, summoned by the voices of three women. A doorway was opened, and he stepped back into the world of the living, again taking his place as a dark god among the weak."

"How do you know all of this?" Ssabra asked, confused.

"Because I came back through the same opening before it closed," he replied. "I know the dark one is back, because I have seen it with my own eyes. I came through the doorway behind the Shiru, following the voices of the three women. I would have warned them of the danger they were in, but it was already too late."

"Too late?"

"The Shiru has already killed. He has taken the life of one of the women, she whose words opened the doorway between the two worlds."

"The Shiru killed someone?"

"Killed and consumed."

"But how? It's a spirit, like you. How can it hurt the living?"

"The Shiru is not like me. It is a thing of evil. The spirit world and this world are almost the same to such a creature. There it was only resting; here it is back at full strength. In this world it can again return to its old ways."

"But why did it kill the women?"

"It killed only one of them. Perhaps it was hungry. I do not know."

Ssabra made herself a cup of instant coffee, noticing that her hands were starting to shake. And why shouldn't her hands shake? It had been one hell of a night. First there was a crazy psychic in her home. Now she was in the middle of a conversation with a ghost, and talking about a spirit-monster eating people. Damn right her hands should be shaking.

"What does the Shiru look like?" she asked, stirring sugar into her coffee.

"The Shiru is a shape-shifter, and can take many forms. It can look like anyone it has killed and eaten, stealing their identity. It can look like a man, or even an animal. That is how the Shirus used to sneak into the villages long ago. They would enter the villages as men to steal the women, taking them back to their lair to mate.

"The Shiru can change its appearance, but it cannot disguise its reflection. Its true form can be seen in running waters, mirrors, and in glass."

"What does its true form look like?"

"Like nothing you have ever seen before, and like nothing you will ever want to see."

Ssabra was silent for a moment, thinking about

what had just been said. "I'll make sure to put a large mirror in my purse before I go out."

"You will need more than just a mirror when you do battle against the Shiru."

"When I do what?" She nearly choked on her coffee.

"When you do battle against the Shiru," Tolomato replied. "When you fight the dark one."

"You're out of your frigging mind. I'm not fighting this god/monster of yours. If you're so worried about the damn thing, then you fight it."

"The Shiru is no longer in my world. It is in yours. Someone among you must destroy it."

"Well, you had better look around for another volunteer, because I'm not your girl. I'm a tour guide; I'm not a monster fighter."

"But I have chosen you."

"Then choose someone else, because I'm not going to fight it."

"It is not so simple. I have chosen you to hear my voice. I cannot choose another. Not now."

"Okay. No problem. Let me just grab my sword and shield, and climb on top of my white horse, then we'll be off to fight the Shiru bogeyman."

"You have a horse?"

She laughed. "Of course I don't have a horse. I was being sarcastic. I live in an apartment. Where in the hell would I keep a horse?"

"I had a horse. He was a gift from the Spanish."

"Enough about horses already. I don't have a horse. Never did and never will. And I really don't want to hear about your horse. I'm also not going to fight any monster for you."

"But you were chosen."

"I don't care if I was chosen. Choose another."

There was a moment of silence, then Tolomato said, "There is no one else I can speak with. I have chosen you. Your people need your help. If we do not do something soon to stop the Shiru, others will die. And if we do not act quickly, then the old ones may return to this world. When that happens the darkness will return, and all of you will suffer."

Ssabra set down her cup of coffee and looked around the room. It was hard enough to believe that she was having a heated conversation with a ghost, but now the spirit of Chief Tolomato was asking her to fight an evil creature that had been released upon the world. A thing of darkness had returned to the land of the living, perhaps hoping to breed with humans in order to reestablish its hideous race on earth.

It all sounded like a really bad fantasy novel, but Ssabra had an awful feeling that what she was hearing was the truth. She really did hear the voice of someone who had crossed back over from the spirit world. And while she would rather go back to her normal life, she knew that nothing about her life would ever be normal again.

"Okay, you win," she sighed. "I'll help. Tell me what I have to do."

CHAPTER
16

It was Monday, and all hell seemed to be breaking loose at the police station. The *St. Augustine Record* had run an article about human remains being found for the second day in a row, suggesting that a homicidal maniac might be stalking the streets of the old city. The article had been front-page news, complete with file photos of the Tolomato Cemetery and the Old Drugstore.

The newspaper had hit the stands early that morning, and the phones had been ringing off the hook ever since. The police department was swamped with calls from upset and worried residents, mostly senior citizens who were absolutely certain something strange was going on in their neighborhood.

But it wasn't just the seniors who were worried. The police had been receiving phone calls from teachers, school kids, taxi drivers, and even fishermen. One man called to say that his wife had been missing for two days, convinced she must be one of the victims, and was actually relieved to learn that she had been sitting in jail after being arrested for prostitution.

In addition to the scores of phone calls they were receiving, quite a few people had taken it upon themselves to come down to the station to pass along information about the crime. Most of them filled out reports about the suspicious activity of a neighbor, or a coworker, suggesting that the particular person or persons just had to be guilty of something.

An elderly woman complained about the teenage boys who lived across the street, handing over a journal she had been keeping on the daily activities of the three young men. A local minister also stopped by the station, pointing his finger at the hard-rock band living down the street from him. According to the good minister, the members of the band were devil worshipers who practiced blood rituals. If there were any murders to be investigated, then the police should start with the band members.

There was also a middle-aged man who walked into the police station that morning, claiming to be the killer and demanding to be arrested. His confession might have been taken seriously, had he not had a history of making such statements on a regular basis. Instead of being locked up, he was put in a taxi and sent home to his wife.

Arriving at work a little before ten that morning, Jack Colvin squeezed through the crowd waiting in the lobby. He deliberately avoided making eye contact with any of them, because he just wasn't in the mood to answer questions. Not that he had any answers to give. It was still early, so the lab tests had not yet come back from the medical examiner's office. However, he did cast a glance toward the besieged desk sergeant as he crossed the room. The sergeant only smiled and shook his head.

Jack thought he was home free when he made it to his desk without being stopped, and he almost risked a smile, but then he spotted the mountain of paperwork awaiting him. It seemed additional reports needed to be filled out about the homicides, in triplicate. There was also a stack of messages from people wanting to talk with him, including two from the chief of police.

The detective coughed and rubbed his throat, feeling the invisible line where the ax was going to fall. If he didn't come up with a suspect and a motive, or at least some serious leads in the case, Chief Harris was going to have his head on a platter. Getting on the chief's bad side was never a pleasant experience, nor were the ass chewings that usually came as a result of it. Chief Harris had already left several messages on Jack's desk, which meant he wanted to see the detective immediately, if not sooner.

This would be a perfect time to be on vacation.

There was no way in hell Jack was going to walk into the police chief's office, not without having something to tell him. Since there were no suspects in the case, or witnesses, or leads, and since the lab reports hadn't come back yet, Detective Colvin decided his best course of action was to become invisible. He needed to make himself scarce, and do it quickly. Anyplace else would be a better place to be than where he was standing.

Looking around the room, he noticed that the desk

belonging to Detective Moats was also covered with paperwork and message memos. The desk was also unoccupied. He didn't know if Bill had come to work that morning, but if he had, then he too had decided to seek refuge elsewhere. Jack would call Bill's cell phone to see where his coworker was hiding, then the two of them could get together to work on the case.

He had just picked up the phone to call Detective Moats, when a striking young woman entered the room. She was tall and thin, with long black hair and dark eyes, her skin a rich tan color. She was dressed in tight black pants and a white blouse, and it looked as if she might be Puerto Rican, Filipino, or maybe even Native American.

Wow. Double wow. Maybe I shouldn't be in such a hurry to leave.

The woman stopped and studied the room for a moment, perhaps unsure of which detective she wanted to speak with. She looked toward Jack for a moment, glanced down at the sheet of paper she held, and then started walking his way. Jack hung up the phone and smiled.

"Yes, ma'am. May I help you?" He recognized the paper in her hand as department stationery, so the desk sergeant must have given her his name.

The woman offered him a faltering smile. "Are you Detective Colvin?"

"Yes, ma'am. In the flesh. Detective Jack Colvin."

She looked back down at the paper she held in her hand, making sure she had the right man, then folded the paper and put it into her pants pocket. "The man at the front desk said you're the one I should talk with. It's about something that happened at the Tolomato Cemetery a couple of nights ago."

"The Tolomato Cemetery? A couple of nights ago?" He played dumb for a moment, but his plan almost backfired.

The woman again glanced around the room, growing agitated. "Maybe I have the wrong person." She turned and started to leave.

"No. No. Please. You've got the right guy. I'm the detective in charge of the Tolomato Cemetery investigation. Forgive me if I sounded a bit standoffish; I haven't had my second cup of coffee yet."

She turned back around and smiled. "I understand completely. It takes several cups for me to get started in the morning."

Jack nodded, pleased he had found something they both had in common. It was always good to quickly build relationships with civilians, especially those who came to him with news about a murder investigation. "Please, have a seat, Ms. . . ."

"Onih. Ssabra Onih." She sat down on the chair on the opposite side of the desk, facing the detective.

"That's an unusual name. Is it French?"

"It's Indian," she replied. "My father's Cherokee."

"Really. That's interesting. You don't find too many Cherokees in Florida." The detective took a seat behind his desk. "Can I get you a cup of coffee, Miss Onih? It is Miss, isn't it? You're not wearing a wedding ring."

She smiled. "Yes, it's Miss. I'm not married. Thanks for the coffee, but I'll pass. I've already had my two cups for the morning. Any more caffeine and I'll be climbing the walls."

"Well, we certainly don't want that. Not in this place. Somebody will think you're trying to escape." Jack laughed and leaned forward in his chair, giving her his undivided attention. "Now, what can I do for you? You said you know something about what happened at the Tolomato?"

Ssabra looked around, making sure no one else was listening to their conversation. Several officers were in the room, but they were all occupied with other business. She cleared her throat. "I know about what happened the other night. At least I know some of it."

The woman hesitated, and fell silent for a moment. It was obvious she was having a difficult time approaching the subject. Perhaps she was even a little bit frightened. Maybe she had seen a homicide take place, or was somehow involved with the crime.

Jack was hoping she wasn't involved, because it would be a damn shame to put someone so attractive behind bars. She would not look good in prison orange.

"Take your time," he said, encouraging her to go on but not to rush.

Licking her lips, she said, "I know someone was killed in the cemetery the other night. A woman. You found her body, but there hasn't been much about it in the paper. There was a short article in yesterday's paper about human remains being found, but all it said was that police were not ruling out the possibility of a homicide."

"No. There wasn't much in yesterday's newspaper, other than a brief write-up about the remains being found," Jack said, nodding.

"Why is that?"

"Truthfully, we weren't sure if a homicide had actually taken place at the cemetery. The remains we found could have come from anywhere."

"The murder happened at the cemetery," she said, looking increasingly more uncomfortable.

"And how do you know that? Were you a witness to the crime?"

"No." She shook her head. "Someone else was a witness. They told me about it."

Jack picked up a pencil, and began jotting down notes on a pad of paper. "And what exactly did they tell you?"

She coughed nervously, and continued. "They told me a woman was killed in the cemetery a few nights ago, and that she was not alone when she died. Two other women were with her, but they ran away."

"Two other women?" Jack stopped writing for a moment. "But no one has called to report a crime. If two women witnessed the murder, at least one of them would have called by now."

"They're scared."

"Scared because they broke into the cemetery?"

"No. Scared of what they've seen, and what they did."

"And what did they do?"

Miss Onih took a deep breath, and slowly let it out. She was obviously trying hard to keep her composure. Jack wondered why she was so nervous. Was she somehow involved in the crime?

"The three women broke into the cemetery to conduct a magical ceremony. They were spiritualists, or maybe witches, and were trying to obtain spirit guides."

"Are you also a witch, Miss Onih?" Jack interrupted.

"No. I'm not a witch."

"Sorry. You just seem to know a lot about what happened that night."

"I'm not a witch. I'm a tour guide. Look, someone told me what I'm telling you. They asked me to bring the information to the police."

"Why didn't they come themselves?"

"They couldn't come here."

"Why not?"

"I'll get to that in a minute. Do you want to hear what I have to say? If not, then I'll be glad to get out of your hair."

"No. Please, go on." Jack almost grinned. Miss Onih had quite a temper. She also knew something, because, so far, what she was saying matched up with some of the evidence found at the Tolomato. A leather bag containing candles, sage, and quartz crystals had been found at the scene, and Jack suspected some kind of occult ritual had taken place. She said three women were attempting to obtain spirit guides from the graveyard, and that would qualify as a magical ritual.

Ssabra continued. "The women were trying to obtain spirit guides, but they accidentally opened a doorway to the spirit world and something evil came through."

"Something evil? You mean like a poltergeist?"

She shook her head. "Much worse than that. I'm really not sure how to describe it. I've been told it's a creature that lived in this area a long time ago. It's called a Shiru."

Jack wrote down the name. "Can you describe this Shiru? How big is it? What does it look like? Does it have any identifying marks or nasty habits?"

"You're being sarcastic."

The detective looked up from his paper. "I'm sorry, but can you really blame me? You just told me that three witches accidentally opened a doorway to the spirit world and let a monster in. I take it this monster ate one of the women; at least it ate most of her, because all that's left are tiny bits of skin, bones, and a few molars. Oddly enough, no one has reported any monsters running around St. Augustine. You'd think something like that would have been on the news by now, but maybe people think it's just another tourist attraction."

"No one has reported a monster, because the Shiru can change its shape. It can even look like a person."

He couldn't help but laugh. "Ah, that explains it. A shape-shifting monster. I should have known."

"This is stupid. I knew you wouldn't believe me."

"You have to admit that your story is a bit hard to swallow. Maybe if you told me where you heard it. . . ."

"Tolomato."

"Excuse me?"

"Tolomato told me."

Jack looked at her, wondering what to write down. "Who?"

"Tolomato. An Indian chief. Leader of the Guales."

"Tolomato, as in Tolomato Cemetery?"

Ssabra nodded.

"I see." He quit writing and put down his pencil. "And when did Chief Tolomato tell you about the murder in his cemetery? Was it recently, or in a past life?''

She glared at the detective. ''Listen, I know you think I'm some kind of flake. I can't blame you. I didn't want to come here today, but he made me. Up until last night I was leading a normal life. I'm a tour guide. I have a nice little apartment. I have no problems in my life. At least I didn't have until recently. Now I've got a dead Indian chief talking to me, and writing words on my bathroom mirror.

''Maybe I am crazy. Tolomato told me about what happened at the cemetery. He says a great evil has been released, and that the Shiru will kill again.''

Ssabra stood up and pulled the slip of paper from her pants pocket. Borrowing the detective's pencil, she wrote her name, address, and phone number on the paper and handed it to him. ''I told you what I came here to say. I know you don't believe me, and I really don't care. I've done my job, and I want no more part of it. You can call me if you need more information, but don't call if you just want to make fun of me.''

With that the young woman turned and walked away, leaving the room. Jack watched her go, and then looked down at the paper lying on his desk. He sighed. ''Why are all the good-looking women crazy in the head?''

CHAPTER
17

A flush of embarrassment warmed Ssabra's face as she left the police station. She looked neither left nor right as she walked across the lobby, avoiding eye contact with the other people waiting to be seen. Pushing the door open, she left the building and headed for the parking lot.

Her embarrassment turned to anger by the time she reached her car, causing her hands to shake and making it hard to put her key into the door lock. She glanced around to see if anyone was watching her, took a deep breath to steady her nerves, and tried again. Finally, she was able to get the key into the lock, and open the door. Climbing into the car, she quickly closed the door, but she didn't start the engine.

Her hands still shook with emotion, and she was worried about her ability to drive. It wouldn't do to get into an accident before she got out of the parking lot, especially since it was the parking lot for the St.

Augustine Police Department. That definitely would not look good on her driving record. If she did get into an accident before leaving the parking lot, she would probably be asked to step back inside the building to fill out a police report.

There was no way she could go back inside the station, not after humiliating herself. Detective Colvin would have already told his fellow detectives and coworkers about the crazy young woman who had paid him a visit. He was probably telling the story right now, clustered with his friends around the office coffeepot, having a good laugh at her expense.

She hit the steering wheel with her fist, a flash of pain shooting up her right arm. "Dumb. Dumb. Dumb. How on earth could I be so stupid?"

It had been foolish for her to go to the police. There was no way anyone was going to believe a story as outrageous as hers. She was damn lucky they even let her leave the station. They could have turned her over to the local mental hospital, where she would have been locked away for her own protection, undergoing a series of shock therapy sessions, and maybe even a lobotomy.

Come on. They don't do lobotomies anymore.

Ssabra let out a sigh and leaned forward, resting her head on the steering wheel. She knew it was a stupid idea, but still she had come. Why? Other than getting laughed at, what had she hoped to accomplish?

The answer to her question was simple: she had come to the police station because Tolomato had insisted that she warn someone in authority about the

Shiru. She had listened to the voice of a dead Indian chief, which, in fact, may be nothing more than the beginning of a brain tumor.

No wonder the detective hadn't believed her. At least he had been patient enough to listen to the whole story. Had the tables been turned, she probably would have tossed him out on his ass at the first mention of ghosts or monsters.

She sat back up and looked into the mirror. Her face was still flushed, but her hands weren't shaking quite so badly anymore. Grabbing a pack of gum out of her purse, she stuck two sticks into her mouth and started chewing. She was still pretty upset, and wanted to calm down a little more before starting for home.

What she should have done was only tell the detective part of the story. She could have said that she overheard a couple of people in her tour group whispering about a homicide, dropping hints about the identity of the victim. She could have passed along some of the information, without having to mention anything about a dead Indian chief. She might even have been able to leave out the part about the Shiru, although she didn't know how she could have warned the detective about the monster without talking about it.

Tolomato had convinced her that the Shiru had to be stopped before it could kill again, and her help was needed to stop it. He had talked her into going to see someone in authority for help, insisting that they would listen to her if her heart was good and her tongue truthful. Tolomato was obviously used to living in simpler times, because a good heart and a truthful tongue didn't always work in the twenty-first century.

"Yeah, the detective offered to help me all right: he offered to help me find the front door."

Maybe she wouldn't feel so bad about the whole thing had she spoken with a fat, balding detective. Ssabra wouldn't have been quite so embarrassed if an old fat guy had laughed at her. But Detective Jack Colvin wasn't fat, or old. He was around her age, in pretty good shape, and rather pleasing on the eyes. He came across as a nice guy, with a smile that made his blue eyes light up. She could almost imagine the two of them on a date, having dinner at some candlelit little restaurant.

Ssabra laughed. "Fat chance of that ever happening. After today, if I come within twenty feet of the guy he'll probably have a restraining order taken out on me."

Detective Colvin's laugh had cut her like a knife, and she had almost run out of the office. She couldn't blame him for laughing at her, but that didn't dull the pain any. He had cut her deeply, and she would never be able to look him in the eyes again.

She let out a sigh and shook her head. Ghost Indian chiefs. Evil monsters. She almost didn't believe the story herself. Maybe she had finally gone off the deep end. She had given one ghost tour too many, and her mind had finally snapped. The voice she heard was only her imagination. Hell, maybe she hadn't even gone to the police. Maybe she was still in her bed, only dreaming that she was sitting inside her stuffy car, working two pieces of Juicy Fruit gum with her back teeth.

The thought that she was safely in her bed had just passed through Ssabra's mind, when she accidentally bit the inside of her mouth, causing her eyes to water. No, the pain was definitely real, which meant she was indeed sitting inside her car, and not just dreaming it.

Starting the car, she backed out of her parking space and started for home. Traffic was light in St. Augustine, so it only took fifteen minutes to make it back to her apartment. Climbing the stairs to the second floor, she hesitated before unlocking the door.

The last few times she had been in her apartment surprises had awaited her, spooky surprises that came close to scaring the hell out of her. She just didn't know if she could put up with such shenanigans today, especially after what she had already gone through.

Putting the key into the lock, she opened the door and entered her apartment. The interior was quiet, the kitchen and living room empty.

She closed the door, almost expecting to see a ghostly shape drift past, or witness another object slide across the room. When nothing happened, she said aloud, "Tolomato, are you here?"

A few seconds passed, but no voice answered her. Ssabra repeated her question, speaking in a louder voice, "Chief Tolomato, are you in here?"

Again no answer. The only sound to be heard was the soft humming of the refrigerator. The chief must be elsewhere, doing whatever it was that ghosts did in the daytime. She wondered if he had been with her at the police station, even though she hadn't heard his voice during the meeting. If he had been there, then he already knew what a dumb idea it was for her to go to the authorities.

"Great. Just great. I do what he wants, and now that I need to speak with him he's nowhere to be found. Typical."

She set her purse on the coffee table. "You had better hide from me, because I'm going to give you an earful when I find you." She laughed, amused by her own statement. "If I can find you. If you really exist."

She thought her last statement, a direct challenge to his existence, might flush out her phantom friend, but the room remained quiet and still. No voices. No sliding coffee cups. No ghost of any kind. Not even the spirit of a little girl, as Claire's supposedly psychic aunt had claimed to have seen.

"One thing for sure, I'm going to start looking for a different place to live. This apartment has become entirely too crowded."

Ssabra crossed the room and entered the bathroom, almost expecting to see words spelled out on her bathroom mirror, but the glass was void of lettering. A quick check of the shower stall also proved to be without words.

"Osiyo," she said, remembering what had been written on the mirror. Tolomato said it was Cherokee for "hello," but it might have been the name of a mixed drink for all she knew. She said the word aloud a second time, but there was no reply.

She left the bathroom and went into the bedroom,

again finding no evidence that a spirit visitor had come to call. Ssabra was beginning to wonder if her encounter with Tolomato had actually taken place. Maybe she had just imagined the whole incident.

"I knew it. I'm going frigging nuts."

Wanting to let a little more light into the room, she pulled the cord to raise the blinds covering the window. She had forgotten what time it was, and that it was a Monday, her embarrassing conference with the police detective throwing her completely off schedule. Therefore, as the blinds in her bedroom were lifted, Ssabra was treated to a spectacular view of the fat man in the next apartment building. The man was on his porch watering his plants, dressed only in a pair of Speedo swim trunks, his enormous butt aimed directly at her.

"Oh, Jesus," she said, jumping back from the window and covering her eyes. "I'm blind."

Her day had just been made complete. Not only had she suffered embarrassment and humiliation, but the retinas of both her eyes were now damaged by a sight too horrifying to describe. If she didn't need therapy before, she would surely need it now.

Still shielding her eyes from the sight that lay beyond the glass, she stepped forward and quickly lowered the blinds.

"Whew. Better. That was a close one. Never raise the blinds on a weekday. You know better than that."

Turning away from the window, she studied the clothes hanging in her closet, trying to decide what she would wear for that afternoon's tour. The weather was going to be warm, so something simple and light would be the obvious choice. Something cheerful and bright to take her mind off laughing police detectives and dead Indian chiefs. But even her most colorful outfit probably couldn't keep the events of the past couple of days from intruding into her thoughts.

She turned and looked around the room, suddenly feeling as if she might not be alone. "Tolomato, are you here?"

There was no reply. The only sound in the bedroom was the soft ticking of her alarm clock. Tolomato obviously wasn't in the room with her, and she was beginning to have serious doubts about his existence. Maybe she had just imagined everything, having given one ghost tour too many. Maybe she was getting as kooky as Claire's psychic aunt.

"That's me, Ssabra Onih. Resident psychic and ghost talker."

CHAPTER
18

After his strange conversation with Miss Ssabra Onih, Detective Colvin grabbed the stack of paperwork off his desk and slipped out the back door. He had too much work to do to be bothered with crazy people, and even crazier stories. He also didn't want to have a meeting with the chief, not until after he had gotten the lab tests on the two victims back from the medical examiner's office.

Checking to make sure the coast was clear, he hurried across the parking lot to his unmarked patrol car. Slipping behind the wheel, he started the engine and drove west, putting distance between himself and those he would rather not talk with. Waiting until he was several blocks away, he called the dispatcher to say that he was following up on a few leads, and would be back later. He was actually heading over to a little bagel place on U.S. 1, and had a sneaking suspicion that Bill might already be there. The two of them often used The Bagel Hut as a makeshift headquarters when they didn't want to be at the station.

His hunch was right on the money, because he spotted Bill's car as he pulled into the parking lot behind the Hut.

"Son of a bitch. I knew it." Jack should have been angry, but he couldn't help but smile. The two detectives were both thinking along the same lines, neither one of them wanting to hang around the police station amid all the confusion, and with the police chief on the warpath.

Grabbing the stack of paperwork off the passenger seat, he climbed out of the car and headed for the restaurant. Bill was sitting at one of the back booths, well away from the other customers, an impressive pile of folders stacked on the table in front of him. Jack was almost to the booth when Detective Moats looked up at him and grinned.

"About time you got here. I was beginning to worry."

"Nice disappearing job you pulled," Jack replied, sliding in on the other side of the booth. "You could have let me know where you were hiding."

Bill faked a frown. "I left you a note. Didn't you get it?"

"No. I didn't get a note. That's because you didn't leave me one."

The frown turned back into a smile. "You're right. I didn't leave a note. Didn't have time. Chief Harris was stomping around the place like an angry bull, so I figured I had better get out of there while I still could. You knew where to find me."

"Yeah, I knew where to look." Jack got up and walked to the counter, ordering a coffee and a toasted cinnamon and raisin bagel. He would have gotten something for Bill, but his partner already had a full coffee and an empty bagel plate sitting in front of him. Paying for the items, he returned to the booth.

"What have you got there?" Jack asked, pointing at the stack of folders sitting in front of his partner.

Bill took a sip of his coffee before speaking. "I was just going over your report from yesterday. Interesting stuff, but I'm glad I had the day off."

"I wish I was off yesterday." He took a bite out of his bagel, nearly burning his tongue on a hot raisin. "By the way, how was the fishing?"

"Not bad. I caught a sea bass that was definitely a keeper."

"Did you keep it?"

"Of course I kept it. It's in my freezer now. I'll give you a call when I decide to cook it. I'll provide the fish, you bring the beer."

"Deal."

"I was also going over the lab reports from the medical examiner's office."

Jack nearly choked on his coffee. "You have the lab reports? How in the hell did you get them?"

"I stopped by the office on my way over here. Figured it would be quicker than waiting around for them to send the reports to us."

"Damn it to hell, I've been waiting all morning for those reports. I even called twice to check on them, and they promised to send them to me as soon as they were finished. I'm supposed to be the lead detective on this case, but a fat lot of good it's doing me. They didn't even bother to tell me that they had already given the reports to you. I swear, I don't get any respect."

Bill leaned forward and patted Jack on the back of the hand. "I still respect you."

Jack snatched his hand back. "Fuck you, Moats. Eat shit and die."

The older detective roared with laughter, nearly spilling his coffee.

"So, what do the lab reports say?"

Detective Moats pulled one of the file folders from the stack, and slid it across the table to his partner. "Here, read it for yourself."

Opening the folder, Jack read through the stack of reports. According to the tests, there were indeed two different victims. Based on bone, blood, teeth, and hair samples, and DNA testing, the forensic examiner had determined that the first victim was a Caucasoid female, between forty-five and sixty years of age, and around five feet five inches tall, with type O positive blood.

The second victim, whose remains had been found in the Dumpster, was a Caucasoid male, between twenty-five to thirty-five years of age, around six feet tall, with type A positive blood. The testing also determined that the second victim had been a heavy user of alcohol and Flexeril.

"Damn, it is two homicides." Jack flipped to the next report and read down the page. "What's this?"

"What's what?" Bill leaned forward, but couldn't read the report upside down.

"It says that a high concentration of hydrochloric acid, along with the enzyme pepsin, was found in the soil sample taken from beneath the remains of the first victim. A similar chemical combination was found on the bone and teeth samples." He glanced through the report about the second victim. "Hydrochloric acid and pepsin were also found on the remains of the male victim."

Jack looked up at his partner. "Hydrochloric acid? You think the perp might have put his victims in an acid bath to get rid of the bodies?"

Bill took a sip of coffee and nodded. "It's a possibility. That would explain why we only have a few pieces of bone, teeth, and skin to go on. Acid can eat a body up pretty fast. But you've got to remember that hydrochloric acid and pepsin also occur naturally in nature."

"Naturally? I'm not sure about where you live, but it doesn't occur naturally in my neighborhood."

"Sure it does, and right in your own body. Hydrochloric acid and the enzyme pepsin make up the digestive juice in your stomach."

"Digestive juice?" Jack frowned. "Jesus, Bill. Are you trying to tell me that the victims died of a massive case of indigestion?"

"I'm not suggesting anything. I was just stating a fact."

Jack was about to make a comment, but was interrupted by the shrill ringing of Bill's cell phone. "Why can't you pick a normal ring?"

"I like to be different." Detective Moats answered the phone on the second ring. It was a short conversation, but Bill was frowning by the time he hung up.

"Bad news?"

Bill nodded. "Finish your coffee, we've got work

Owl Goingback

to do. That was the station. A third body was just discovered."

"Another victim? Jesus, that makes three in three days." Jack downed his coffee and stood up. He also unhooked his cell phone from his belt, wondering why it hadn't rung. "But why did the station call you? Don't they know that I'm lead detective on the case?"

"Yes, but they also know we're working together, so it doesn't really matter who they call first. But if it makes you feel any better, I'll let you answer my phone the next time it rings."

Jack laughed. "Bite me, Moats. Just bite me."

The remains of the murdered woman had been found behind a gift shop in the old section of town, only a few blocks from the bay. The owner of the gift shop lived above the store, and she had found the body after letting her little dachshund out to pee that morning. The wiener dog had actually been rolling in the remains when the owner came out to call her back inside.

At first the dog's owner didn't know what her puppy had been playing with. The remains were scattered around the alley that ran behind the gift shop, and it was hard to make out what it was. She thought someone had dumped food scraps in the alley, or maybe something had fallen off a truck. There were several restaurants in the area, so it might have been garbage meant for a Dumpster.

But then she saw the naked lower torso of a woman. Just the legs and pelvis, vagina, and part of one hip. Nothing more. The feet were also missing, torn off at the ankles. Scattered around the torso were pieces of flesh and bone, ranging in size from a few inches to half a foot in length.

Jack Colvin looked down at the remains of the dead woman and felt his stomach do a slow roll. It looked as if she had been shoved headfirst into a wood chipper, or as if a pack of wild dogs had ripped her to pieces.

They also found the victim's tattered clothing and shoes in the alleyway: black work shoes, black slacks, and a white, long-sleeve shirt. It was the kind of clothing waiters and waitresses often wore, which might mean the victim had been employed in one of the local restaurants. The pants and shirt were torn and dirty, but they did not have any bloodstains, so the victim had not been wearing the clothing when she died.

A purse was discovered lying a few feet away from the shirt. The contents of the small leather purse included a driver's license, several credit cards, money, makeup, a pack of chewing gum, a roll of breath mints, a couple of paycheck stubs, birth control pills, and four condoms. Ribbed.

For the first time in days, they might actually have a name to go along with the remains. At least they had a possible name, because there was no way to be one hundred percent certain of the victim's identity without further tests. A photo ID wasn't nearly as useful when the victim didn't have a head.

According to the driver's license, homicide victim number three was Cindy Hawkins, age twenty-four, of 1921 Palmetto Drive, St. Augustine, Florida. The paycheck stubs indicated that she was employed as a waitress at Harry's Seafood and Grill, a restaurant located only a few blocks from the crime scene.

Jotting down the information from the license and check stubs, Detective Moats called the police station and requested a unit be sent to the victim's address. He wanted to know if anyone was home at the residence: a husband, boyfriend, roommate, or relative. If so, then he also wanted to know if anyone was missing. He sent a second unit over to Harry's to find out if Ms. Hawkins still worked for the restaurant, and when she had last been seen.

While Detective Moats was making the phone calls to the station, Jack walked back over to take another look at the body. He didn't take a long look, because just a glance was enough to make his breakfast want to come back up on him. But a quick glance was all that was needed for what he wanted to know. The woman's vagina was badly lacerated, indicating she had been violently raped prior to being murdered.

Despite the grisly nature of the homicide, there was no blood to speak of on the cobblestone street. It should have been splattered all over the place, bucketsful of it, but the street and the surrounding buildings were damn near spotless. Only a few drops were to be found on the bricks, looking as if the perpetrator took time to mop up after murdering and mutilating the young woman.

The lack of blood led Jack to believe that Cindy Hawkins was murdered somewhere other than where her body now lay. But, unlike the two previous homicides, there was clear evidence to suggest that this crime had taken place in St. Augustine.

Cindy was a resident of the old city, and she apparently worked in one of the local restaurants. She had not been killed in some other town, in some other state, with her remains dumped in the alley for a little wiener dog to find. She had been raped and murdered in her hometown, which meant there was indeed a killer stalking the city.

Detective Moats walked up to where Jack stood. "I once saw something like this. Years ago, when I was in Alaska."

Jack turned to look at his partner, but didn't say anything.

"I was on a two week vacation with a couple of old friends. We were out salmon fishing, and came across a camper that had been attacked and killed by a grizzly bear. The bear had eaten most of him: legs, arms, internal organs. All that was left was the head and chest, the bony parts that the bear probably didn't want.

"The grizzly had eaten its fill, leaving the remains for the three of us to stumble upon—the naked upper torso of a man, still warm and steaming on a cold October morning. I had nightmares for a year."

"Jesus, Bill. You never told me that story."

"It's not something I like to think about." Bill looked up from the body. "I only brought it up now because there's something similar between the bear attack and what we have here."

Bill pointed at the body of Cindy Hawkins. "Look at her ankles. Look at how ragged the flesh is around the bone. Her feet weren't cut off, not with any knife. They were either torn off, or they were chewed off."

"Chewed off?" Jack was surprised. "You're not suggesting we have a grizzly bear running around St. Augustine, or some kind of wild animal?"

"I'm not suggesting anything," Bill replied. "I'm just making an observation. The body of this young woman looks a lot like the camper we found in Alaska. Another thing, there's not much blood."

"Which means she was murdered someplace else, and her body was dumped here."

Bill nodded. "That's probably the case, but there wasn't much blood with the camper either. The bear had licked up damn near every drop."

Jack felt his stomach rumble, and knew the cinnamon bagel he had for breakfast was about to do a slow march back up his throat. "Dammit, Bill. You're playing hell with my indigestion. I need a cigarette."

He walked away from the crime scene, ducking under the yellow barrier tape that had been strung around the area. The body of the murdered woman was hard enough to look at without getting sick, but Bill had just made things worse with his story about bear attacks and half-eaten campers. Detective Moats must have an ironclad stomach to be able to think of such things at a time like this.

Choosing a place to stand that was out of everyone's way, he lit up a cigarette and turned to watch the other officers hard at work. One thing for sure: the three homicides that had taken place in St. Augustine would no longer be just a local case. The State Police would want to get involved in the investigation, maybe even the FBI. Police Chief Harris was probably on the phone at that very moment, calling in the big guns.

Jack sighed. He didn't mind it so much that other agencies were going to get involved. Truthfully, he could use the help. The FBI had equipment and connections not available to local cops. They also had some of the finest laboratories in the country.

The National Center for the Analysis of Violent Crime was based at the FBI Academy in Quantico, Virginia. The Bureau also had a rapid response unit known as the Child Abduction and Serial Killer Unit (CASKU), which was designed to assist local law enforcement agencies with investigative support and technical coordination. He just hated the attitudes of some of the federal agents, who acted as if local police units were nothing more than clubhouses for country bumpkins.

If only he and Detective Moats could solve the homicides before any outside help arrived. It would be a real shot in the arm for their careers. When word got out about the third murder there was going to be one hell of a panic in the old town. The mayor and city leaders were going to be screaming for answers, and he just didn't have any to give them.

Think, man. Think. You've been a detective for years. Use your mind. What are you missing here?

The clues might be lying right before him, but damned if he could put them together. The first two homicides had certain similarities, but they were nothing at all like the third. But maybe they did have something in common, maybe his partner's bear story had some merit after all.

The body of Ms. Cindy Hawkins looked like it had been attacked and partially eaten by a wild animal, and the remains of the first two victims contained a high concentration of hydrochloric acid and pepsin. Hydrochloric acid and pepsin, two chemical substances commonly found in stomach acid.

Could all three homicides have been the result of an animal attack? Were the first two victims eaten, and the third victim partially eaten, by the same beast? Surely not, for even the largest grizzly bear couldn't consume two and a half full-grown people in just three days. But what if there was more than one animal?

A pack of dogs. Rottweilers, or maybe pit bulls.

Still, Jack didn't know of too many animals smart enough to toss their leftovers into a Dumpster, like what had been found at the second crime scene. Nor did he know of any animals that raped their victims prior to eating them. But what if they were dealing with some new kind of animal, something completely alien to Florida.

Alien.

Maybe something had escaped from a zoo, or a wildlife refuge, or perhaps something exotic and deadly had been smuggled in aboard a ship. They had been looking for a crazed murderer, when maybe they should have been searching for a land shark, or perhaps a polar bear with a misguided sense of direction, or some other kind of monster.

Monster.

The detective felt his heart skip a beat, an image suddenly coming to mind. Not the horrific image of mutilated bodies and pieces of flesh, or of grizzly bears and dead campers. On the contrary, what he thought of at that particular moment was rather pleasing to the senses, for it was an image of an attractive young woman with long black hair, big eyes, and a great figure.

Ssabra Onih had come into the station early that morning to see him, with a crazy story about a strange creature stalking the streets of St. Augustine. The young woman claimed she had gotten her information from a dead Indian chief, which only added to the incredibility of the tale she told.

Jack had dismissed Miss Onih as just another nut case, attractive but insane. He had even laughed at her story.

He felt a funny sensation start to settle into the pit of his stomach. What if there were more truth to the woman's story than he was willing to admit? What if she actually knew something? Could it be possible that some kind of beast was running around the old city, an animal no one had ever seen before? If so, then how long did he have before it claimed another victim?

Jack wasn't sure if he believed in monsters, but he wasn't about to take any chances. He had three vicious homicides on his hands, and he damn sure didn't want any more. Ssabra Onih might have a screw loose, but that didn't mean she might not be useful. One thing for sure, he was definitely going to give her a call.

CHAPTER
19

Ssabra went through the motions of a tour guide that afternoon, reciting memorized speeches with little or no emotion, her mind preoccupied with thoughts of ghosts and her visit to the police station. Luckily, she had done the tours so many times she really didn't have to concentrate on what was being said. Here was the old Spanish quarters, blah, blah, blah. And over here used to be the military hospital, la de da.

None of the group complained about her abilities as a tour guide. They were quite content with the memorized speeches she spouted at the various historic sights. Nor did they ask too many questions, for which she was extremely grateful. Her mind was so rattled from the day's events, she probably couldn't have answered any questions had they been asked. She could barely remember her own name, let alone answer a question posed by some smart-ass history buff trying to impress his fellow coworkers.

The afternoon tour wrapped up just as the sun was starting to set, casting long shadows over the old plaza. Ssabra had a couple of hours to herself before she needed to get ready for the evening's ghost tour. She thought about going home for dinner, but she just wasn't in the mood to go back to her apartment.

Nor was she in the mood to eat at one of the restaurants in town. She had just spent two hours with a large group of noisy people, so the last thing in the world she wanted was to sit inside a crowded diner.

Walking through the Plaza de la Constitución, giving the antique brass cannons little more than a passing glance, she found a bench sitting empty in the shade of a towering oak tree. Glad to find a place to sit down, Ssabra plopped down on the bench, stretching her legs out in front of her.

At one of the benches on the other side of the plaza sat a middle-aged Hispanic couple, obviously worn out from too much walking. The man was short and ruddy, but he had a smile that looked to be a permanent fixture on his face. His wife was tall and thin, with long dark hair that seemed to glisten in the light of the setting sun. She was massaging her husband's shoulders, at the same time keeping an eye on the three small children playing nearby on one of the old cannons. Every once in a while she would shout a warning in Spanish, advising the children to be careful so as not to get hurt.

The sight of the happy but tired couple and their three children pulled at the heartstrings deep inside of Ssabra's chest. She and Alan had talked about having children once they were married. They wanted a matched set, a boy and a girl, and wanted to have them while they were still young enough to enjoy being parents.

They had spent long hours debating what they would name their children, where they would send them to school, and what sports and activities they would be involved with. Alan would be the ideal dad, planning family outings on the weekends, and taking part in all evening activities. Ssabra would be the world's greatest mom, packing lunches for the children before they left for school, doctoring cuts and scrapes, listening to stories of their adventures over home-cooked meals, and helping them with their homework in the evening.

Everything would have been perfect, but fate had pointed a cruel finger at them one gray November afternoon on a rural Iowa road. Ssabra had told Alan it was much too cold to go riding in his Fiat Spider convertible, especially with the top down, but he wanted one final spin before storing the little sports car for the winter.

About five miles out of town, they came upon a wooded lane where shadows lay heavy upon the road. Alan never saw the patch of black ice, and didn't realize they were in trouble until the car started to slide. He immediately lifted his foot off the accelerator, but was too late. The little car missed the curve and went airborne over a drainage ditch.

On the other side of the ditch was a fence of wooden posts and barbed wire. The car hit the fence at an angle, shearing off two of the posts.

There was a high-pitched twang as the strands of barbed wire snapped like guitar strings. One of those strands whipped back as it broke, catching Alan around the throat and cutting his flesh to the bone. He died within minutes, drowning in his own blood.

Ssabra shook her head and blinked her eyes, pushing back the memories before the tears came. She looked around the plaza, noticing that the Hispanic couple were no longer sitting on the bench across from her. They had gathered their three children, and were now making their way across the street to the church. She watched them until they vanished from sight, then turned to see who else was walking through the area.

She remained sitting on the bench for another hour, then decided to grab a bite of food before heading back to work. She didn't want much, so she purchased a club sandwich from a little coffee shop on St. George Street. It was still early in the evening, but a couple of street musicians had already taken up position on the narrow avenue, risking a run-in with the local authorities and the possibility of being arrested.

Giving a couple of dollars to each of the musicians, she took her sandwich back to the plaza to eat it. Unfortunately, someone had already claimed the bench she had been sitting on, so she was forced to eat her dinner seated on the ground next to one of the old cannons.

Finishing her meal, Ssabra slowly strolled back to the office to get ready for her ghost tour. She was giving a tour of the south side of the city that night, which was usually a little less hectic than those given on the north side. It was also a lot less crowded.

Arriving at the office, she went into the bathroom to slip into her costume. Once dressed, she put a new candle into her lantern, checked to make sure she had a lighter with her, and then headed out the front door to meet her group.

The south side tour started at nine p.m., with the participants gathering together in front of the Lightner Museum. Since she had time to kill, Ssabra chatted with some of the tour members while she waited for everyone to arrive. She never knew who would end up in her group. Once she had half a dozen horror writers in her party, who were in town for a book signing at the local Barnes & Noble.

By nine o'clock all but two of the twenty-five people in her group had shown up. She stalled for a couple more minutes, then decided to get the show on the road. The missing two people had either changed their minds about taking the tour, or they were hopelessly lost. If they did show up at the office after the tour had started, one of the employees would help them to catch up with the group.

Ssabra led her group away from the museum, traveling down unlit cobblestone streets that were just perfect for the telling of ghost stories. Slipping into her role of spooky storyteller, she described the various hauntings that were starting to make St. Augustine famous. She talked about the bed and breakfasts where guests checked in, but they never checked out. She pointed out the lighthouse across the bay, informing her audience that the ghost of the old keeper still climbed the spiral staircase each and every night. And she told the group about an un-

solved murder that had taken place in the city several
years earlier.

The tour concluded on St. George Street, with Ssabra making a point of ending in front of a fudge
and candy shop. There was nothing like a slice of
homemade fudge to top off the evening. Many of the
people in her group agreed, hurrying inside the store
to purchase a late-night treat.

The tour guide was just saying her good-byes,
when a couple of the members in the group asked if
she would take them to the cemeteries on the north
side of the town. Apparently, they had read the
morning paper, and knew about the human remains
that had been found. Ssabra hadn't read the paper
that morning, and was surprised to learn more remains had been found behind the Old Drugstore.

She wondered if the remains found in the cemetery, and those found behind the Old Drugstore,
were from the same victim. Ssabra was also concerned about how safe it would be to take someone
to the Tolomato, but the police were probably keeping a close watch on the area. The eight o'clock tour
groups had already been to the old cemeteries, and
there had been no reports of danger.

Even though she was fairly sure the area was safe,
Ssabra tried to beg off from doing additional duty as
a tour guide. It had been one hell of a day, and all
she wanted was to go home. But one of the men
offered to pay an extra forty dollars for her time. He
even promised a generous tip.

As tired as she was, she should have turned the
offer down. But forty dollars plus tip was good

money for a presentation that would probably only take fifteen minutes. Besides, both the Tolomato and the Huguenot cemeteries were only a short walk from the north end of St. George Street. She could pay the graveyards a quick visit and then be done for the night, with a little extra money in her pocket.

Ssabra realized she had made a mistake when they arrived at the Tolomato Cemetery, because everything Chief Tolomato had said to her came back in a flash, causing goosebumps to break out along her arms. She had been trying all day not to think about the dead Indian chief, or the Shiru. But now, as she stopped in front of the cemetery, she couldn't help but wonder what kind of evil creature might be lurking in the darkness.

Swallowing hard to keep her voice from trembling, she turned to the others and told the ghost stories connected with the ancient burial ground. She only told two stories, and she talked faster than she normally did, wanting to be done with her tales and away from the spooky graveyard.

Finishing up at the Tolomato, she led her handful of thrill seekers to the Huguenot Cemetery. The Huguenot wasn't as dark as the other cemetery, and she didn't feel isolated and alone when standing in front of its gates. No matter where she stood at the Huguenot, she could still see traffic moving along San Marco Avenue, giving her the feeling that others were just a scream away.

Telling her final story for the night, she gratefully accepted the money placed into her hands. She even told the remaining tour members about the local bars in the area, pointing out which served the best and the cheapest drinks. The tour members were delighted with the information, scurrying off to continue their night of fun.

"Whew. Finally. Now I can go home." Ssabra stuffed the money into the pocket of her dress. She thought about crossing the street to the Irish pub, maybe having a beer or two before heading home, but decided against it. She was tired, and a couple of beers might put her to sleep. Better to do her drinking back at the apartment.

She had just turned her back on the Huguenot Cemetery, when she heard laughter coming from above her.

Startled, she spun around, shocked to see a man sitting on the lowest branch of an oak tree. He was of average height, with a slightly muscular build. The front of his head was shaved bald, while the hair on the back of his head was long and tied into a braid. Several earrings adorned each of his ears, and a strand of beads circled his neck. He was dressed in a long white shirt, and matching pants, with shoes and socks almost the same color.

The man was sitting in the oak tree, holding what looked to be a long-stemmed clay pipe. He was looking down at Ssabra with a smile, apparently amused that he had surprised her. He was there, and yet he wasn't, because some of his features were not clearly defined. She could see him, but she could also see right through him.

The sight of the semitransparent man startled Ssabra, causing her to stumble back and trip, landing on her butt with a dull thud. The lantern she held hit the ground harder than she did, one of the panes of glass breaking in two.

"Ow." She picked up her lantern and examined the damage. "Look what you made me do. I'll have to pay for this, and these things are not cheap."

She looked back up to the oak tree, but the man was no longer sitting on the branch. Instead, he now sat on the stone wall a few feet in front of her. He was still smiling at her, and she suddenly realized who he was.

"Shit!" Ssabra quickly got back to her feet, forgetting all about the broken lantern. "You're Tolomato. You really do exist. You're not a brain tumor. I can see you."

"Of course you can see me," he answered, his grin growing even wider.

"But this can't be possible. It can't be real." She shook her head.

"Why not?"

"Because you're dead."

"Dead and buried for many years." He placed his hands on his chest. "I look pretty good for a dead man."

"No. No. No. This can't be happening." Ssabra looked around to see if anyone was watching, but there was no one else in the area. Even the last members of her tour group were long gone, on their way in search of alcoholic beverages to kill their thirsts. She also needed a drink. A really strong drink.

She turned her attention back to the stone wall surrounding the Huguenot Cemetery. Tolomato still sat upon the wall, smiling at her. She started to argue the possibility of his existence, but she really didn't see much point in it. Either she had just suffered a massive brain aneurysm, and was lying in a coma in some hospital, or she really was having a one-on-one conversation with the ghost of a dead Indian chief. Since the thought of a brain aneurysm depressed the hell out of her, she decided to go along with the ghost theory.

"Okay then, answer me this: if you're a dead Indian chief, and you died over two hundred years ago, then how come you're speaking perfect English? How about that?" Ssabra smiled, thinking she had come up with a very good question. A dead Indian from some long vanished tribe should not have been speaking her language. He should have been speaking a tribal dialect, maybe with a few words of Spanish scattered in. But Tolomato spoke English with very little accent. She could understand everything he said.

His smile did not falter. "Are you sure I am speaking English?"

Ssabra nodded. "I hear you. You're speaking perfect English."

"And how are you hearing my voice?"

"What do you mean? I don't understand."

"Are you hearing the sound of my voice with your ears, or are you hearing it inside your head, as you heard it earlier?"

She had to stop and think about it a moment. "You're right. I'm still hearing your voice inside my head."

The Indian nodded. "Then you are not hearing my voice. You are hearing my thoughts. Thoughts have no language."

"But I see your lips moving," she argued.

"My lips are moving because it is easier for me to speak and think at the same time. This is the first time I have tried to speak with the living since I crossed over, so it is very difficult for me."

"The first time?"

Tolomato nodded. "You are the first."

"But why couldn't I see you before?"

"You were not able to see me, because the veil was still over your eyes."

"Veil?"

He nodded. "The living cannot see the dead, unless they are made to see. Or unless they learn how to see through years of spiritual training, meditation, and fasting. We do not have years to wait, so I have used my energy, and all of my power, to touch your spirit and open your eyes. I have removed the veil that blinded you, allowing you to see things as they truly are."

"I'm not sure I understand. You mean I can see spirits?" Ssabra turned around, looking up and down the street. "Where? I don't see any other spirits. Only you."

Tolomato shook his head. "Stupid woman. You do not see any spirits, because there are none to be seen. You think a parade is going to be held just for your amusement? Even with the veil lifted, most spirits cannot be seen unless they want to be seen."

"How long will I have this gift of sight?"

"Forever. Once the veil is removed it cannot be placed back. Your spirit now knows how to see other spirits, and it would not be happy being blind again."

A nervous sensation danced across her stomach. She was almost afraid to look around, fearful of what she might see. "But what if I don't want to see such things?"

Tolomato's smile failed. "You no longer have a choice. The veil has been removed, and things cannot be put back the way they were. I am sorry, but I need your help. You will now see the world with new eyes, your gift growing stronger with each passing day. Soon the spirit world will be as real as the world you already know."

Ssabra was silent, not knowing what to say. A very special gift had just been given to her. She had also been handed a huge responsibility, and the weight of it was heavy on her heart. She didn't know if she was ready to have the veil lifted from her eyes, but the choice was no longer hers to make.

"Did you do as I told you to do?" Tolomato asked, changing the subject. "Did you go to see those in charge?"

She quickly told him about her experience at the police station that morning. The Indian was greatly disappointed to learn that Detective Colvin had not believed her story.

"Maybe you can talk with the police yourself," she suggested. "Surely they will believe you."

The chief shook his head. "Because of your heritage you are more open to the visits of spirits than others. A white person would hear my voice and blame it on bad food."

She laughed. "Yes, but you picked an Indian that doesn't know much about her ancestry."

"True. But I did not know that when I picked

you," the ghost replied. "Maybe there is someone still who can help us. Have you any money?"

"Some." Ssabra nodded.

"Enough to stay in one of the city's smaller inns?"

"I'm not sure. Maybe. If not, I have plastic."

"Plastic?"

"Never mind. It's a long story." She didn't want to explain credit cards and the new American banking system. "I have enough money."

"Good." Tolomato's image faded, but his voice was still heard. "Then let us go. I think I know someone who can help."

CHAPTER
20

The voice of the dead chief was still with Ssabra as she slowly walked back to her car, even though his image had disappeared back at the Huguenot. It was a pity the voice didn't also disappear for a while, for it seemed Tolomato never grew tired of talking. Maybe it had something to do with his being dead for so long, perhaps he didn't have anyone to talk with on the other side. Whatever the reason, the Indian kept up a continuous dialogue as she walked along St. George Street, making comments on this and that, and poking fun at things he found amusing.

Of course, Ssabra could not reply to any of his comments, for then it would look like she was talking to herself. She didn't want to be labeled as a crazy woman so she remained quiet, not even giving a reply when he directed a few of his comments at her.

"This place has changed a lot since I was alive," Tolomato said, continuing his one-sided dialogue.

"When I was here most of the buildings were made out of wood, with roofs of palmetto fronds. There were a few buildings made from shell stone, but that was not until after the fort was built.

"There were a lot of soldiers back then too. Not too many today. That is good. My people didn't like the Spanish soldiers. They were afraid of their guns, and their dogs. The Spanish soldiers were quite mean to the native people of this land; sometimes they fed our women and children to the dogs."

Ssabra stopped walking. She looked around to make sure no one was watching, then whispered, "The Spanish soldiers fed Indian women and children to their dogs? That can't be true. Can it? This town embraces its Spanish heritage. Surely the soldiers couldn't have been that bad."

Tolomato's voice grew harsh. "This city embraces its Spanish heritage because it has forgotten how cruel the Spanish soldiers really were. They did not come to this land to explore it, they came to conquer and destroy. They claimed this land as their own, even though thousands of people were already living here. Those you know as brave explorers are known to my people as butchers.

"De Soto, Pánfilo de Narváez, even Ponce de León. Their names struck fear in the hearts of the native people living in this land, because they brought with them death and destruction. They destroyed our villages, stole our land, murdered our women and children, and enslaved our men. They did all of this in the name of their king, and in search of the precious yellow metal."

"Gold?"

"Yes, gold. A useless metal. They thought this land was littered with the yellow metal, but what was truly valuable was the land itself. Look at it now. What was once forest is now covered with stone and buildings."

Ssabra looked around, seeing the city of St. Augustine in a different light. What she had always thought of as Europe's first foothold into an untamed new world, might actually have been the first nail driven into the coffin for the native people who already lived in America.

She had always considered the early Spanish explorers to be brave and noble men, spreading culture and civilization throughout the world. She had never looked upon their arrival in Florida as anything else. Living in St. Augustine, it was easy to get swept up in the love affair the locals had for the old Spanish settlement.

She spotted a couple of tourists walking her way. Not wanting it to appear that she was talking to herself, she turned and pretended to be reading a historic marker on one of the buildings. "But if the Spanish were so bad, why did so many of the Indian tribes make friends with them?"

"Did we have a choice? The Spanish were looking to make inroads into our world. They were looking for food and supplies, and they were looking for labor. If we did not provide these things, they would have destroyed our villages and enslaved our people. Some tried to stand against them, but were slaughtered by guns and cannons. By being friendly to the Spanish our villages and people were spared.

"It wasn't just the soldiers that conquered our people. The Spanish also sent their priests among us, trying to change our ways of belief. They said it was for our own good, that we needed to believe in their God. We tried to tell the priests we already had a God of our own. Maybe it was the same god, but with a different name. The priests would not listen. They built their missions among us, so they could control our people, and our land. The priests brought their religion, but it was my people who dug the stones and cut the trees to build the churches. We were called their children, but we were really only their slaves."

"I had no idea the Spaniards were so bad," Ssabra said, still pretending to read the sign before her.

Tolomato laughed. "It wasn't just the Spanish. The French and English were no better. Even the Americans did their best to eliminate the native people of this land. But the Spanish were the worst."

The voice of Tolomato fell silent. Maybe he had finally run out of things to say, or maybe he was thinking of all the terrible things that had happened to his people. A tribe that no longer existed.

Stepping away from the sign, Ssabra continued on her way down St. George Street to the plaza. In front of one of the local restaurants two police officers were arguing with a street performer about why he could not play his violin in public. She gave the argument little more than a passing glance, her mind filled with thoughts of Spanish conquest and the genocide of indigenous tribes.

Tolomato didn't speak again until she reached her car. She had just started the engine, when he gave her instructions on where he wanted her to go. She easily recognized the building he spoke of, so it was only a few minutes later that they arrived at their destination.

She pulled the car into a tiny parking lot and switched off the engine. Across the street stood a three-story building that had been built as a private residence back in 1791. The building had changed ownership several times over the years, and in 1845 it had opened to the public as an Inn. That made the St. Francis Inn the oldest existing bed and breakfast in St. Augustine.

Ssabra knew the story about the St. Francis Inn by heart, because it was one of the stops on the ghost tour. According to the legend, General William Hardee had owned the building back around 1855, before being sent to West Point as officer in charge of cadets. The General's nephew, who lived with him in the house, fell in love with a young black slave named Lily. Because such relationships were forbidden back then, their love was kept a secret, with the young couple meeting whenever possible in the attic. But the general found out about his nephew's interracial affair, and threw the young black woman out of the house.

Heartbroken that the love of his life had been taken away from him, General Hardee's nephew hung himself in the attic, committing suicide on the very spot where the young couple used to secretly meet.

Around 1888, the attic was converted into additional guest rooms for the Inn, and it wasn't long after that when people started to notice that Room 3A was haunted. The room was the place where the general's nephew hung himself, but it was the ghost of the young slave who haunted the Inn. She has been seen so many times over the years, room 3A was now known as Lily's Room.

A businesswoman checked into the room a couple of years ago, having no idea the room she rented was haunted. During the night, she awakened from a sound sleep to find a black woman standing beside her bed, crying. Thinking the management had given a spare key to someone else, she hurried down to the front desk to complain. It was only then that she learned the story about Lily, shocked to discover she had just had an encounter with the Inn's ghost. The woman checked out immediately, seeking accommodations elsewhere in the old city.

"We're here to see a ghost. Right?" Ssabra asked, looking through the windshield at the old Inn.

"You are not as stupid as I thought," Tolomato replied, breaking his silence.

"Lily?"

"You know her?"

"No. I just know the stories. This place is one of the stops on my ghost tour."

"Good. Then you will not be too upset by meeting her."

"But what if someone is already staying in the room?"

"No one is staying there," he replied. "I visited the room earlier tonight, and it is empty."

Ssabra got out of the car and locked the door behind her. Crossing the street, she walked past a decorative courtyard to the front door of the Inn.

A feeling of history enveloped her as she entered the Inn, making it seem as if she had gone back in time. The reception area was small and cozy, with the warmth and charm of old Europe. The front desk sat to the right of the door, tucked beneath a wooden staircase leading up to the second and third floors. Beyond the reception area was another room, filled with antique chairs and a sofa, a place for guests to sip coffee and get acquainted.

An attractive, middle-aged woman stood behind the registration desk. She smiled as Ssabra entered the Inn. Perhaps she was smiling at the way Ssabra was dressed, because the tour guide still wore her historic reproduction dress with layered petticoats.

"Yes. Can I help you?" the woman asked.

"Yes, ma'am. I would like a room for the night," Ssabra answered, glancing around at her surroundings. "I would prefer to stay in 3A, if it's still available."

The receptionist laughed. "You're in luck. Lily's Room is still available. It's usually booked weeks in advance, but we had a cancellation."

"Good. I'll take it."

The receptionist filled out a form for the room, asking to see Ssabra's driver's license. Ssabra handed the receptionist the license, along with her credit card to pay for the room. Signing the form, she was given a key to room 3A. She was also informed that a free breakfast was served each morning downstairs in the dining room, and that there was still free coffee in the silver urns. She thanked the receptionist for the information, then proceeded up the stairs to her room.

As she climbed the stairs to the third floor, Ssabra became aware of just how low the ceiling was on each of the floors she passed. She also noticed that the entire building appeared to be tilted to one side.

The tilting was especially noticeable when she stopped on the second-floor landing. The wooden floor seemed to slope severely away from the fireplace, as if the whole building were in danger of falling over on its side. It reminded her of the sloping floors in the old carnival fun houses.

At the second-floor landing there was a door that opened onto a small balcony overlooking the courtyard. Several chairs had been placed on the balcony, so it was obviously a favorite place for the guests. Ssabra was tempted to open the door and step outside for a few minutes, to take in the view and the night air, but decided against it. Instead, she continued up the wooden staircase to the next level.

She arrived on the third floor, only a little out of breath. Room 3A was tucked back into the corner of the building, and she had heard that it was one of the smaller rooms at the Inn. Slipping the key into the lock, Ssabra opened the door and stepped across the threshold.

Lily's Room was indeed rather small, but it was also quite charming in a storybook sort of way. The walls were painted white, as was the textured ceiling. An antique, four-poster bed sat at one end of the room, against a wall adorned with built-in bookshelves and a small collection of books. On the other side of the room were several chairs, a dresser, and a small television set. Several old paintings and potted ferns decorated the room, giving it a comfortable feeling.

There were two large windows in the room, both covered by movable wooden shutters. One of the windows overlooked the building and parking lot across the street, while the other offered a view of the courtyard and fountain. A smaller row of windows ran along the wall nearest the door, facing out on the main staircase. They were covered with a set of curtains that could be opened or closed to block out the light.

Opposite the bed, a green door with glass window-panes opened onto the bathroom. The bathroom was small, but it featured everything one needed to start their day, including an antique bathtub.

Ssabra was delighted with the room, and chided herself for never having stayed at the Inn. She had been missing out, but she never considered the bed and breakfasts of St. Augustine to be places for the locals. Nor had she ever considered one to be within her price range, but the room didn't cost much more than what many of the local motels charged.

Closing the door, she crossed the room and sat down on the bed. The antique bed sat high off the floor and was covered with plenty of pillows, sheets, and homemade quilts. Kicking off her shoes, she stretched out full length and closed her eyes.

"This is no time for sleeping."

Tolomato's voice popped into her head, startling her. She sat up quickly, surprised to find that the Indian chief had again materialized, and was sitting in a chair at the opposite side of the room. He was frowning, so he apparently wasn't too happy about finding her lying down on the job.

"Sorry," she said, a little sheepishly. "I've never stayed in a room this nice, and I just wanted to see what it felt like."

The chief looked around the room. "It is very nice here."

"Can we spend the night?" she asked. "I mean, I paid for the room. We are going to stay here tonight. Aren't we?"

"Yes, you can spend the night if you want, but business first. Now go wash the paint off of your face."

"My makeup? You want me to remove my makeup?"

"Yes."

"But why?"

"Because the spirit you are going to meet tonight is very jealous of pretty women."

"You think I'm pretty? Really?" She smiled.

"Yes. You are pretty. But do not get a big head about it. Now, go clean your face."

"Wow. This is the first time a ghost ever gave me a compliment."

Tolomato shook his head. "It may also be the last time."

Ssabra got up off of the bed, still smiling. She thought it was funny that Tolomato had a sense of humor. She had never thought of ghosts as being anything other than scary, or maybe a little lonely. But apparently not all ghosts fit that description. Except for his little rant against the Spanish explorers, and his concern about the Shiru, he seemed to be in rather good spirits for a ghost.

In good spirits for a ghost. Ssabra laughed at her own thoughts.

Slipping into the bathroom, she turned on the water in the sink, grabbed a bar of lavender scented soap, and started removing all of her makeup. She didn't wear much makeup, only powder, lipstick, and a little eyeliner, so it didn't take long to get it off.

Removing the last of the makeup, she dried her face with a small towel. She would have brushed her teeth, but she hadn't brought along a toothbrush. Nor had she brought a fresh change of clothing, or a nightgown. The clothes she had worn earlier that day were still at the tour office, and she had forgotten to pick them up before coming to the Inn.

Stepping out of the bathroom, she found Lily's room to be empty. Tolomato had disappeared again.

Now where did he go? "Tolomato, are you still here?"

A few moments passed, then the chief appeared again. He was stretched out on the bed, smiling at her. "You are right. This is very comfortable."

"Hey. No fair," Ssabra protested. "You said no lying down on the job."

"I said that for you, but not for me." He pointed at the chairs on the opposite end of the room. "You will sit over there. Stay at that end of the room until I tell you otherwise."

She reluctantly did as she was told, choosing the most comfortable chair at the opposite end of the room. Tolomato again vanished from sight, but she could still hear his voice. He was calling to Lily, trying to make contact with the spirit of the young slave

woman who haunted the room. Ssabra tried to listen
to all the things the Indian was saying, but it had
been a long day and she soon found herself drifting
off to sleep. Laying her head back against the wall,
she closed her eyes and rested.

"Wake up. Hurry, wake up."

Tolomato's voice startled her, causing her to wake
from a sound sleep. Ssabra blinked and looked around
the room. Nothing had changed, except she now had
a kink in her neck from sleeping in the chair. Glancing at her watch, she saw it was already three in
the morning.

"What? What is it?" she asked, rubbing her eyes.
She was still sleepy, and her vision was blurry.

"Shhh . . . be quiet. We have company."

A cold shiver walked down her spine, bringing her
fully awake. She knew what Tolomato meant, and
looked around to see who else was in the room. At
first she didn't see anything, but then she noticed a
strange blurring in the air at the opposite end of the
room, between the bed and an antique washbasin. It
looked like heat waves rising up from a radiator.

Remaining perfectly still, she focused her gaze on
the other end of the room, watching as the swirling
vapors continued to appear. A few moments later
she saw something a little more solid, and had to
bite her tongue to keep from crying out.

Something small and black floated from the wall
near the washbasin to the bed, and back again. It
moved across the open space in front of the window
several times, hovering a few feet off the floor. At
first Ssabra wasn't sure what the object was. The only
light coming into the room was through the row of

windows above her head, so it was fairly dark. She
watched the floating object for almost a full minute
before realizing what it was.

*A hand. My God, that's a woman's hand. I can see it
now. A black hand. Lily's hand.*

The hand was Lily's ghostly trademark. Other
guests had seen the black hand of a woman going
down the banister on the back staircase, a stairway
formerly used by servants of the house. Ssabra
wished she had brought along a camera to take a
picture, but she hadn't. Not that she would risk taking a snapshot, fearful of scaring off the spirit they
had come to talk with.

She watched the hand for another minute or so,
and then suddenly there was a woman standing at
the other end of the room. Lily had appeared so
quickly it looked as if she had always been standing
there, and Ssabra had to blink twice to make sure
she was not seeing things. But her imagination was
not playing tricks on her. A black woman stood at
the opposite end of the room, her left hand resting
on the bed's headboard.

Lily was short and slim, probably no more than
five-foot-six-inches tall. She also appeared to be quite
young, and may have only been in her twenties when
she died. She was dressed in a white dress and
apron, her head covered with some kind of scarf.
Unlike the spirit of Tolomato, Lily's ghost was quite
solid. It looked as if a real person stood in the room,
and not just an apparition.

The young woman looked at Ssabra, but made no
attempt to move away from the corner of the room.
Ssabra wanted to communicate with her, and was

grateful when Tolomato suddenly materialized on the bed.

The Indian chief spoke with the former slave, gesturing to himself and to Ssabra. He was obviously making introductions to the other spirit, but it was several minutes before Ssabra could hear either of their voices. Finally the conversation began to come through to her; she heard Tolomato's guttural voice first, followed by the softly spoken words of the slave girl.

"This is a friend of mine," he said, pointing to where Ssabra sat. "Her name is Ssabra Onih. She is an Indian woman. She has come with me to ask your help."

"She is not white?" Lily asked, looking at Ssabra.

"Her mother was white, but her father was Cherokee."

Lily looked at her for a moment, then nodded. It seemed to be important to the young woman that Ssabra was not white.

"Hello, Lily," Ssabra said, risking Tolomato's scolding for speaking. "I'm very happy to meet you."

The chief turned toward Ssabra and smiled. Apparently her greeting had been the right thing to say. Lily also smiled, but it was slight and fleeting, as if happiness did not know her face.

Tolomato turned back to face the black woman. "Lily, we have come here tonight to ask for your help. It is said that you have certain powers, as well as a knowledge of this city. A great evil has been released from one of the burial grounds in this town, the one that bears my name. It is an evil that has not been seen in the world of the living for a long time:

a dark god that may attempt to breed with others. We need your help. Is there anything you can tell us that might help fight this evil one?"

Lily was silent for a few moments, apparently thinking things over, and then she spoke. Her voice was soft, and almost musical to the ears. "I know of the monster that has been called into this world, the thing you call the Shiru. I too have seen it. The three women who set the beast free were very foolish. They played with magic they did not understand. One of the women paid for her foolishness with her life.

"The Shiru now walks among the living, and with each passing day in this world it will grow stronger."

"Is there any way to destroy it, or send it back?" Tolomato asked.

Again Lily was silent for a few moments before speaking. "Once there were people who knew how to destroy a Shiru, but that was long ago. I have never met any of those people, even though I have been in this city for a long time. But I have read the words they put to paper.

"There is a library in the old church that contains many books. Among the books you will find a journal written by a Spanish monk named Father Sebastian Diaz. It is a small book, bound in green leather. The pages are yellow and brittle, but the words can still be read. In this book you will find what you are looking for. You will find how to destroy a Shiru."

With those words Lily fell silent. Ssabra expected the young black woman to tell them more about the book, but she didn't. Instead, she vanished quickly from view, leaving Ssabra to wonder if she had ever been there at all. A few moments later Tolomato also disappeared, his voice slowly fading out.

"Sleep here tonight, if you wish. You will need your rest. Tomorrow we will search for the book."

Ssabra looked around, but the room was empty. She was completely alone, or at least the only one visible. Getting up from the chair, she slipped out of her dress and lay down on the antique bed. It had been a long day, and she was too tired to get underneath the covers. She was asleep a few minutes after her head touched the pillow, unaware of the black servant girl who reappeared a short while later to stand watch over her.

CHAPTER
21

By Tuesday morning, things had gone from bad to worse at the police station. In addition to the worried, upset, and slightly crazy citizens of St. Augustine, the lobby was jammed with reporters and news crews, standing around waiting for the latest updates on the homicides, or trying to get an interview with Chief Harris or one of the detectives on the case.

Spotting the news vans parked in front of the station, Jack decided to park down the street and sneak in through the back door. He had stayed up late the night before filling out paperwork, and carefully going back through all of the lab reports, and he really wasn't in the mood to do any kind of interview. Not that he was ever in the mood to do interviews. He had a deep distrust of the news media, and only tolerated reporters because they could sometimes be useful when the police wanted to release information about a suspect for whom they were searching.

Additional police units were needed yesterday to keep the news crews from getting too close to the crime scene. Someone had accidentally leaked information about the third homicide over the police radio, and two different television crews had shown up to cover the story. Jack was not about to let them get a picture of the dead woman's lower torso, nor would he release any information on the case.

He tried to keep the owner of the gift shop away from the news media, but one of the reporters had grabbed her before he could warn her to keep quiet about what she saw. The owner was obviously quite happy with all the free publicity, and had described in gory detail what her little dachshund had discovered that morning. The brief interview had run on the six and eleven o'clock news, and the owner's picture had appeared on the front page of the morning paper, along with a detailed description of what she had seen.

If there hadn't been a panic in St. Augustine before, there probably would be one now. It was one thing for the press to say that pieces of bone had been found in the Tolomato Cemetery, and the police were not ruling out the possibility of a homicide. It was quite another to report that the naked, mutilated lower torso of a young woman had been found in the historic district.

Walking to the station from where he parked his car, Jack spotted Sergeant Steve Avery standing just outside the back door, smoking a cigarette. The sergeant shook his head and smiled when he saw Colvin approaching.

"You think that trick is going to work?"

"What trick?" he asked innocently.

"Parking down the street so no one will see your car, then sneaking in the back door."

"Steve, I'm surprised you would even suggest such a thing. I'm not trying to sneak in; I just felt like walking this morning. It's great exercise." Jack reached out and patted him on the stomach. "You should try it sometime."

The sergeant coughed. "I'll have you know that I wear the same size pants now as I did twenty years ago."

"Yeah, but you wear them a few inches lower now than you did back then."

"Are you really going in there?" asked the sergeant. "I wouldn't if I were you."

"That bad?"

Steve nodded. "The lobby is filled with upset citizens and reporters, and the rooms are crowded with feds and FDLE agents. They're taking over everything."

Jack sighed. "I was afraid of that. When you ask the FBI and the Florida Department of Law Enforcement for assistance, you might as well hand them the case and step back. I knew the shit was going to hit the fan when we found that third body."

"Hit it, bounced off, and spattered all over the ceiling and walls. St. Augustine is still a small town, so this is big time. In New York City it would probably be just another day at the office."

"I suppose it's too late to request a transfer to the Big Apple?"

"Transfer? What, and leave all this?"

Detective Colvin sighed again. "Well, I guess I had better go in and face the music."

"Chief Harris has been looking for you."

"No surprise there. He was also looking for me yesterday."

"And you still showed up this morning? Man, you've got balls."

"I may not have them much longer," he replied. "Has Detective Moats come in yet?"

"He's been here and gone. Signed out and left with one of the federal agents, said he had a couple of leads to run down."

"Knowing Bill, he and the fed are probably sitting over at The Bagel Hut."

"Maybe that's where you should be."

"Can't. I have too much work to do today. I also need to use the office computers." He gave a final look around, then nodded to Sergeant Avery. "I guess I had better go in. Talk to you later."

To his surprise the hallway was empty as he entered the station, and he didn't see his first federal agent until he reached his office. He actually saw two of them; they were standing just inside the doorway engaged in a quiet conversation. Jack nodded to the two agents, but they only stared at him.

Jerks.

There was another federal agent sitting at Bill's desk, using the phone. He couldn't help but smile, knowing that his partner would have a fit if he knew someone else was sitting at his desk. Detective Moats did not tolerate anyone using his desk, not even the boys from Washington. It was a good thing for the agent that Bill had already been there and left, otherwise he would have gotten an earful. He might have gotten more than that, because the last guy who made the mistake of using Bill's desk without permission had been physically removed by the scruff of his neck.

The detective had just sat down at his desk when the phone rang. He was reluctant to answer it, suspecting the call might be from a reporter, or another upset citizen. Bracing himself for what could be a tirade from a scared resident, Jack put aside the stack of folders he had brought to work with him and picked up the phone. "St. Augustine Police Department. Detective Jack Colvin speaking. How may I help you?"

The line was silent for a moment, and Jack thought the person on the other end had hung up. He was about to hang up himself, when a woman's voice came on the line. She was speaking slowly, carefully choosing her words.

"Detective Colvin? Yes, my name is Louise Fowler. I'm calling on behalf of myself and my sister, Jane."

"Yes, Ms. Fowler. What can I do for you this morning?"

"Well, I'm not really sure if you're the person I should be talking to, but they patched me through to your number. My sister and I are calling because we're concerned about a friend of ours. We haven't seen her for several days, and we think something bad might have happened to her." The woman cleared her voice. "I mean, we know something has happened to her."

He picked up a pen, and slid a pad of paper in front of him. "What is your friend's name?"

"Her name is Sanchez. Maria Sanchez. She lives here in Cassadaga, as do my sister and myself."

"Cassadaga? Then shouldn't you have called the Cassadaga Police Department?"

"I thought about that, but the last time we saw Maria was in St. Augustine. That's why I decided to call you."

"I see," he said, nodding to himself. "Go on. When and where was the last time you saw your friend?"

"Friday night, at the Tolomato Cemetery."

Jack stopped writing, the skin at his temples pulling tight. "The Tolomato Cemetery?"

"Yes, sir. I know this is going to sound funny, but please don't hang up on me. This isn't a joke."

"Don't worry. I'm not going to hang up on you."

"Thank you. My sister and I went with Maria to the Tolomato Cemetery in search of spirit guides. We're spiritualists. Jane and I are still students; Maria is our mentor. She said we would get our spirit guides that night, but something bad happened instead. Something really bad."

"Yes, ma'am. I'm listening. What happened?"

"I'm not sure, but I think we opened a doorway to the other side and something came through."

"The other side?"

"The spirit world. We each wanted a spirit to help guide us in this world, but something bad came through instead. Something dark."

Jack glanced around the room. He wanted someone else to hear what was being said over the phone, but there was no one else in the room he trusted.

All of his fellow detectives were in other parts of the building.

"Do you know what came through the opening from the other side?" he asked, choosing his words carefully. The detective didn't want to sound as if he was mocking the woman, fearful she might hang up on him. Ordinarily, he would have been the one hanging up, but he had seen too many strange things in the past couple of days to do that now. What he was being told over the phone sounded an awful lot like the story of Ssabra Onih.

"I'm not sure what it was," she replied. "It was dark, and it came out of the ground like black fog. You're going to think I'm crazy, but it changed shapes. One second it was just fog, but the next it looked like a giant spider, or maybe an octopus. And then it changed again, looking like a man."

"A man?"

"Yes sir. One moment it was just fog, the next it was a giant spider, and then it was a man. And then it changed back again."

"How many times did this thing change appearance?"

She hesitated for a moment. "I can't be sure. It kept changing shapes, from one thing to the next, and it was never very solid. All I know is that it was evil, and we summoned it."

"What happened after you saw this fog thing in the cemetery?"

"We ran," Louise answered. "We were all pretty scared, and Maria told us to run. She's our teacher, and she knows all about the spirit world. She was scared too. And when she said to run, I ran."

There was a moment of silence on the phone; then Louise came back on the line. Her voice was unsteady, and it was obvious she was crying. "That was the last time either of us saw Maria. We made it back to where the car was parked, but Maria never showed up. I had an extra set of keys, so we got in and drove off. Maybe we shouldn't have driven away, maybe we should have gone back to look for her, but we were both terrified."

"And you haven't heard from Maria Sanchez since then?"

"No, sir. Not a word." Louise sniffed. "No one's seen her. She has a little shop here in Cassadaga, but it's been closed."

"If your friend has been missing for several days, and if what you say happened at the Tolomato Cemetery is true, then why didn't you or your sister call someone before now?"

Louise was crying again, no attempt to hide the waver in her voice. "We were both afraid. We did something terrible that night. Something bad got Maria, and we were afraid it was coming after us. We haven't been outside of the house in three days."

Jack wrote a few notes on the pad of paper, trying to figure out what really happened to the missing woman. "Can you give me a description of your friend? What does she look like, and what was she wearing the night she disappeared?"

He started to jot down the description of Maria Sanchez, but stopped when he heard what the woman was wearing. Louise Fowler said her friend and mentor had been wearing a black dress the night of her disappearance. She had also been wearing sil-

ver jewelry, including an ornate ring with an oval
blue stone. The description of the clothing and ring
matched the items he had found at the Tolomato
Cemetery.

"Was there anything else?" he asked. "Did Maria
have a purse, or a bag? Maybe she brought along a
few items when the three of you went to the
cemetery."

Louise thought for a moment. "No. I don't think
so . . . wait a minute. Yes, Maria did have a bag. A
leather shoulder bag. That's what she used to carry
her crystals and candles."

The noise around him seemed to fade out to nothingness as he listened to the description of the bag
and its contents. He had found a leather bag just
inside the front gates of the Tolomato Cemetery, containing several quartz crystals, candles, and a sage
smudge stick. A black dress, an ornate silver ring,
and a leather bag. The items being described over
the phone matched those he had found at the cemetery. Which meant that Maria Sanchez was no longer
just missing; she was dead.

And if what Louise Fowler said was true, then Ms.
Sanchez had been killed by something not of this
world. A door had somehow been opened to a world
beyond the living, and something evil had come
through. Something evil and deadly.

Detective Colvin did not tell Louise her friend
might be dead. Nor did he mention the grisly remains that had been found in the Tolomato Cemetery. Instead, he listened to all she had to say, taking
careful notes on the pad of paper. When she was
done speaking, he wrote down Louise Fowler's

phone number and address, promising that someone would be getting back in touch with her real soon.

Hanging up the phone, the detective stared at the notes he had taken. He now had a name to go with the remains found at the first crime scene. He also had a story that just happened to match what Ssabra Onih had previously told him.

Witches, spells, spirit guides. The case was becoming more and more strange by the minute. One thing for sure, he was definitely going to pay a little visit on Miss Onih. Jack had tried to call her the day before, but she hadn't been home. He was now determined to have a face-to-face meeting with the young woman, even if he had to sit in front of her apartment all day.

CHAPTER
22

Ssabra awoke with the first rays of sunlight filtering into the small bedroom. She stirred slowly, fragments of a strange dream sinking back into her subconscious: something about tragedy and ecstasy, love and suicide. Opening her eyes, she stared up at an unfamiliar ceiling of textured tin painted white. It took a few moments to realize where she was, and then the memories of the previous night came flooding back to her.

"Lily." She sat up and looked around, almost expecting there to be someone else in the room with her, but she was alone.

"God, what a night," she lay back down on the bed, allowing her head to sink into the feather pillow. Her sleep had been so sound, she had completely forgotten about the events of the previous evening. She had expected to wake up in her own bed, and was surprised to find that she was not in her apartment.

As she lay there, her mind becoming more fully awake, she began to remember the things that had transpired a few hours earlier. She had finally gotten to see Tolomato, his appearance convincing her that the voice she heard was not her imagination.

Seeing the spirit of the Indian chief had only been the first surprise of the night. She had also seen Lily, the resident ghost of room 3A at the St. Francis Inn. Not only did she see Lily, but she had actually spoken with her. The former slave had told them about the journal of Father Sebastian Diaz, which might provide information on how to destroy the Shiru.

The journal was important, and Ssabra had to go to the church to see if she could locate it. She knew the task would be difficult, if not downright impossible, because such a book would not be available to the general public. It would be kept in a private library, safe from harm or theft.

Ssabra stretched and sat back up. She needed to locate the journal of Father Diaz, but she didn't need to find it at that very moment. The Cathedral-Basilica didn't open to the public until later in the day, so she was going to make the best of her stay at the St. Francis Inn.

Climbing out of bed, she walked across the room and entered the bathroom. The antique bathtub looked inviting, but she hadn't brought along a clean change of clothing or a toothbrush. It would be stupid to take a bath and then slip her dirty undergarments back on again. Not that they were really dirty, but they were definitely less than fresh.

Looking into the mirror, she remembered that Tolomato had ordered her to scrub off all of her makeup.

"I look like hell."

Luckily, she had brought along a few basic makeup items in her purse: lipstick, powder, and mascara. She never went anywhere without them, because she never knew when such things might be needed in an emergency. Afternoon thunderstorms and high humidity were common in Florida, and she often had to reapply her makeup between tour groups. Ssabra also had a roll of breath mints in her purse, which would take the place of toothpaste.

Washing her face in the sink, she retrieved the makeup items from her purse to reapply her war paint. She also ran a brush through her hair, sorting out the tangles. With makeup and hair taken care of, she turned her attention to getting dressed. The only clothing she had was the historic dress she had been wearing for the ghost tour. Anywhere else she would have felt funny about wearing such a dress out in public, especially in the daytime, but not in St. Augustine. There were always people walking around in costumes in the old city, so her appearance would be nothing to stare at.

Putting on the dress, she turned to look at herself in the oval mirror that hung above the washbasin in the bedroom. Satisfied everything was in place, she slipped on her shoes. She also took out two five dollar bills from her purse and left them on the dresser as a tip for housekeeping.

She smiled. "Now, I believe someone said something about free breakfast."

Leaving the room, she closed the door and started down the stairs. It was early, so the Inn was still quiet. Most of the guests were probably sleeping, although there was one young couple sitting out on the second floor balcony. They were probably newly-weds, enjoying every waking moment together.

Descending the stairs to ground level, she entered the dining room, surprised to find it empty. Not that she was looking for company; she was looking for food. The sandwich she had for dinner the previous evening was a long-gone memory, and her stomach was starting to announce its anger over being empty.

The dining room was light and airy, with several windows facing out toward the street. A low ceiling, adorned with heavy wooden beams, and a collection of antique furnishings, gave the room a real feeling of history, making it seem much older than the rest of the Inn.

Giving the decorations little more than a passing glance, she focused her attention on the serving stations that had been set up along two of the walls. There were silver trays containing scrambled eggs, sausages, bacon, pancakes, even gravy. There was also fresh orange juice, and a bottle of opened champagne for making mimosas. Filling a plate, and grabbing a cup of fresh coffee, she sat down at a vacant table in the corner of the room.

She was just about to take a sip of coffee when Tolomato suddenly materialized in the chair on the opposite side of the table. His unexpected appearance was so startling, she nearly choked.

"What are you doing?" Tolomato asked, apparently upset over something.

Ssabra coughed, wiping her mouth with her napkin. "What do you think I'm doing? I'm eating."

She looked around to make sure no one had heard her. "You damn near gave me a heart attack. Next time give me a warning before you pop in. You're lucky I didn't spill coffee all over my dress. Do you have any idea how much it costs to dry clean this thing?"

"What are you doing here?" he repeated.

"I'm eating. That's what people do in the morning. It's called breakfast."

"You should not be here."

"And just where should I be?" She was beginning to get annoyed with her ghostly guest. Her eggs were getting cold.

"You should be out trying to stop the Shiru before it can kill again."

She shook her head and took a sip of coffee. "Sorry, but I never do battle with monsters on an empty stomach. And I never do battle before my first cup of coffee."

The Indian chief was not amused with her answer. "Have you learned nothing? Did you not listen to what Lily said last night? You should be at the church, looking for the journal of Father Sebastian Diaz. Lily said the book might help us defeat the dark one. We need to find it before the Shiru grows too strong."

Ssabra smiled and leaned forward, keeping her voice low. "I did indeed listen to everything Lily had to say. And I plan on going to the church to look for the book, but not now. First I am going to have breakfast, and I fully intend to enjoy every bite."

Tolomato glared at her. "There is not time."

"There is always time," she retaliated. "Can I get you something? Eggs? Juice perhaps?"

"I am a spirit. I do not eat or drink."

"That's a pity." She ate a forkful of eggs. "The scrambled eggs are really quite good. It's a shame you can't have any."

"Why are you doing this to me?" he asked, his voice almost a whine.

"Why am I doing what?" Ssabra asked innocently, still chewing.

"Why are you tormenting me?"

"Am I tormenting you?" She swallowed. "Sorry, I didn't realize that I was."

"Yes, you are, and you know it. We have to go to the church, and here you sit eating."

"And enjoying every bite." She tried one of the sausage links. It was also delicious, and she let Tolomato know it.

She put down her fork and wiped her mouth with a napkin. "Look. It wouldn't do me any good to go to the church now anyway."

"Why not?"

She started to answer, but suddenly realized that someone was standing in the dining room doorway. It was one of the Inn's staff, probably a kitchen worker checking to make sure everything had been set up for the guests. The woman stood in the doorway, watching with obvious concern. There was no telling how long she had been there, probably long enough to witness Ssabra having an argument with an empty chair.

Ssabra felt her face go red with embarrassment. She smiled, thinking quickly of some way to explain her actions. "Good morning. You're probably wondering why I'm talking to myself. I'm an actress in a local theater group, and I was just rehearsing my lines for a play. It must have looked like I was crazy, talking to myself and all."

The woman gave a half smile, and a slight nod, and then stepped back out of the doorway. Ssabra watched her walk away, breathing a sigh of relief. She didn't know if her story had been believed, and would have to be more careful about such things in the future.

"See what you did?" She turned back to Tolomato. "That woman probably thinks I'm crazy, because I'm sitting here talking to myself."

"She thinks you are crazy, because the veil has not been lifted—"

"Don't you start with that veil stuff again. I don't want to hear it. I didn't ask to be sitting here having a conversation with an overbearing ghost, nor did I ask you to do anything to my eyes. Veil or otherwise." She took a sip of coffee, setting the cup down hard on the table.

"As I was saying, I am going to enjoy my breakfast. Period. If you don't like it, then that's too bad. There is no reason for me to go to the church this morning, because it is not yet open to the public. I can't get in, which means I can't look for the book you want. I will go to the church when it opens, after I have had my breakfast, and after I have gone to work."

"You are going to work too?" Tolomato threw his hands into the air, unable to believe what he was hearing.

"Yes, I am going to work. I have to make a living, which means I have to go to work. Unlike you, I have to eat. I also have to pay for staying in this place, which was your idea, so I have to go to work. I will go to the church this afternoon, and not before. Now, if you don't mind, I would like to finish my breakfast in peace. So will you please leave me alone."

The chief looked at her in stunned silence for a few seconds, then burst out laughing.

"What's so funny?" she asked, still ready for a fight.

"You say you know nothing about your heritage, but you have an Indian temper. You are definitely Cherokee."

Ssabra tried to keep her anger, but failed. She also laughed. "Maybe I do."

"Your eggs, are they good?" he asked.

"Very good," she replied, still laughing.

"And the little sausages?"

"Quite tasty."

"Can I please smell them?"

"Smell them?"

He nodded. "I cannot eat food, but I can smell it. The smell brings back happy memories."

She pushed her plate across the table, watching as the spirit leaned forward and lowered his face toward the food.

"Ah, that does smell good. Very good."

She started to retrieve the plate, wanting to eat her breakfast before it got completely cold.

"Please, just a little more," Tolomato said, stopping her. "Ah, it is good."

"I can get you a plate of food if you like."

"No. No. Don't do that. I cannot eat food. I can only smell it."

A few more moments passed with Tolomato sniffing her food, showing no sign of his wanting to stop. Annoyed, Ssabra slid her chair back and stood up.

The chief looked up from the plate. "What are you doing? I told you I cannot eat. There is no reason to get me a plate of food."

Ssabra smiled. "Who said anything about getting you a plate? I am getting one for me."

Tolomato grinned and nodded, then went back to sniffing the breakfast.

CHAPTER
23

The land had once been covered with endless forests, filled with places of shadows and great mystery. It was a world of fauna and fowl, of the predator and the hunted, where death often came without mercy or warning. And in those shadowy places his people were the strongest of the strong, hunters feared by all creatures of feather and fur.

But then the two-legs came to the land, building their villages among the original inhabitants of the forest, bringing with them their fears and weakness, taking without asking, and shunning those not of the light. The new arrivals also brought with them a cunning unknown among the simple forest dwellers, making them a very dangerous enemy.

One by one his people had been conquered and killed by the new arrivals, their offspring put to death under a sharpened blade or cast into the burning flames of fire. He too had been hunted down and killed, crossing over to the eternal darkness of the spirit land. But now he was back, summoned by the voices of three females. A doorway had opened, and he had stepped back into the world of the living, taking his place as a dark god among the weak.

The Shiru made a soft hissing sound, angry at the thought of what the two-legs had done to his people. He would like nothing more than to watch their miserable race suffer and die, as his people had suffered and died. Still, he knew the weak ones were a necessary evil. If he wanted to reestablish his race upon the world, then he needed their females for breeding stock. The offspring of human and Shiru were far from perfect, but they were better than no offspring at all.

At first, he thought the three females who had summoned him wanted to breed, seeking his power for their children, but they had all fled from him. One of the females had not gotten away, but she was of such a weak mind and frail body that he had dispatched her to the other side without even trying to copulate. Instead of a mate, she had ended up as food for a god.

Perhaps the females had been frightened by his appearance, which is why they had run away. Since they had summoned him from the other side, he had honored them by appearing in his true form. Sensing their fear, he had changed shape to that of a human male: a Spanish priest he had consumed when he last walked the earth. He could assume the appearance of anyone he had ingested, but the Spanish priest was the form that came quickest. Still, the females had been afraid of him.

The Shiru was puzzled as to why the females remained frightened. They should not have feared a priest, but maybe such men no longer existed in this world. Deciding that a new human shape was needed to wear as an identity, he had killed and consumed a male who walked funny and smelled of strong drink. Now he was able to walk among the two-legs without detection, as long as he did not come in contact with anyone who knew the face he now wore.

He also had to avoid water, mirrors, and glass, for such things always cast a true reflection. His true appearance had been seen in a mirror by a young female in the food place, which is why he stalked and killed her. He had tried to breed with her, but, while touching her mind with his, he learned that she was incapable of reproducing.

Standing in the shadows of a narrow alleyway, waiting for the coming of night, the Shiru watched as a group of two-legs moved slowly past. They were mostly old and feeble, and not of much interest to him as potential breeding stock. Still, there was one among them, a leader, who caught his attention.

She stood tall and straight, with long black hair that reached to the center of her back. Her eyes were dark and intelligent, and her voice sounded like soft music. He carefully studied the female, reaching out to mentally probe her subconscious, discovering that her bloodline was old and strong, and that she was capable of giving birth.

Yes, that one. She will make a fine mate. The perfect female to bring my race back to this world. She is the one I will breed with.

As he stood there, watching, the young woman

turned and looked in his direction. The Shiru thought he had been spotted, but then realized that he was well hidden in the shadows. Still, the female had looked his way, as if searching for him.

She knows I am here. The female has felt my touch upon her mind, and is looking for me. Wonderful. She has the gift. This is better than I had hoped. She will make a fine mother for my offspring.

The female did indeed have powers, something lacking in other humans, but he felt those powers were not yet fully developed within her. Her eyes were open, but she was just learning to see. He would follow this woman, and learn more about her. When the time was right he would take her, making her a breeder for the gods.

He watched as she turned away from him, leading the older two-legs down the street. As she left, he reached out and touched her mind once more, learning what the female called herself.

Ssabra.

Ssabra decided to lead only two tour groups that day, switching work schedules with another employee so she could get off early and go to the Cathedral-Basilica when it opened. The groups she led had, for the most part, been boring and uneventful. There was one moment, however, when something interesting had happened, in an odd sort of way.

She was standing on Charlotte Street, pointing out one of the local historical attractions, when an intense chill came over her. The feeling spread outward from her stomach to her fingertips, causing her to become somewhat light-headed. At first Ssabra thought she might be coming down with a cold, or maybe a virus, but the feeling only lasted a few minutes, leaving as quickly as it had appeared.

With the chill came the sensation that she was being watched. So strong was the feeling, she found herself turning to face an alleyway across the street.

There was no one standing in the alley, at least no one she could see, and she wondered if it had been Tolomato's presence she felt.

Arriving back at her apartment, a little after three p.m., she changed out of her work clothes and donned a pair of shorts, sandals, and a knit top. She had just finished dressing when a strange tingling touched the back of her neck. A voice followed, announcing that Tolomato was in the room with her.

"Osiyo."

Startled, Ssabra spun around, angry that he might have been in her bedroom while she changed clothes. "Where are you, and how long have you been here? I hope you got yourself an eyeful. Did you like seeing me naked?"

Tolomato slowly began to materialize. He was standing in the corner of the room, smiling at her. "Naked? You were naked? That would have been something to see, but sadly I only arrived at this moment. If you would like, I can leave and come back again when you have less to wear."

"You weren't in here a few moments ago?"

The Indian shook his head. "Do you think I have nothing else to do but sit around and wait for you in your bedroom? I have been busy elsewhere."

"And you didn't see me naked?"

"No. Why? Do you want me to see you naked?"

"Of course I don't," she snapped.

"Good. Then you have your wish." His grin widened. "Now, if you have no other reason to stay here, maybe we could go to the church."

Ssabra held up her hand. "Not so fast. I think it's time we established a few ground rules in this screwy relationship of ours. If you're going to be a part of my life, which you seem to be, then I want you to make me a few promises."

"Promises?"

She nodded. "Promises. For one, I want you to give me your word that you will stay the hell out of my bedroom. I don't like the idea of having a man, even a dead one, watching me when I'm sleeping or changing clothes."

Tolomato laughed. "You are being foolish. I am just a spirit. You are in no danger with me."

"I don't care. Promise me that my bedroom will be off limits to you."

The Indian sighed, and held up his right hand. "I promise that I will stay out of your bedroom. Now can we go?"

"I haven't finished yet. I also want you to promise me that you will stay out of my bathroom. I don't want you popping in when I'm taking a shower, or doing my business."

"I will also stay out of your bathroom."

"Good. Finally, I want you to promise not to spy on me if I'm ever with a man. Not that I date very often, but I don't want to worry about someone looking over my shoulder if such an unlikely event should happen. I don't need a ghost chaperon."

"Very well. I promise. No bedrooms, no bathrooms, and no dates. Are you happy now?"

"It's a little better," she smiled. "At least I won't have to worry about you spying on me all the time, like you spied on me this morning."

"This morning? What are you talking about? I did not spy on you this morning."

"That wasn't you I felt this morning, over on Charlotte Street?"

"No. Not me." He shook his head. "I told you I was busy. Perhaps you should tell me what happened."

She explained about the weird sensation that had come over her that morning, describing the chill and the feeling of being watched. Tolomato waited until she was done with her story before making comments and asking questions.

"This chill, did it make you feel sick to your stomach, or give you a headache?"

Ssabra nodded. "It gave me a headache. Why? What does having a headache mean?"

"The chill you felt, and the headache it gave you, could mean that you came in contact with evil. Perhaps it was lurking in the alley you spoke of, watching you."

"Evil? What do you mean? What kind of evil?"

"I am not sure, but your reaction is typical of someone who can see. Remember, your eyes have been opened. Even though you cannot see everything yet, you are still a threat to the darkness. Something was obviously lurking in the alley, because you felt its presence. Your headache means it was a thing of evil. Something of the light might have given you the tingling sensation, but it would not have made you feel sick."

"What was it?"

The chief shook his head. "Maybe it was the thing we are hunting."

"The Shiru?" Ssabra inhaled sharply. "The Shiru was in the alley, watching me?"

"Perhaps. I do not know."

"But why was it watching me?"

"Maybe it was trying to find out more about you. It may even be scared of you."

"Scared of me?"

Tolomato nodded. "The Shiru might not be able to hide its true form from you. That makes you a danger to its existence here in this world."

"The Shiru considers me a danger? Great. Just great. It also knows who I am. At least it knows what I look like. What if it decides to eliminate the threat, and comes hunting for me?"

"That could happen, which is why we need to find a way to destroy it." He grinned. "But do not worry about the Shiru, I will be here to protect you. You will be safe, as long as the dark one does not attack you in your bedroom, your bathroom, or when you are on a date."

Tolomato's laugher floated on the air as his figure faded from view. "It is getting late, we must go to the church."

She took a last look around the room to make sure she wasn't forgetting anything. Grabbing her purse and car keys, she left her apartment and headed down the stairs to the parking lot. The drive to the Cathedral-Basilica wasn't a long one, but she drove it alone. Tolomato did not speak to her on the trip, and she wondered if he had gone on ahead of her. If so, he would probably be waiting for her when she got there.

As was the case with most days, parking places in front of the church, or around the plaza, were impossible to find. Ssabra was forced to park in a metered space behind the Casa Monica Hotel and walk back to the Cathedral-Basilica.

Formally known as the Cathedral of St. Augustine, the Basilica was a towering structure of stone and poured concrete, complete with an impressive bell tower, and topped by a Spanish-style terra-cotta roof. The interior of the church had been gutted by a fire back in 1887, but most people would never have guessed, for the inside of the stately building was even more beautiful than the outside.

Ssabra opened one of the massive wooden doors and entered the church, stopping to allow her eyes to adjust to the sudden change in lighting. The interior of the church was quiet and cool, a blessed relief from the afternoon heat. In front of her, rows of pews stood like soldiers at attention, leading down to the main altar. Above the pews arched a high ceiling, decorated with ornate wood and a Spanish seal. Hanging from the center of the ceiling was a crude wooden cross, like the kind that might have been carried by the first Spanish explorers to the New World.

The cross may have been an original, for the stained-glass windows to her right showed a similar cross. In the paintings of colored glass, Spanish explorers and settlers knelt on the sandy shore of the New World, listening to a prayer of thanks being offered up by a priest. The stained-glass windows were quite unusual for a church, for they told the story of the discovery of America, and the founding of St. Augustine, rather than depicting scenes of Jesus, God, and the apostles.

At first she thought the building was empty, but

then she encountered an elderly custodian. The man was scarecrow thin and gray-haired, dressed in blue jeans and a tan work shirt. Ssabra asked if she could speak to one of the priests, or a church officer, and was disappointed to learn that they were all in a meeting.

"Perhaps there is something I can do for you?" asked the custodian.

"Perhaps there is." She smiled warmly, hoping to put any suspicions the man might have at ease. "My name is Ssabra Onih. I'm a tour guide with First City Tours. I want to add the church to the places I visit on my afternoon tour, but I'm afraid I really don't know a lot about its history. I pride myself on being a very knowledgeable tour guide, and I was wondering if you might have a library I could use to do a little research."

"Well, we have a library, but it's only for the church officers. Perhaps you could try the public library, or the Historical Society."

"I've already been there," she lied. "And they just don't have anything of value. You would think that a building this important would have more things written about it, but my search so far has been terribly disappointing. If I could only have access to your library for a few minutes, I'm sure I'll find something I could use for my tour."

"I'm not really supposed to let outsiders use the library. I might get into trouble. Maybe you could leave me your name and phone number, and I could speak with someone in charge."

Ssabra had a feeling that she was butting heads with a brick wall, but she was not going to give up without a fight. "Couldn't you make an exception just this one time? I'll be as quiet as a mouse, so no one will ever know. Besides, I'm Catholic, so it's not like I'm an outsider. If I do make this one of my stops, it could mean extra revenue for the church. The people on my tours are very generous when it comes to making donations. I'm quite sure they'll want to contribute something toward the upkeep of this magnificent building."

He looked around the room, nervously checking to see if anyone was watching. "I'll tell you what, I'll let you into the library for a little while—thirty minutes, and no more—but you have to be real quiet. If you can't find what you're looking for in that time, you'll have to come back and talk with one of the officers."

"Great. Thank you." She smiled. "I really do appreciate it."

The custodian led her away from the main altar, to the far left side of the church, stopping in front of a door opposite the small Altar of the Blessed Virgin. A giant wooden spear hung from the ceiling above the door, symbolic of the weapons carried by the natives that once lived in Florida. The door was opened to reveal a small room crowded with bookshelves, each shelf containing countless volumes of dusty, hardcover books. There was also a small wooden desk and chair in the room, along with a lamp for reading.

"Remember, thirty minutes and keep it quiet."

"I'll remember," Ssabra replied. "Thank you."

She waited for the custodian to walk away, then turned her attention to the shelves. A frown unfolded on her face as she realized there must have been thousands of books in the room. There was no way she was going to find the journal she was looking for in only thirty minutes.

Peeking out to make sure the custodian was nowhere close, she whispered, "Tolomato, are you here?"

"I'm here."

Even though she heard the voice inside her head, she knew the Indian was behind her. Turning, she saw him sitting on the small desk. He was smiling at her, and making a clapping gesture with his hands.

"You did very well; I am proud of you. You are a great liar."

"Thanks." She turned and studied the bookcases. "How are we ever going to find the journal with so many books to look through?"

"That is easy. The journal we want is not here."

"Not here? What do you mean it's not here? Lily said it was in the church library."

"Yes, but it is not here."

"You mean I went through all this trouble for nothing? If the journal isn't here, then where is it?"

Tolomato pointed to her left, at a small door set in the wall between two of the bookcases. "What we seek is there, in another room."

"Then why didn't you just say so?" Ssabra crossed the room, and tried the door. "Great. It's locked. Now what are we going to do?"

"We? I am afraid that I cannot be of much help. I can walk through doors, but I cannot open them. You will have to open the door yourself."

"With what?"

"With your imagination, and a little luck," he replied. "But first I suggest closing the other door so the guard does not see what you are doing."

She crossed the room and closed the library's outer door, then turned back to face her ghostly companion. "Now, how am I supposed to get this other door open?"

"The door is old, and the lock weak. Use one of the metal things in your hair to open it."

"My bobby pin? You think I can open a lock with a bobby pin? I don't think so. Maybe a professional thief could do it, but not me."

"You worry too much. Give it a try; I will help to guide you. In the past, I have watched slaves open the locks of the Spanish with tiny pieces of metal. And I can now see into places where you can't."

Ssabra reluctantly removed one of the bobby pins from her hair and approached the door. She glanced back over her shoulder to the desk, but Tolomato had again disappeared. "You better not have abandoned me."

"Fear not, I am still here," he replied.

"I wish you would quit doing that."

"Doing what?"

"Here one moment, gone the next. You're starting to get on my nerves. A few more disappearances and I will be on Prozac."

"Prozac? What is Prozac?"

She shook her head. "Never mind. It's a long story, and I've only got thirty minutes to pick this lock."

The chief instructed her to straighten the bobby pin and insert it into the lock. He told her which way to turn as she jiggled the pin back and forth. A few moments of frantic fumbling was rewarded with a soft click. Straightening up, she tried the door. It was unlocked.

"Tolomato, you're a genius," she whispered.

"I know."

She opened the door and entered the room she had just unlocked. It was a very small room, no windows, containing several glass-front cases filled with antique books and moldering journals.

Locating a light switch, she closed the door behind her, fearful that the custodian might come to check on her. He might get mad if he found her in the second room, especially if he knew the door had been locked. If he didn't see her in the main library, then he might just assume she had already left.

"Which one is it?" she asked, keeping her voice a low whisper. She was searching through the books in the cases, looking for the journal Lily had described. The ghostly maid had said the journal of Father Diaz had a green cover, but there were quite a few books with green covers.

"Wait a minute, I am still looking," Tolomato answered, his voice as loud as ever. Ssabra started to shush him, but remembered that only she could hear his words.

"Ah, there it is. This one."

"Where?" She turned around, trying to determine which book he was talking about.

"To your right," he answered. "No, left. Dammit, woman. Hold still a minute."

Ssabra froze in place.

"That is better. The book is behind you, in the smaller case. Top shelf on the left."

She turned and looked at the bookshelf behind her. There was a narrow book with a green covering sitting on the top shelf. She stepped forward and tried the glass doors, happy to find that the case was unlocked.

"This one?" she asked, opening the doors and removing the book from the top shelf.

"That is the one," Tolomato assured her. "The journal of Father Sebastian Diaz."

The book was quite old and smelled a little of mildew, and the pages were yellow and brittle, appearing to be made out of some kind of parchment, rather than paper. The words were handwritten in faded black ink, probably scripted by a quill. They were also written in Spanish, and difficult for her to read. She could speak a little Spanish, could even read a word or two, but word usage and language had changed quite a bit since the sixteenth century. The journal might not be easy to read for someone fluent in the language.

"Take the other book too. The white one, next to the book you just took."

She turned back to the bookcase, picking up the book to the right of where the journal had been. It was a modern book, with typed words. She opened the second book and read the introduction, discovering that it was an English translation of Father Diaz's journal.

"It's a translation of the journal," she said, surprised at the find. "Perfect. We won't need the original if we have this."

"You had better keep the original," warned the chief. "Maybe the whole journal was not translated. If something was left out, it might be the part we need to read."

Ssabra thought about it for a moment, then nodded. She glanced at her watch. "I've only got fifteen minutes left before I have to get out of here. There's no way I can read either one of these books in that little time. And the custodian will have a fit if he finds out that I took them out of the case."

"He is not going to find out."

"Why not?"

"Because you will be gone before he returns."

"What about the books?"

"You are going to take them with you."

"You want me to steal the books?"

"Not steal. Borrow. You are going to borrow the books, and then you will return them when we no longer have need of them."

"What about the door? It was hard enough to unlock; I'm not sure if I can lock it again using a bobby pin."

"Close the door. Maybe it will lock by itself."

Ssabra turned off the light in the little room and pulled the door shut, breathing a sigh of relief when she heard the lock click back in place. She tried the door and found that it was again locked.

"Now hurry, hide those books in your purse before the guard comes back."

Opening her purse, she tried to conceal the two books. But the books were too large for the tiny purse she carried, and there was no way she could fit them inside and close the zipper.

"This isn't going to work. My purse is too small; the books will stick out of the opening. I'll get caught for sure."

The sound of a door slamming echoed from the other end of the church, followed by approaching footsteps.

"Shit, someone is coming."

"It is the guard."

Ssabra felt a panic attack coming on. "Is he coming this way?"

"Yes. You must hurry."

She grabbed the two books and tried to pull them back out of her purse, but they were stuck tight.

"Shit. Shit. Shit," she said, struggling to get the books out of her purse.

"You must hurry."

"I'm trying."

"The guard is coming."

"I know. I know. I can hear him. This stupid purse is too small and now the books are stuck. You could help, you know."

"Help? How?"

"Go make some noise. I need a distraction, something to keep the custodian from coming in here."

"A distraction. That is a very good idea."

"I know it is. Now, go do it before it's too late."

"Consider it done."

Ssabra didn't know if Tolomato had left the room, nor did she know if the ghost could create such a distraction. She didn't have time to think about it, because she had to get the books back out of her purse before the custodian returned to check on her. He would be none too happy to discover that she was trying to steal a rare church artifact.

"Come on, you stupid bastard," she whispered

under her breath. "Loosen up so I can get these books out. Cheap leather. I swear, this is the last time I'm going to shop at a flea market."

Grabbing the purse in her left hand, she attempted to pull the books free with her right. She was trying to be careful not to damage the books, but she wasn't having much luck removing them.

"Come on, you stupid purse. Give them up."

Desperate now, she put the purse between her knees and pulled on the books with both hands. The position was awkward, and the purse kept slipping, so she decided to sit down on the chair and have a go at it. She had just sat down when she again heard the sound of approaching footsteps.

I'm caught.

The footsteps were no longer on the other end of the church. Instead they sounded as if they were right outside the door, and she knew that at any moment the custodian was going to step into the library to check on her. Ssabra thought about hiding the books on one of the shelves, but she would have to get them out of her purse to do that. The two books would blend in with the others, and not look out of place to the custodian, but the purse sitting on the shelf would stick out like a sore thumb.

Damn you, Tolomato. This is all your fault. You had better do something to help me. I don't want to go to jail.

The footsteps grew louder. There was no longer time to get the books out of the purse. Nor was there time to hide the purse and its contents. She didn't even have time to slip the purse into the desk, or grab another book off the shelf in an attempt to look as if she were reading. She was caught, red-handed, with a priceless journal stuck in her handbag.

I'm screwed.

She looked up, knowing the custodian was about to step into the room. But just as the footsteps appeared to reach the door, there came the sound of glass breaking from the other end of the church. The footsteps stopped, then hurried off in the opposite direction to check out the noise.

"Oh, thank God," she whispered, breathing a sigh of relief. Her hands were shaking, and she was on the edge of having a nervous breakdown. But the sound of glass shattering had distracted the custodian, giving her a few more moments of freedom. With a Herculean effort, she slipped her hands down inside her purse beside the books and pulled in opposite directions to stretch the leather. She pulled until her arms strained, and something popped like a rubber band in her neck.

"Ow." Ssabra ignored the sudden pain that shot down her spine. Pulling her hands back out of the purse, she tried again to remove the books.

Stretching the leather had done the trick, and this time she was able to remove both volumes. "Yes. Yes. Yes. Thank you. Thank you. Thank you. I did it."

"We did it," corrected Tolomato.

She spun around, startled by the voice. There was no one else in the room to be seen. Tolomato was back, but he had not materialized.

"What did you break?" Ssabra was worried about the sound she had heard.

"Nothing important," the Indian assured her, "but it will keep the guard busy for a few minutes. If you are done playing around, this would be a good time for you to leave."

"I'm way ahead of you." Pulling up her shirt, she slipped both books into the waistband of her shorts. She pulled the shirt back down over top of the books, attempting to conceal them.

"How does this look?"

"It looks like you have two books hidden under your shirt."

"Really?"

"Yes. You have obviously never stolen anything before."

"You said we weren't stealing these books; we were only borrowing them."

"I say borrowing, the police will say stealing."

Worried that the books beneath her shirt were noticeable, Ssabra looked around the room for a mirror. But there was none to be found. "What should I do?"

"Try sucking in your stomach, and bend over a little so your shirt is not so tight."

She did as the chief suggested, bending over and sucking in her stomach.

Tolomato laughed. "Aieee. You are quite a sight. Now you look like an old person trying to steal two books."

"This isn't funny," she snapped, angry.

"It is to me," he chuckled. "You should see how you look."

"Will you quit laughing and help out?"

"I have already helped you, but I will be happy to break something else if you like."

"No. No. Not that. I mean help me to get out of here without getting caught."

"I will do my best."

Uncomfortable with her new position, she straightened up a little. "Where is the custodian now?"

"He is still busy."

"Good. Is there anyone else around?"

"No. Not now."

"Then I think I had better get out of here while I can."

"That would be a good idea," laughed the chief.

Doing a quick double-check to make sure the books would not slip down her shorts as she moved, Ssabra stepped toward the doorway. She opened the door and peeked out to make sure no one was around, then left the library and hurried through the church. She tried to move quietly, but her footsteps sounded excessively loud. She was certain someone would intercept her before she could reach the front doors.

But no one tried to stop her as she made her way toward the front of the church. The custodian was apparently still busy, and she wondered what Tolomato had caused to break. Reaching the front of the church, she yanked open one of the heavy wooden doors and stepped outside. Pulling the door closed behind her, she hurried off down the sidewalk, trying to put as much distance as possible between her and the custodian. She expected someone to call after her, but the only voice she heard as she hurried away from the crime scene was Tolomato's, and he was laughing at her.

CHAPTER
25

Ssabra kept looking back over her shoulder as she made her way down the sidewalk, terrified the church custodian was going to discover her theft and come racing after her. Crossing the street, she hurried past the Casa Monica Hotel to where she had parked her car.

Once past the hotel, she paused to look around again. Satisfied that no one was watching, she reached a hand under her shirt and removed the two books. Now she could walk faster, without having to worry about the books slipping. She also didn't have to worry about getting perspiration on them, a definite concern because she was sweating with fear.

"Much better," she whispered to herself. She almost expected Tolomato to make a reply, but the Indian spirit was silent. Or maybe he was gone, taking off somewhere and leaving her holding the bag. Or in her case, holding the books.

She reached her car without incident, and without

being stopped. Unlocking the driver's door and sliding in behind the wheel, she hid the books under the
seat and started the engine. A few seconds later she
drove out of the lot and headed for home.

The young woman felt a little like Jesse James as
she sped along the narrow streets of the old city, and
she kept glancing into the rearview mirror to see if
a posse was pursuing her. Luckily, no posse gave
chase. Nor did any police cars come speeding up
behind her with sirens blaring. As a matter of fact,
it was a rather uneventful drive back to her apartment. Still, that didn't relieve the butterflies in her
stomach. She had never stolen anything, other than
an occasional piece of candy as a child, and she did
not like the sensation of being one of the bad guys.
No, the life of crime was definitely not for her.

Arriving back at Cypress Pointe, she parked the
car and hurried up the stairs to her apartment. It
was only when she was finally inside, with the door
double-locked behind her, did she start to calm down
a little.

"Well, young lady. What does the book say?"

Ssabra nearly screamed at the sound of Tolomato's
voice. She spun around, angry at being startled.

"Dammit, will you stop doing that."

"Doing what?" he asked innocently.

"Popping in unannounced, scaring me half to
death."

"But we are not in your bedroom, or in the bathroom. You said—"

"I don't care what I said. Just quit doing it."

"Oh, I see. Perhaps this would be better." He made
a coughing sound. "Ladies and gentlemen, please

make ready. Tolomato, chief of the Guales, is about to make his appearance." With those words the chief slowly materialized in the center of the living room. He was watching her with a crooked smile on his face, his head cocked to one side.

"You're a regular comedian." She set the books down on the kitchen counter and picked up her coffee cup. "You really should be in show business."

Tolomato just laughed.

"I'll look at the books in just a minute, after I make a cup of instant coffee. My nerves are shot."

"Make one for me too."

"You want a cup of coffee?"

The spirit nodded.

"But you can't . . . oh yeah, I forgot. You like to smell things."

"Make it black, and strong."

"Got it." Ssabra took another cup out of the cabinet, and made two cups of instant coffee. She watched with amusement as Tolomato appeared to sit down on the couch. She wondered if he was really sitting on the couch, or hovering over it. Maybe he was just projecting the image of sitting on the furniture. She didn't know a lot about ghosts, so she wasn't sure if they could sit like normal people.

"What have I gotten myself into?"

"What was that?" He turned to look at her.

"Nothing. I was just talking to myself." She set both cups down on the living room table, sliding the cup of black coffee over to where he was sitting.

The Indian looked at her for a moment, then nodded. "Crazy people often talk to themselves."

She coughed. "I am not crazy."

"Sure you are," he laughed. "It is the middle of the day, and you are having coffee with a spirit. And you are wondering if I am sitting on your sofa, or hovering above it."

Ssabra was shocked. "You can read my thoughts?"

"Thoughts and words are the same to me. There is no difference between the two. As I told you before—"

"Please, don't start explaining things again. You are giving me a headache."

"You have too many headaches for someone so young. Maybe you should see a doctor. The medicine man of my village would have put leeches on your ears to stop your headache. You should try that."

She laughed, nearly spilling her coffee. "That's a great idea. I think I'll rush out and buy some leech earrings."

"Do it later," he said, very serious. "Now we must read the books."

"Okay, you win. Let's look at the books." Ssabra decided the best way to do it was to place the books side by side on the coffee table, and attempt to go through them at the same time. She was concerned that the English translation of the journal might be abridged, and some of the priest's original notes might have been left out—especially if anything had been written about the Shirus. She didn't know where the Catholic Church stood when it came to talk about monsters and ancient gods. There were also several pages of hand-drawn maps and illustrations in the old journal that didn't appear in the translation.

Pushing her coffee cup back out of the way, she

opened the journal of Father Sebastian Diaz. She also opened the English translation of the journal, which was written by a university professor named John Willis. According to the books, Father Diaz had lived in St. Augustine during the early 1600s, and he was very much involved with the Indian tribes in the area.

"Did you know him?" Ssabra asked, turning to Tolomato.

He shrugged. "Maybe. All priests look alike to me."

"But when were you born?"

"In the summer."

"No. I mean what year?"

Again the Indian shrugged. "I do not know. Our calendars were different than yours. Our years were listed by major events, not by numbers."

Turning her attention back to the books, Ssabra continued reading the translation. She referred back to the original as she went along, looking for similar words, names, or dates. It was a tedious process, for the original journal was handwritten in Spanish and the script was old and faded, making it very difficult to read. Still, she could pick out enough key words and phrases to let her know that nothing had been left out when the journal was translated.

The first fifty pages of the journal were about Father Sebastian Diaz's arrival in the New World. He spoke of the long voyage he had taken from his native Seville, and the terrible journey across the Atlantic Ocean. He wrote how the crew and passengers aboard the tiny wooden ship had faced rough seas, and suffered from sickness. The food and water had been foul, and they had existed mostly on rum and salt pork. Several people had died during the journey, and Father Diaz had been responsible for receiving their last confessions and sending their spirits on to God.

After a stop in Cuba, the priest had arrived in the New World on April 15, 1602. His first impressions of America were not good, describing St. Augustine as a miserable little hamlet infested with vice, savages, and mosquitoes. He was dismayed to find that most of the town resembled the neighboring Indian villages, with houses made of wood and palm frond roofs. He compared St. Augustine with peasant squalor, unlike the beautiful city of Seville he had left behind.

Still, despite his dismay at the living conditions, Father Diaz was anxious to get started with his work. He was to bring the word of God to the New World, attempting to save the souls of the local heathens. If they had souls, and if they could be saved.

Many of the Indian tribes living in Florida at that time were still untouched when it came to the religious teachings of the Old World. There had been some progress made in the conversion of the local tribes, and a few missions had already been established, but Florida was a vast uneasily traveled wilderness, so the going had been slow. Not only did the priest, and those who traveled with him, have to worry about making their way through thick forests and dense swampland, where infectious mosquitoes, poisonous snakes, and alligators, awaited around every turn, they also had to be wary of the various warlike tribes that dotted the landscape. Many a Spaniard had ended up with body parts hanging as trophies on village walls.

Father Diaz had first traveled north to the Jacksonville area, establishing a tiny mission on the coast. He had stayed there for almost four years before returning to St. Augustine, working with the Indians living in the surrounding wilderness.

The relationship between the priests and natives could be called shaky at best. The Indians wanted to trade with the Spanish, in order to obtain metal tools and other items. Some even allowed themselves to be baptized into the new religion, hoping to become better friends with the white man. There were also a few Spanish men who took Indian women as wives, but this was not a common practice.

For the most part, however, the Indians were looked upon by the Spanish as little more than slaves or cattle, something to be claimed with the land and forced into servitude for the Crown. Father Diaz had accompanied several military expeditions into the interior of Florida, and he wrote openly about the cruelty of the Spanish soldiers. He told how he was witness to the rape and murder of native women, and how he had watched entire villages burned to the ground.

Unlike the priest, the soldiers had no interest whatsoever in saving the souls of the indigenous peoples. Instead, they were looking for gold, wealth to increase the storerooms of the Crown. The Indians who weren't killed outright by the soldiers were often forced into slavery. They became the workers in the fields, and the laborers to build St. Augustine into a real city.

Despite what he wrote in his journal, Father Diaz

never protested aloud the incidents of cruelty that he saw. Instead, he stood silently by, watching as helpless natives were put to death or forced into servitude. After all, the military was in charge, and it would be foolish to stand up against such power. Even God might not be able to come to his aid in the middle of a hostile wilderness.

Ssabra was halfway through the journal before coming upon what she was looking for. It seemed Father Sebastian Diaz was one of the few priests who had actually taken the time to learn the customs and folklore of the native tribes. He had even written down some of their legends, concerned the stories might be lost once the Indians converted to Christianity.

The priest described the native practice of lighting a new council fire each year in the village, and then carrying a flame from that fire to light the smaller cooking fires in each household. The term he wrote in his journal was *Tacachale*, which, in the native tongue, meant to light a new fire. It was a ceremony of rebirth, with a cleansing fire giving life to a new year while the ashes of the old year were swept away.

He wrote about the superstitions of the various tribes living around St. Augustine, and he also described their creation myths. Some of the natives believed their people had originally descended from the heavens, while others were absolutely certain their ancestors had climbed up from the underworld through a tiny hole in the ground. Some even claimed that the world rested on the back of a giant turtle.

Father Diaz was obviously amused by the stories he gathered in his journal, but he did not try to edit or ridicule them. Instead he recorded each story as it was told to him, adding his personal comments and thoughts at the end. Ssabra was just skimming through one of the last legends, when she came upon the word "Shiru."

"Bingo," she said, backing up to reread the page.

"What is it?" asked Tolomato.

"I think I have something here. I just came upon the word 'Shiru.' "

"What does it say?"

"Shhh . . . give me a minute. I'm still reading."

She reread the page, and then went on to the next. According to what was written in the journal, the Indian tribes living along the east coast believed that dark gods walked the earth, and these gods, called Shirus, often mated with humans in order to ensure that their bloodline continued on in the world of the living. The Indians feared these living gods, and would put to death any child with characteristics that led them to believe it was born of human and Shiru.

When the Spaniards first arrived in the area, the natives were terrified of the stories about Jesus Christ. The Bible said Jesus was born of God and woman, so the Indians believed him to be one of the dark ones. They would often run away and hide when the priests recited aloud a prayer, terrified the white men were calling upon a Shiru to visit.

Father Diaz was apparently fascinated by the Shiru legends, and had devoted several pages in his journal to the subject. He had talked with the natives of different tribes, finding out that they all had similar stories about the Shirus. They also all feared the monsters.

The priest also wrote about a hideously deformed child being born in a neighboring Indian village, said to be an offspring of a Shiru. The villagers were terrified of the child and wanted to put it to death, but Father Diaz managed to hide it for several years. The Indians eventually found out where the child was hidden, killing it one night while the priest was asleep.

The Indians wanted to cut up the murdered child's body, for they believed its bones were magical and could be used as weapons against the dark gods, but the priest took the body and buried it in a secret plot. Father Diaz hinted in his journal that the burial plot of the deformed child was somewhere in old St. Augustine, marked by a small stone bearing a Spanish cross.

The last few pages of the journal contained several crude drawings made by the priest, showing what the Shiru offspring looked like. The images were frightful, showing a child with an oversized head and multiple arms, like a mad cross between a human baby and an octopus.

"Good Lord." She glanced up to see if Tolomato could see the illustration, but the Indian was no longer visible.

"Hey, where did you go?"

"I am still here," he replied.

"I wish you would stop doing that, popping in and out all the time."

"It is quite difficult for me to make myself visible to your untrained eyes. I tire easily."

"I thought spirits didn't get tired."

"You will think otherwise when you get on this side."

"Can you see the drawing?"

"Yes. It may be an offspring. I do not know. I have never seen one before."

Ssabra pointed to the opposite page. "Look at this. It's an old map of St. Augustine. The details aren't the best, but the X marks where Father Diaz buried the offspring.

"The natives living back then believed the bones of an offspring could be used as a weapon against the dark ones. They had experience in fighting Shirus, and probably knew what they were talking about. If we can find the remains, we can make arrows, or even a spear. We might be able to stop the Shiru before it can kill again."

"Then we should start looking."

"I agree. Just give me a minute to—"

She was suddenly interrupted by the ringing of her doorbell. The sound was unexpected and nearly caused her to jump. "Who could that be?"

"You have company."

"You think?" Ssabra asked, sarcastically. Getting up, she made her way to the door, looking out the peephole to see who it was. At first she didn't recognize the man standing on the other side of the door, because his face was in profile to her, but then he turned back around to ring the doorbell a second time. It was Detective Jack Colvin.

The books. Someone must have reported them missing. Turning away from the door, she hurried back through the living room and snatched the books off the coffee table. She carried the journal and its translation into her bedroom, hiding them in a dresser drawer, then started back toward the front door. The detective rang the bell a third time, and knocked, obviously growing impatient.

"Just a minute. I'm coming." Unlocking the two locks, Ssabra pulled open the door.

The detective nodded and smiled, his eyes darting past her to see who else was inside the apartment. "Miss Onih, I'm Detective Colvin. We spoke the other day."

"Yes, Detective, I remember you. Forgive me for taking so long to open the door, I wasn't expecting anyone. What can I do for you?"

"I was wondering if I could talk with you for a few minutes. I tried calling you earlier, but you must not have been home."

The detective seemed somewhat embarrassed. Perhaps he was feeling guilty for being so rude to her during their first meeting.

"Get rid of him." Tolomato's voice popped into her head. The Indian was obviously quite unhappy with the detective interrupting their plans to search for the offspring.

How? Ssabra formed the words in her mind. Tolomato had said that thoughts and words were the same to him. If so, then he might be able to read her mind.

"Tell him you are about to leave."

That won't work. He's a cop. He won't care if I have plans. He'll be suspicious.

"You do not know unless you try."

"What's this about?" Ssabra asked, trying to keep her voice friendly.

"If you don't mind, I would like to talk to you about a few things you said at the station the other day."

"Oh? I was under the impression that you didn't believe what I told you . . . that you thought I was some kind of mental case."

Detective Colvin cleared his throat. "I won't lie to you; I did find your story a little odd. But there have been a few developments since then, and I would really appreciate it if you would take the time to speak with me again."

"Get rid of him!" Tolomato said, his voice almost a shout. "There is no time for this."

Ssabra glanced down at her watch. "Gee, I would really like to help, but I'm running late for a very important meeting. I was just about to head out when you rang the bell. What if I called you first thing in the morning?"

"Can't you spare a few minutes now?"

She glanced at her watch again. "No. Sorry. I wish I could, but I can't. I took time out to see you the other day, and I've been running behind schedule ever since. Now, if you will excuse me, Detective. I simply have to get ready for my meeting. I promise I'll call you first thing in the morning. Good night."

With that, Ssabra closed the door on Detective Jack Colvin. She expected the man to get mad at her, yelling that he was the police and she had better talk with him right then and there. She even expected him to put his foot in the door, like detectives always did in the movies. But he didn't do either of those things. Instead, he said good night, adding that he looked forward to speaking with her in the morning.

She double-locked the door, breathing a sigh of relief. Ssabra listened to the detective's footsteps as they descended the steps. Even though she had done nothing wrong, other than steal a priceless journal from the church, she was still uncomfortable in his presence. She hoped he had believed her story about being late for a very important meeting.

Fighting monsters, stealing from churches, and lying to the police. Tolomato, what have you gotten me into?

CHAPTER
26

Detective Colvin returned to his car, but he did not drive away. He had been a law officer long enough to know that Ssabra Onih had been anxious to get rid of him. But why? The day before she had wanted to talk, but now it seemed his presence made her nervous. Suspecting something was amiss, he decided to keep an eye on the young woman to see if she really was going to an important meeting.

Less than thirty minutes later, he saw Ssabra coming down the stairs from her apartment. Jack glanced at his watch; it was nearly seven p.m. Sliding down in his seat to keep from being spotted, he watched as she crossed the parking lot to a blue Ford Escort. In her hands, she carried a leather purse and a small green book. If she was going to a meeting, then, judging by the way she was dressed, it must be a casual affair. Definitely not a business meeting, or a date.

"Okay, lady. What are you up to?" He pulled a

cigarette from the pack on the seat beside him, but he did not light it. He didn't want the sudden flaring of a butane lighter to get the woman's attention; he did not want her to know that she was being watched.

Ssabra Onih climbed into her car, started the engine, and drove out of the parking lot. Jack sat up straight in the seat and started his vehicle, but gave his quarry a few seconds' head start before following after her. He had tailed many a suspect, and knew all of the tricks to keep from being spotted.

The Escort headed south toward the city's historic district. Traffic was heavy along Avenida Menendez, due to the evening influx of tourists crowding the restaurants and bars, so parking spaces were at a premium. Jack thought Miss Onih might be heading for one of the side streets to park, but a green pickup pulled out of a space on the opposite side of the street, and she did a quick U-turn in order to grab the parking space before anyone else could take it.

The detective suddenly found himself in somewhat of a predicament. There were no other spaces along the street, which meant he would have to drive past Ssabra in hopes of finding a place to park. He might be seen while driving past. He also might not find a spot right away, and would lose sight of the woman. There were dozens of restaurants, bars and shops in the historic area, any one of which could be where she was going to meet someone.

He ducked down as he drove past the blue Escort, looking away to avoid eye contact. In his rearview mirror, he saw Ssabra climb out of her car and lock the door. She obviously intended to cross the street, and would probably disappear before he could find a parking place.

But luck must have been on his side that evening, for he suddenly spotted an empty space in front of him on the same side of the road. A Dodge Caravan was backing into the space, but the driver was obviously not very good at parallel parking and had overshot his first attempt. The driver pulled forward to try again, but Jack jerked his steering wheel to the right and whipped into the parking place, cutting off the van.

The van's driver slammed on his brakes and hit the horn. Jack put his car in park, killed the engine, and climbed out of the vehicle. He looked around and saw that Ssabra Onih had already crossed the street and was heading away from him.

"What the hell are you doing?" The driver's door of the mini van popped open and a tall, well-dressed, slightly overweight man climbed out. "You son of a bitch, you saw I was trying to back into that space."

Jack shrugged and half smiled. "Sorry. You snooze, you lose."

The big man's face went beet red with anger. "You son of a bitch. I'll call the fucking cops on you."

Jack grinned, pulling out his badge and displaying it. "You go ahead and call the cops. While you're at it, you might want to also call your lawyer. I'm on official police business, and if you call me a son of a bitch once more I'll lock your ass up for public profanity and threats against a police officer. Any questions?"

The big man stopped, not sure what to make of the situation. "That's not a real badge."

"Oh, it's a real badge." Jack reached under his jacket and slipped his handcuffs out of the leather case on his belt. "And these are real handcuffs." He dangled the cuffs so they could be seen. "I also have a real gun, but I'm hoping I won't be needing that tonight. 'Cause if I have to pull my gun, then you're going to jail. Or maybe to the hospital. Now, I suggest you climb back into your vehicle, and find yourself another parking spot."

The man stared at the detective for another moment, made a sputtering sound that might have been a curse word, then climbed back into his van and drove away. Jack would have enjoyed the moment, might even have laughed out loud, but Ssabra Onih was already halfway down the street and about to disappear from view. Slipping badge and handcuffs into his jacket pocket, he hurried after her.

If Miss Onih was late for an urgent meeting, as she claimed, then she was taking her sweet time about getting there. She moved at a slow pace down the sidewalk along Avenida Menendez, turning left on Cuna Street. Occasionally she would stop to study the book she carried, as if looking up a particular address.

"What are you up to, lady?" Jack stayed back, far enough to blend in with the crowd without losing sight of his quarry. But the path she took was through some of the quieter sections of the old city, down narrow streets and alleyways where few tourists traveled. Soon it was only the two of them on the street, and the detective knew he might be spotted if Ssabra was to turn around. Luckily, it was already getting dark, and there were few streetlights along the avenues they walked.

They had just turned onto an unlit narrow side street, passing a deserted lot overgrown with weeds, when he suddenly realized that Miss Onih was no longer alone. A man now followed about twenty feet behind the young woman, moving along at a pace matching hers.

Where did he come from?

The man must have come out of the deserted lot. Perhaps he was lurking there in the darkness, or he might have been using the lot as a shortcut from one street to another, and just happened to appear as Ssabra was walking past. His sudden appearance behind the woman could be perfectly innocent, but Jack had been a detective long enough to suspect the worst in people. And right then, he was thinking that the man following Miss Onih was up to no good.

The man might be a robber, or a rapist. One thing for sure, he moved with too much grace to be a drunken tourist. He also moved at a pace that matched Ssabra's, stopping when she did, and keeping to the left side of the street where the shadows lay heaviest.

Knowing his plans for secretly trailing Miss Onih were about to be dashed to the winds, Jack decided to make the first move. Wanting to run a little interference on the stalker, he quickened his pace. The man was so intent on watching the woman he followed, he never heard the detective until he was right behind him.

Not wanting Ssabra to know he had been following her, Jack spoke in a low voice to keep from being
overheard, "Okay, buddy. That's far enough. I think
we need to have ourselves a little talk."

The stalker spun around, startled to find someone
behind him. The detective already had his badge out,
and had one hand on his holstered automatic.

Jack's eyes must have played a trick on him, because, for a split second, it appeared as if the man
changed shapes as he turned, his features blurring
and then becoming clear again.

The detective blinked and shook his head. What he
had seen, or what he thought he saw, was probably
nothing more than a trick of the eyes. Even though it
was rather dark where they stood, there was still
enough light to clearly see the man he had stopped.
He was Caucasian, about six feet tall, with sandy
brown hair and a full beard. He was dressed in blue
jeans, boots, denim jacket, and an unbuttoned black
shirt. The man's features seemed vaguely familiar, and
Jack wondered where he had seen him before.

The man took a step back, apparently trying to read
Jack's badge. As he moved, his shirt opened to reveal
a dark tattoo on the left side of his chest: a tribal image
of a turtle. It was the same tattoo that had been on
one of the pieces of human skin in the Dumpster behind the Old Drugstore.

Jack glanced at the tattoo, then looked back up at
the man's face, realizing his features were identical to
the face found at the second crime scene. Same colored
beard, same wide nose and heavy lips. Hell, the guy
even had the same fucking tattoo. He was damn near
a perfect match for the remains they had found.

A twin brother? A member of the same gang? Or maybe this guy just goes around shedding his skin from time to time.

Detective Colvin was about to ask for the stalker's identification, when he happened to catch a glimpse of the building to his right. Housed in the building was a gift shop that sold antiques and collectibles, some of which were displayed in a large window. The building was closed for the night, its interior dark and the OPEN sign unlit, but he could still see his reflection in the glass. He could also see the reflection of the man standing before him. Or rather, he could see the reflection of the monster standing before him, because what he saw in the window was anything but human.

Instead of a bearded man, dressed in jeans, boots, and a jacket, Jack saw a shimmering black blob with long tentacles, a creature made of smoke whose shape and appearance constantly changed. The image in the mirror was a nightmare beyond words, causing the skin at his temples to pull tight.

The man standing before him also turned his head and looked at the window, seeing what Jack was staring at. He saw the reflection and smiled, then he lunged at the detective.

"Son of a bitch!"

Jack went down hard, a mass of twisting blackness on top of him. He was no longer facing a man. Instead, he was fighting a creature that must have been spewed from the very bowels of hell. A misshapen thing, multilegged, with long ropelike tentacles, more spider than human.

The detective tried to get free, but a tentacle wrapped around his throat and squeezed tight. He heard a strange clacking sound and was terrified to see a large beaked mouth only inches from his face. The beak was opening and closing, the creature attempting to get close enough to bite him. Knowing that serious injury, and perhaps even death, was only moments away, he managed to draw his pistol from its holster and fire a single shot.

The gunshot startled her. It was loud and close, and might have come from the next street over. In most cities the sound of gunfire would be cause for alarm, but that wasn't always the case in St. Augustine. Historical reenactments were held quite often in the old city, everything from Drake's pirate invasion to the British Night Watch, so the sound of flintlock rifles and pistols being fired, or the booming roar of an old cannon, was not uncommon.

Ssabra didn't know of any historical events scheduled to take place that night, but someone might have decided to put on a show at the last minute. Curious if some kind of pageantry was indeed taking place, she turned and started in the direction of the shot.

She had only taken a few steps, however, when a feeling of icy numbness came over her. It was the same sensation she had experienced earlier in the day, a feeling that Tolomato said was caused by evil. Ssabra froze and looked around, but she was alone in the alley.

Where was Tolomato? She did not see the Indian spirit anywhere. Nor had she heard his voice since starting out on foot to look for the place where the offspring might be buried. That was just like him, never around when she needed him most.

Dammit, Tolomato. Where are you? And what is causing this feeling?

The icy sensation continued to grow, bringing with it a painful throbbing behind her eyes. She blinked and shook her head, but the pain did not go away. Whatever was causing the feeling had to be close, too close for comfort.

Ssabra was suddenly aware of just how alone she was, and how dark it had already gotten. Night had descended over the area without her notice, her attention completely occupied with her search for the offspring. It wasn't safe being out by herself at night, especially with a dark god on the loose.

Damn, you're an idiot. What were you thinking? You should have waited until morning to start the search.

If there was evil nearby, then she sure as hell didn't want to face it on her own. And if that evil happened to be the Shiru, then she wanted to have as many people around her as possible for protection.

Deciding that a group of historical reenactors might provide some level of safety, even if their guns were only loaded with black powder and no bullets, Ssabra hurried toward the noise coming from the next street. A few more steps brought her to the intersection of two narrow alleyways.

She hurried around the corner only to stop dead in her tracks, horrified by the sight before her. There were no reenactors dressed in historical military costumes. No Spanish soldiers, British troops, or bloodthirsty pirates. There weren't even any buckskinners, with their greasy leathers and tattered furs. There was only one man, and he was on his back in the middle of the alley, fighting for his life.

It wasn't muggers or bad guys the man did battle with. No one was trying to rob him, beat him up, or settle an old score. On the contrary, on top of the man was something far worse than mere criminals, a hideous creature that looked like a giant black octopus. Or maybe a spider.

The octopus-spider thing was obviously winning the fight, dozens of long black tentacles wrapping around the poor man trapped beneath it. The man held a pistol in his right hand, but he was having a hard time aiming it for another shot.

It only took a moment for Ssabra to realize that the thing in the alley was the Shiru. It was the same monster she and Tolomato had been looking for, the creature of darkness whose very presence sent waves of cold shooting through her body.

Here was the beast Tolomato was convinced they could destroy, but how on earth could they hope to defeat such a monster? It was bigger and stronger than what she had imagined. Just seeing the Shiru in its true form caused her to go numb with fear, and nearly sent her running in the opposite direction. Had it not been for the man trapped beneath the monster, she would have fled for her life.

As she stood there, the man turned his face toward her and mouthed a silent cry for help. There was something compelling about the look of terror in his eyes, like a kitten trapped in the topmost branches of a high oak tree. There was also something familiar about his face, as if she had seen him somewhere before.

Ssabra watched the man voice the silent words, suddenly realizing where she had seen him. She did indeed know the Shiru's unfortunate victim, and had spoken with him less than an hour earlier. It was Detective Jack Colvin who did battle with the ancient god, and who was about to lose his life.

She didn't know what the detective was doing in the same part of town, but suspected he had been following her. Perhaps he was still hoping to talk with her, or maybe he was spying on her. Whatever the reason, he was now fighting the very thing he had refused to believe existed.

Not only was Detective Colvin in the same area of town, but so too was the Shiru. Perhaps if he had not been following her, the monster might have found itself a different victim. She might have been the one fighting for her life.

Discovering that she knew the man beneath the monster, and just how close she had come to bumping into the Shiru, brought an involuntary scream to her lips. Ssabra had never been much of a screamer, but she did herself proud at that particular moment.

Much to her surprise, the scream had an unexpected effect on the battle taking place, actually causing the Shiru to stop its attack on Detective Colvin and turn toward her. Apparently, she had managed to get the monster's full attention, whether she wanted it or not.

"Now I've done it." She stumbled backward a step or two, but was much too frightened to run away. Not that running was really an option. She was quite sure a multiple-legged dark god could easily outrun a terrified tour guide. Nor did she have the courage needed to turn her back on the monster long enough to make a run for it.

Her scream had gotten the Shiru's attention, and she expected the monster to come after her. But instead of lunging toward her, the creature disengaged itself from the detective and scurried away in the opposite direction. The dark god magically changed shapes as it fled down the alley, transforming from a monster into a man.

Ssabra stood and watched the Shiru as it ran away, mesmerized by the transformation. She then turned her attention to the detective, hurrying to help him to his feet.

"Are you hurt?"

"I'm okay. I'm okay," Detective Colvin replied, getting to his feet. He looked around, eyes wide, his pistol still gripped firmly in his right hand. "Jesus Christ, what is that thing? Where did it go?"

"It's called a Shiru, and it's what I tried to warn you about," Ssabra answered. "It took off down the alley. I think it's gone, but I'm not sure for how long."

Jack lowered his pistol, but did not put it away.

"Now do you believe my story?" she asked.

He turned to her and nodded. "Miss Onih, from now on I will believe anything you tell me. I think maybe we had better have that little talk, but let's do it someplace else. I don't want to be standing here if that thing comes back."

Ssabra glanced down the alley, but there was no sign of the Shiru. "How about my apartment? I've got booze, and I think we can both use a drink."

"I hope you've got a full bottle, because I damn sure need more than just one drink."

CHAPTER
27

Detective Jack Colvin had just been up against something that could not be explained in logical terms, a shape-shifting creature that had nearly taken his life. Nothing in all his years of law enforcement had prepared him for such an encounter. They did not teach Fighting Monsters 101 at the police academy, nor were there any training manuals on the subject. Hell, as far as he knew, he was the first cop ever to have such an experience.

At least he thought he was the first cop ever to be attacked by a monster, not that he was going to ask any of his fellow officers if they ever had a similar experience. He didn't dare breathe a word about his little encounter, because there wasn't a man or woman on the police force who would believe him. Not even Bill Moats.

At that particular moment, however, Jack wasn't too worried about being believed. Sitting on the living room sofa in Ssabra Onih's apartment, a tumbler filled with vodka and ice clutched tightly in his right hand, he was more concerned about getting his heart rate to slow down.

As the detective sipped his vodka, Ssabra repeated the story she had told him at the police station, adding what she had learned since her visit. Jack let her talk uninterrupted, listening carefully to everything she said. Her story no longer sounded quite so far-fetched, at least it didn't sound any crazier than the story he now had to tell.

"And you stole this from the church?" he asked, looking through the journal written by Father Sebastian Diaz.

"I borrowed it," Ssabra frowned. "I'm not a thief."

Jack nodded. "Sorry. I didn't mean that the way it sounded." He took another sip of vodka and looked around. "Is Tolomato in the room with us now? I mean, can you see him?"

Ssabra glanced over by the television. Tolomato stood leaning against the wall, watching them. He made a funny face, which made her smile. "Yes. He's here with us."

He looked toward the television, but didn't see anything. If it wasn't for his encounter with the Shiru, he never would have believed her story about being able to speak with a dead Indian chief. One thing for certain, he was not about to call her crazy after what he had seen in the alley.

"Forgive me if I still sound skeptical," he said, shaking his head. "I've been a cop for too many years to change my way of thinking overnight, and I'm having a hard time dealing with all of this."

"It hasn't been easy for me either. Just the other day I was leading a normal life, now I'm talking with dead Indian chiefs, stealing books from a Catholic church—excuse me, I mean borrowing books from a church—and trying to find magical bones so we can kill some kind of evil god."

"We?"

She nodded. "You're now a believer, so there's no way in hell I'm going after the Shiru by myself. As far as I'm concerned, my job is over: I finally got someone in authority to listen to my story. You're a cop; it's your sworn duty to protect the citizens of St. Augustine. So go protect them."

"I can't do it by myself."

"Who said anything about doing it by yourself? Get on the phone and call your cop buddies. Hell, call in the army. You're going to need them."

Jack shook his head. "No one would believe me. You're the only help I've got."

"I hate to say this, but you don't have me. I've seen the Shiru, up close and personal, and there's no way I'm going to go after that thing."

"I need you."

"No, you don't," she argued.

"You're right, I don't need you. But I need Tolomato, and the two of you are a team. I'm not any more anxious than you to go back out on the streets with that thing walking around. Your spirit sidekick might be able to watch my back, keep an eye on the Shiru while I'm trying to find a way to kill it."

She thought about it for a minute, then nodded. "Okay. You made your point. I guess we're both in this together. But do not expect me to stand my ground if that monster shows up again. Battling evil is your job, not mine."

"Agreed." Jack set his drink down on the table.

"What about using heavy firepower to stop it? Would that work? I could get some shotguns and stun grenades. I could probably even get my hands on a few M-16s, and armor piercing rounds. That ought to send the Shiru back to where it came from."

Ssabra shook her head. "Tolomato doesn't think conventional weapons will do much good. The Shiru is a dark god, and has returned from the land of spirits. It is a thing of evil, and that has to be taken into consideration when trying to stop it. Only strong medicine can stop evil, which is why I was trying to find out where the offspring was buried."

Jack flipped to the back of the journal, studying the crude map drawn by Father Sabastian Diaz. "Were you able to locate the remains?"

"I didn't have time. I was out looking tonight, but I got sidetracked trying to save your ass."

The detective looked up at her and smiled. "Thank you."

He turned his attention back to the journal. "Even using this map, it's not going to be easy to find the remains of the offspring, if there are any remains left to be found, especially with the Shiru out there hunting in the old city. And there's no telling how much time we've got before that thing decides to kill again.

"I'd call the station to report what happened tonight, maybe even ask for a curfew to keep people off the streets, but I'm not sure what to say. They're not going to believe a story about a shape-shifting monster, and I need a damn good reason to request a curfew. The homicide investigation has pretty much been handed over to the FBI, and I doubt if the feds would believe my story. Luckily, we've already got extra patrols out on the streets."

Jack closed the journal. "One thing bothering me about tonight: how is it the Shiru happened to be in the same section of the city as you? Was it just dumb luck, or did the monster know where to look for you? I mean, does that thing know that you're hunting for it? If so, is it now hunting you?"

"But the Shiru didn't attack me," she corrected. "It attacked you."

"True enough, but it was following you. Had I not stopped it, you might have been the victim."

Her eyes went wide. "Oh, my gosh. That's right. You said I was being followed. That means you might actually have saved my life. Thank you."

"You're welcome." He continued. "I would like to know how you and the Shiru ended up in the same alley at the same time. Does Tolomato have any thoughts about it?"

She turned her attention to the corner of the room, but Tolomato no longer stood there. "Damn, I wish he would quit doing that."

"Doing what?"

"Disappearing on me."

"He's not there?"

"No. Not now. At least I can't see him anymore."

"Relax, young one," Tolomato said, his voice popping into her mind. "I am still here."

Ssabra smiled. "He's still here."

"Where?" asked the detective.

She shrugged. "I don't know. I don't see him; I just hear his voice."

"Did he hear the question, or should I repeat it?"

"I heard it," the chief replied. "I am dead, not deaf."

Ssabra burst out laughing.

"What did he say?" Jack asked.

She held up her hand and shook her head. "Nothing. Wait a minute."

The smile slowly melted off of her face, as Ssabra listened to what the chief had to say. A few moments of awkward silence passed in the room, and then she turned her attention back to the detective.

"Well, what did he say?" Jack asked, impatient for the news.

Ssabra cleared her throat. "Tolomato said the Shiru was following me because it knows who I am. It made contact with me earlier in the day, while I was leading a tour group around the city."

"The Shiru made contact with you?"

She nodded. "I didn't mention it to you, because I didn't think it was all that important. I was out with a tour group this morning, and I had an icy numbness come over me when I was on Charlotte Street. I also had the strangest feeling that I was being watched.

"I told Tolomato about my encounter, and he said I had come in contact with evil. The Shiru is a creature of darkness, and apparently knows that my eyes have been opened."

"Is that what Tolomato just told you?"

"No. That's what he told me earlier today. What he just told me is that the Shiru might consider me a threat, which may explain why it was following me. There's another reason why it might have been following me. . . ."

He leaned forward on the sofa. "What?"

Ssabra swallowed and continued. "I'm different, so the Shiru might think I'm the perfect choice for a mate."

"A mate?" Jack was horrified.

She nodded. "The Shirus that lived here before attempted to breed with humans. Tolomato thinks this one might be trying to do the same."

"Dear God."

"But that's not the worst part."

"There's more?"

"When the Shiru made contact with me this morning he touched my mind, maybe even touched my soul. The link is still there, like a fine thread. He knows who I am, and may come looking for me."

The young woman was obviously distraught by the information given to her. She leaned forward and grabbed Jack's drink off the table, taking a sip of the vodka. "Great. I go dateless for almost a year, and now I've got a freaking monster hitting on me. We've got to do something."

"There's only one thing we can do," replied the detective. "We need to find the bones of the offspring so we can kill the Shiru, before it has a chance to kill someone else. And before it can track you down."

"It's not safe for me to go back out there," she protested. "Not with that thing looking for me."

"If you two are somehow linked, then it won't be any safer for you staying here. The Shiru still might be able to find you. Your best bet is to keep moving.

"But we won't start looking tonight," Jack continued. "From what you've told me, and what I've seen so far, I'm pretty sure the Shiru is nocturnal. At least it's done all of its killing at night. We'll go looking for the offspring at first light, when it's safer."

Glancing at the clock on the far wall, she said, "Listen, it's late, and you've been drinking. Why don't you stay here for the night? You can sleep on the sofa.

I'll feel better having someone here tonight, especially someone who has a loaded gun and knows how to use it."

"And where will you be sleeping?" he teased.

"I'll be sleeping in my bedroom, with the door locked. I'll also have an Indian spirit standing guard, just in case a certain houseguest has the nasty habit of walking in his sleep."

Jack laughed. "No need to worry about me. I'll be the perfect gentleman." He looked around the room. "Now, if you don't mind, will you please get out of my bedroom. I have a busy day ahead of me, and I must get my rest."

Kicking off his shoes, he stretched out on the sofa and pretended to go instantly to sleep. Ssabra watched him for a moment, then turned off the lights and went into her bedroom. She felt safer having an armed police officer sleeping in her living room. But even though she felt safer, she still locked her bedroom door.

Maybe I should leave it unlocked. It's been a long time since I've had a little romance in my life.

That may be true, but her idea of romance wasn't making out with a drunken detective. Slipping into her nightgown, she switched off the lamp and climbed into bed. She had just turned out the light when she heard the gentle snores of the detective. He really had fallen asleep instantly. She also heard the laughter of Tolomato, who seemed to be quite amused with the situation.

CHAPTER
28

Dawn came far too early the next morning, and it was with great effort that Ssabra climbed out of bed. Though she had done nothing extremely physical the previous day, she awoke with sore muscles and a general feeling of tiredness. Her aches and weariness could probably be attributed to her encounter with the Shiru the night before, and a great fear of coming face-to-face with the monster again. Better to be safe in bed than out looking for a dark god, especially when the Shiru was also looking for her.

Slipping into a comfortable combination of jeans, sneakers, and T-shirt, she crossed the room and unlocked the bedroom door. She was surprised to find that Jack was already awake, considering the amount of vodka he had consumed the previous evening. Not only was he awake, but he had already made a fresh pot of coffee and was reading through the translated journal of Father Sebastian Diaz.

The detective looked up from the journal as she entered the room. His hair was still uncombed, and his clothes were rather rumpled from having slept in them. He also needed a shave. "Good morning. I'm sorry if I woke you. I've always been something of an early bird. I made coffee. Hope you like it strong."

Ssabra smiled and nodded as she crossed the room to the bathroom. "No, you didn't wake me; I usually get up around this time. The coffee smells great. I'll be out in a minute."

She closed the bathroom door and ran water in the sink. Washing her face and brushing her teeth, she ran a quick brush through her hair and then turned off the water. Any other physical maintenance would have to wait until after she had her coffee.

The detective was still studying the journal when she stepped out of the bathroom, not even bothering to look up as she staggered her way to the coffeepot. Ssabra poured herself a cup of coffee, added cream and sugar, grabbed a box of vanilla wafers out of the cabinet, and then joined him on the sofa.

"I thought you might be hungry." She set the box of cookies down next to the journal. "I can also cook breakfast if you like. I have bacon and eggs, or pancakes."

Jack looked up from the journal, and smiled. "You'd cook me breakfast? That's awful sweet of you. But no, these are fine. No sense going through all that trouble, especially seeing how you just got up. I'm not a big eater in the morning anyway."

"Me neither," Ssabra grabbed a cookie from the box and dunked it into her coffee. "Find out anything new?"

"Not really. I was just going through the journal to see if we missed anything. This map is kind of crude, but there's still a chance we might find where the offspring is buried.

"We'll need to get started as soon as possible. I've already called the station to let them know that I won't be in today. Said I was running some leads about the homicide, which I technically am. We'll get going once you've finished your breakfast."

She popped another cookie into her mouth, speaking around the food. "Be done in a minute."

It only took Ssabra twenty minutes to finish her breakfast and get ready to leave the apartment. She had just stepped back out of the bathroom, after applying a little makeup, when Tolomato announced his presence. The spirit had been out scouting the area, looking for the Shiru. Ssabra was delighted to hear that the monster was nowhere to be found.

"Does this mean it's gone?" she asked, hopefully.

"No. It means the Shiru is not around now," Tolomato answered. "I am sure it will be back later."

"Great." She was less than thrilled with the information. "What about the offspring? Have you been able to locate where it's buried?"

"Not yet."

She opened the translation of the journal and started reading the passages about the offspring, searching for information about a possible burial site.

"What?" Jack asked, wanting to know what she was looking for.

"I'm trying to find any information about where the offspring might be buried."

He cleared his throat. "I don't want to jinx our chances of success, but it's been over three hundred years since the offspring was killed and buried. Bones just don't last that long, especially when buried in the humid wet soil of Florida. If we do find the grave, odds are there will be nothing left of the remains."

"I thought about that," she replied, glancing up from the book. "But that would only apply to human bones. Right? What if the bones of a Shiru were made of sturdier stuff, then something of the offspring might still remain. You have to think positive on this, and quit being so negative."

"I'm a cop, being negative is part of my job."

"Maybe it's time you thought about a career change." Ssabra smiled and went back to studying the book.

"According to the journal, the body of the offspring was buried in a small plot of land on the north side of the plaza. That might mean the offspring was buried on land where the Cathedral-Basilica now stands."

"The offspring is buried at the church?"

"Maybe, at least according to what I'm reading here." She put the translation down and picked up the original journal, flipping to the map in the back of the book. "Look at this, there's a small X drawn on the map, and a few words in Spanish that I can't make out. I guess I looked at the map wrong last night, because I was way off on my search. I was several blocks north of where I should have been."

Jack leaned forward and studied the map. "You're

right, the X does seem to be just north of the plaza, about where the church would be. Maybe the two of us should pay a little visit to the Cathedral-Basilica."

She glanced at her watch. "They're not open yet."

"I'm a cop. They'll be open for me." He grinned. "I would suggest, however, that you leave the journal and translation in the car. It might be hard to explain what they're doing in your purse."

Her eyes went wide. "What if they've already discovered that the books are missing, and know I'm the one who took them?"

"Don't worry. If anyone points a finger at you, I'll just say that you've already been arrested and are now in my custody. Maybe I'll even tell them that you wanted to come back to the church to confess your sins."

"Thanks a lot," Ssabra laughed. "Do you think that will get me off the hook?"

"Of course it will. Catholics are big believers in redemption. They'll jump at a chance to save another soul."

"Well, let's not tell them that story unless we have to. I'm not sure if I want to be saved anytime soon."

"Got it. No soul-saving unless absolutely necessary."

They arrived at the Cathedral-Basilica less than thirty minutes later, but didn't attempt to enter the church right away. Instead they walked around the building, hoping to find a hidden courtyard, or a small cemetery, where the body of the offspring might be buried. There might once have been such a courtyard, or cemetery, back when the church was first built, or back when it was considerably smaller, but the church had grown over the years and it now covered nearly a city block.

Having no luck on the outside of the church, they attempted to enter the building but found the front doors locked. A few minutes later they found a side door that had been left open, and entered the cathedral. Ssabra was a little nervous about sneaking into the church, but Jack told her to relax, for she was in the company of a police officer.

Gaining entrance into the building did little to help them in their search. There were no tombs or crypts within the church, and nothing to point them in the direction of the offspring's remains. Frustrated at the hopelessness of the situation, they were just about to leave when an elderly priest suddenly appeared from one of the side rooms.

The priest was suspicious of them at first, but seemed to relax a little when Jack showed his badge. Detective Colvin quickly made up a story about how he was investigating a string of church burglaries that had occurred in the area, and was worried about the Cathedral-Basilica. He asked if the church had ever been robbed, and then suggested they might want to keep their side door locked in the future.

Ssabra was amazed at the detective's ability to fashion a believable story so quickly, and wondered if being a convincing liar was standard requirement for all police officers. She was even more amazed when Jack started talking about his love of history, and the research he had done on the cathedral.

Then, with great craft, he worked in the story about a deformed child being buried on property where the church now stood, wondering if there was any truth to the old legend. Much to their surprise, the old priest's eyes seemed to light up at the mention of a deformed skeleton.

"Yes, yes. The story is true, but not many people know about it. A child's body was unearthed when they started to build the Cathedral in the late 1700s. No one knew who the child was, so the bones were kcpt in storage for a year. They were later reburied in a small crypt within the church."

"Was the child deformed?"

"Oh yes, terribly deformed. At first they didn't even know if it was human. The skull was misshapen, and there looked to be too many bones for just one body. Even the rib cage looked different. Poor child. How he must have suffered when alive."

"Are the remains still here?"

"No, I'm afraid not. The remains were here for hundreds of years, so long that everyone had forgotten all about them, but they were rediscovered about forty years ago when a new section of flooring was being installed. Created quite a stir when the crypt was uncovered."

The old priest looked around, as if worried about being overheard. "When they uncovered the crypt, some of the priests thought the skeleton was an abomination, and wanted nothing to do with it. Others said we should rebury it, and forget we had ever seen it. It was finally decided that it should not be buried in holy ground."

"They didn't rebury the body?"

The priest shook his head.

"Then what did they do with it?"

"As I said, the child's body was looked upon as something unclean. Instead of reburying it, some of the church members hid it in the middle of the night. They put the bones into a small casket, and then lowered the casket into one of the old Spanish wells."

"A well? They hid the remains in a well? Which well?"

"I don't know." The priest shrugged. "I didn't go with them that night, and all who did are now dead. All I know is that the remains of the child were put in one of the wells in the old section."

Ssabra and Jack were both silent as they walked back to his patrol car, each thinking about the nearly impossible task that now faced them. They knew the location of some of the old Spanish wells in St. Augustine, but there were probably just as many that had been filled in and forgotten, or covered up, during the last forty years. No telling how many old wells were now located under streets, parking lots, and modern buildings.

Reaching the car, Jack walked to the rear of the vehicle and opened up the trunk. "We'll leave the car here and search for the old wells on foot."

"On foot?" Ssabra looked around nervously. "Do you think it will be safe?"

"I'm guessing the Shiru is probably nocturnal, at least its victims have all been killed at night. We still have plenty of daylight left before it gets dark, so we should be safe. Even if it isn't truly nocturnal, the streets are pretty crowded in the daytime and there's safety in numbers. Besides, I'll protect you."

She laughed. "Gee, thanks. I feel much better. But I seem to remember that the Shiru got the better of you the last time you two tangled, and I was the one saving *your* butt."

"Old history. I didn't know there was such a thing as a Shiru last night, but now that I do I'll be ready for it. You also have Tolomato to warn you of danger. He is still around, isn't he?"

"I don't know. I haven't seen him all day, but he doesn't always show himself. Says it wastes too much energy. Tolomato, are you here?"

Ssabra stood silent for a moment, but there was no answer.

"Tolomato?"

Again, no answer. The voice she heard inside her head was silent.

"Great. Just great. When we need him most, he's off running around somewhere."

"Maybe he's out scouting the location of the well, trying to save us some time. Or maybe he's keeping an eye on the Shiru." Reaching into the trunk, Jack removed a map of the historic area of St. Augustine and a flashlight. He also took out a coil of sturdy rope, and a tire tool.

"What's the rope and tire tool for?" Ssabra asked, curious.

"The tire tool is in case any of the wells have lids that need to be pried off."

"And the rope?"

"If we do find the offspring, one of us will have to climb down into the well to retrieve it."

"One of us?" Ssabra asked, horrified by what he was suggesting. "You mean me?"

He nodded. "You're a lot lighter than I am, and I seriously doubt if you would be strong enough to pull me out of a well."

She stared at the rope for a minute, then looked him in the eyes. "I'm beginning to like our relationship less and less."

"We have a relationship?" The detective grinned.

"Don't get funny. You know what I mean."

Jack slipped the tire tool under his belt, and handed the flashlight to Ssabra. He unfolded the map and studied it for a moment, then folded it up and stuffed it into his back pocket. Carrying the rope, he started to walk away from the patrol car, but then remembered they had left the journal of Father Sebastian Diaz, and the English translation, hidden under the passenger seat. Opening the door, he grabbed the journal and handed it to Ssabra.

"I'm not sure if all the old wells are marked on the new map, so we may need the journal. The map the priest drew is pretty crude, but I think he marked the location of some, if not all, of the old wells."

Closing the driver's door and locking it, they started off on foot for the heart of the historic district. The first of the old Spanish wells was located northwest of the plaza, near the intersection of St. George and Hypolita Street. Jack was hoping the area would be devoid of tourists and curious onlookers, but the well was located in a heavily traveled area. He almost had second thoughts about prying up the coquina lid, because it was stamped with a Spanish seal and obviously was quite old. He would catch hell if he broke the lid while attempting to remove it.

"You know, I'm probably going to get my butt in

trouble for this," he said, squatting down to study the lid.

"You can explain everything later," Ssabra replied, kneeling beside him.

"Oh, right, I'm sure my boss would be interested in a story about hidden coffins and monsters."

"I know I would," she laughed. "I could use a story like that on my ghost tour."

"By the time we're done with all of this, you should have plenty of stories you can use." He wedged the tire tool under the lid. "This is going to be a bitch to get off. Keep an eye out and let me know if I attract any unwanted attention."

Ssabra watched the people who walked past as he struggled with the lid. They did attract a few stares, but for the most part the people seemed only mildly curious. At least no one started shouting and pointing a finger, or threatening to call the cops. She expected the lid to be sealed in place and impossible to get off, and was pleasantly surprised when Jack was able to remove it after only a few minutes of effort.

Setting the lid to the side, the detective switched on his flashlight and aimed it down into the well.

"Do you see anything?"

"No. Nothing. How about you?"

"Nothing."

It was more of a cistern than a true well, a deep shaft lined with stones, used by the city's original inhabitants to catch rainwater. There was actually an inch or two of water standing in the bottom of the well, but not enough to make much of a splash when Jack dropped a small rock into the opening.

"That's what I thought," he said. "The water's not deep, so it's not hiding anything. No offspring here. Let's recap this thing and find the next one."

The second well they located was also empty, as were all the others they found that day. They spent hours searching for the remains of the offspring without having any luck. They checked almost every well marked on the two maps, and were beginning to believe it was a hopeless situation.

The hour was drawing late, the sun already starting to set in the west, and there was still one more well left to be searched. The last well was in the historic district, but they weren't having much success in finding it. It took them nearly an hour of searching before they finally found the location of the well, but someone had gone and built a restaurant over it.

The Sword and Cross Restaurant was housed in a two-story, redbrick building, and was one of the most popular eateries in St. Augustine. Owned and operated by the same family for over twenty years, the restaurant was always busy, even during the middle of the week.

"Now, what do we do?" Ssabra asked. They stood across the street from the restaurant, looking in at the dinner crowd.

"I'm not sure. I'm thinking."

"Well, think fast. In case you haven't noticed, it's already getting dark." She looked around nervously, fearful of what the night would bring.

Jack also looked around. "What's the matter? Do you feel something?"

"No. And I don't want to either. Nor do I want to

see anything," she answered. "You're a cop. Instead of us standing out here in the dark, waiting for you know what to show up, why don't you just walk into the restaurant and flash your badge at the manager?"

"And say what, that I'm hunting for a dead body in a well? I don't think that would go over too good."

"It was just a suggestion," she said. "Got any other ideas?"

"Just one." Jack smiled. "Are you hungry?"

"Starved."

"Good, then let's eat. We're not going to be able to get to that well until after the restaurant closes for the night, but we can look around and see if we can find where it's located. And the best way to snoop around a restaurant is as a hungry customer. Don't you agree?"

"Absolutely."

"If you're good, I might even buy you dessert."

"I'll be real good."

"Okay, then. Let's go eat." Switching the coil of climbing rope to his left hand, he took Ssabra by the arm and led her across the street. The restaurant was crowded, but they were lucky enough to get a small table in the back room. They wouldn't have gotten that if Jack hadn't casually pulled his jacket back to reveal the badge on his belt. It was an old trick to impress hosts and hostesses, and it almost always worked.

During dinner they took turns looking around the restaurant in hopes of locating the old well. Jack used the excuse of going to the bathroom twice, and once he walked through the lounge area to supposedly check on the score of a ballgame. Ssabra was more direct in her snooping, telling her waiter that she had never been in the restaurant before and wanted to look around. She also pretended to be interested in the paintings that hung on the wall, when she was actually more interested in what might be underfoot.

Dessert came and went and they still had not found the well. It wasn't anywhere in the dining area, or in the lower level rest rooms, which meant it had to be in the kitchen, or in one of the storage rooms. It was doubtful if the manager would let them have a peek in the kitchen, especially if they told him what they were looking for. Jack could flash his badge and explain that he was in the middle of an investigation, but it might result in a call to his superior at the police station.

Stalling as long as possible, Jack paid the bill and the two of them left the restaurant. They didn't go far, just across the street to sit on a bench and wait for The Sword and Cross to close for the night.

Ssabra was rather uncomfortable, remembering her previous encounter with the Shiru. If the monster was stalking her, then she didn't want to be sitting out in the open after dark. She felt like fresh bait on the end of a hook, waiting for a large fish to come along and take a bite. Jack must have felt the same way, because, as they sat there, he removed his pistol from its holster and set it beside him on the bench.

She wondered if the Shiru had attempted to breed with any of its recent victims, or if she was the only one who held a special place in the monster's heart. Would the dark god even be interested in her if her eyes had not been opened by Tolomato? Had her new gift put her in a world of danger?

"Thanks, Tolomato," she whispered, trying to fight off the fear that was slowly seeping into her body.

"What was that?" Jack asked, turning to face her.

"Nothing. I was just talking to myself."

"You said Tolomato. I thought maybe you were talking to your spirit friend."

She shook her head. "No. He's not around. At least he hasn't said anything lately. He likes to talk, so if he was here he'd be talking my ear off."

Jack frowned, looking around at the darkness surrounding them. "He hasn't been around all day, and I thought he was supposed to help us find the well. We would have saved a lot of time with his help. I wonder where he's gone off to?"

"I don't know, but I don't think he would have deserted us without a good reason. He must be off doing something important."

A sudden movement in the darkness caught their attention. Jack jumped up, pistol gripped firmly in his right hand. But it was only a cat, probably out roaming the streets in search of food.

"I hope Tolomato comes back soon," he said, sitting back down on the bench.

Maybe the reason the chief hadn't been around to help them look for the wells, as promised, was that he was no longer in the land of the living. Maybe he had been summoned back into the spirit world by a higher force, or he had gone back for a visit and was no longer able to return. That would mean she and Jack were now on their own to face the Shiru.

Ssabra had never wanted a wisecracking Indian ghost as a constant companion, but the thought of Tolomato no longer being around to help troubled her deeply. Hopefully his absence was only a temporary thing, and he would soon be making his presence known.

Glancing at her watch, she was shocked to see that it was almost midnight. Midnight. The witching hour. The time when ghosts and goblins were said to walk the night. Was it also a time for dark gods to be out prowling, hunting for their next victim? More than anything, Ssabra wanted to be home at that moment, safe and sound in her little apartment, with the door and windows locked. She did not want to be sitting out in the open, even if the man beside her carried a loaded gun.

Dammit, Tolomato. Where the hell are you? Don't do this to me.

She didn't know Jack was looking at her as she wrestled with her thoughts, nor did she realize that she was shivering. It might have been the night chill causing her body to shake, or it might have been due to a growing feeling of hopelessness and doom.

"You're shivering. Here, take my jacket." Jack removed his suit jacket and wrapped it around her shoulders. She was grateful for the extra warmth, noticing the faint scent of cologne that clung to the material. She leaned her head on the detective's shoulder, allowing him to put his arm around her.

She had just closed her eyes for a moment, enjoying the sensation of sharing a quiet moment, when the sound of laughter startled her. It was the laugh of someone well-pleased with himself, and the sound came from deep inside her head.

"Tolomato!" She sat up straight on the bench. "He's back. I just heard him."

Jack looked around at the surrounding darkness. "Where? I don't see him."

The young woman spotted a faint shimmering glow just to the right of a nearby palmetto tree. As she watched, the glow grew more solid and took on shape, becoming less transparent and a little less shimmering. Tolomato was standing beside the tree, a big grin on his face.

"He's there. By the tree." Ssabra pointed to where Tolomato stood, even though she knew Jack couldn't see him. "Where in the hell have you been? I've been calling you all day."

The chief laughed. "I was doing as you told me to do."

"Doing as I told you? What do you mean?"

"You told me never to bother you when you were on a date, and that is exactly what I was doing. I was not bothering you."

"On a date? I'm not on a date."

"Oh?" Tolomato made a funny face. "You are with a young man. You have just had dinner, and now you are sitting there with his arm around you. If it is not a date, what would you call it?"

Ssabra started to argue, but stopped. Tolomato had left the two of them alone to share each other's company. It was not a real date, but it was the closest thing to a date she had had in almost a year.

You're right, I am on a date. She formed the words carefully in her mind, hoping Tolomato could read her thoughts. *Thank you.*

"You are most welcome." The chief nodded.

Turning, she saw that Jack was grinning at her. Her face warmed with embarrassment:

"Not a bad first date, huh?" he said, his grin growing wider.

She tried to act indignant, but failed miserably. "We are not on a date."

"Tolomato thinks we are."

"Well, Tolomato is wrong."

"If you say so," Jack laughed.

"I do say so. . . ." Ssabra was interrupted by the sight of Tolomato making a hugging motion, as if he were hugging a woman and kissing her. "Stop that!"

"Stop what?" Jack asked. "I'm not doing anything."

"Not you. Him." She pointed at the tree, forgetting that the detective could not see the apparition.

"What's he doing?" Jack asked.

"He's—" She didn't want to describe Tolomato's action, for fear of being laughed at. "Nothing. It's nothing."

"Doesn't sound like nothing to me."

"Well, it is." She stood up and stripped off Jack's jacket, throwing it in his lap. "Oooo . . . I swear. The two of you are more than I can take."

The detective laughed. "Why? What did I do?"

"Nothing. Just forget it." She looked across the street, not wanting to look back to where Tolomato stood. "That restaurant should be empty by now. How about doing what we came here to do?"

"Sounds good to me." Returning his pistol to its holster, he stood up and slipped his jacket back on. "I think I saw the manager leave a few minutes ago. That should be all of the employees."

"How are we going to get inside?"

"We're going to break in."

"What about the alarm?"

"One of the things about being a cop is that you learn how crooks operate. Before I became a homicide detective, I worked in the burglary division for a couple of years. I learned all the tricks to get past alarm systems."

"You definitely are a fun date," she said.

Jack turned and looked at her. "I thought you said we weren't on a date."

"We're not. I'm just taking notes for the future."

The detective located an outside control box for the alarm system, cutting through the wires with a pocketknife. He then led Ssabra to a small door on the back side of the building, away from the street and the possibility of prying eyes, and broke out one of the door's glass panes with a brick. Pausing to make sure no alarm would sound, he reached in and opened the door.

The restaurant remained silent and cloaked in darkness, with only a few lights left on inside the building for security. The lights were not very bright, so the two of them would probably not be seen once inside. Switching on his flashlight, he entered the restaurant with Ssabra close at his heels.

Jack wanted to split up to look for the well, but he only had one flashlight, so they had to stay together. They had already looked through the dining area, and the lounge, so they began their search in the kitchen. If the old Spanish well had been located where the kitchen now sat, then it was completely covered over, for there was no sign of it. There were no breaks in the tile flooring to indicate the presence of a well, nor any odd deformities along the wall.

They searched through the storerooms next, even looked in the cooler, but with no results. If the restaurant had been built over the old well, then the building completely covered it.

"Damn, it's not here," Jack said, sweeping his flashlight around the kitchen for a second time. "The map must be wrong."

Ssabra studied the crude map of Father Sebastian Diaz, straining to see it in the semidarkness. "It has to be here. All the other wells were marked in the right locations."

"We've already been through this place twice. It's not here. We're just wasting our time."

"Let's look again," she said. "I don't want to give up so easily."

He sighed. "Okay, if it will make you happy, we'll go back through this place one more time. But that's it. I want to get out of here before someone sees my flashlight and reports a break-in."

They went back through the kitchen, but didn't have any better luck than the first time. They also searched the two back storerooms, but their effort was fruitless. They were just about to leave the storeroom, when Tolomato spoke up.

"Look around, woman."

Ssabra jumped, startled by the voice. "Wait a minute." She placed a hand on Jack's arm.

"What?"

"Tolomato just spoke to me. I think the well is here. He told me to look around."

The detective swept the flashlight around the contents of the room. The storage room was about fifteen by twenty feet, crowded with beer cases and other boxes. "Where? I don't see it."

"It must be hidden. Maybe it's behind the boxes."

"Here, hold this. Shine it where I can see." He gave her the flashlight and started moving the cases and cardboard boxes out of the way. He went through several stacks, and then he noticed that the next stack of empty beer cases was higher than the previous two, even though the stacks contained the same number of cases. "Son of a bitch. I think we've found something."

Jack pulled the empty cases out of the way, and let out a whoop. The stack had been sitting on top of a round well cover. The Spanish emblem carved into the stone identified it as one of the old wells.

"Bingo. We've found it." He pushed the other stacks of empty boxes out of the way and pulled the tire tool from his belt. "Tell Tolomato thank you."

"He heard you," Ssabra said, holding the flashlight steady. "He says you're welcome."

Knowing the storeroom was not visible to anyone outside the restaurant, Jack found a switch and flipped on the single lightbulb hanging from the ceiling. It took a few minutes of fumbling and prying before he managed to get the lid off the well, and he nearly smashed two of his fingers in the process. Setting the lid to the side, he took the flashlight from Ssabra and shined it down into the opening.

The well was about twenty feet deep and three feet in diameter, and had probably once been used to catch and store rainwater. The water had dried up long ago, but the well was anything but empty. At the bottom of the shaft, standing almost straight up, was a rectangular container that looked to be made of wood and brass. It was nearly black with mildew, but there was still no mistaking that it was a small casket.

The two of them were speechless for a moment, then Jack said, "Done any rope climbing lately?"

"Not since high school gym class, but I probably remember how to do it."

"Good. Get yourself ready while I find something to tie this rope to." He walked back into the kitchen and tied off one end of the climbing rope to a sturdy steel counter that was fastened to the floor. The rope was one hundred feet long, so he would have more than enough to reach the bottom of the well and tie up the casket.

He walked back into the storage room, where Ssabra stood waiting for him. "Okay, I'm going to wrap this around your waist and through your legs to make a sling. That way I'll be able to lower you down slowly, rather than risk having you climb down on your own. Once I get in position, I want you to sit on the edge of the well and then slowly lower yourself into the opening. Keep hold of the rope and use your feet for breaks. I'll try not to let you drop too quickly. Take the flashlight with you; turn it on and slip it into your belt."

He finished tying the rope around Ssabra, fashioning it into a crude harness. Once everything was tied in place, he tugged on the rope to make sure the knots would not come undone. "Good thing you're as skinny as a rail, otherwise this rope might not hold you."

Ssabra favored him with a smile. "Are you always so flattering to your dates?"

Jack returned the smile, then he leaned forward and kissed her lightly on the lips.

"What was that for?" she asked, surprised by the gesture.

"In case I accidentally drop you."

Ssabra leaned forward and kissed him back, her lips lingering on his for a few moments.

"And what was that for?" he asked, genuinely pleased.

"Just because." She stepped back and sat down on the edge of the well, waiting while Jack got into position. He sat down at the opposite edge of the well, facing the opening, using the raised stone lip to brace his feet against. Ssabra waited for him to give her a nod, then slowly lowered herself into the opening.

It took a lot of courage for her to let go of the lip and trust the rope, but Jack had her and she did not fall. Instead, she was slowly lowered down into the ancient stone shaft. When she neared the bottom, she let go of the rope and pulled the flashlight from her belt. She wanted to see where she was going, and didn't want to land on the casket. Once she was safely down, she untied the end of the rope from around her and fastened it around the casket. The casket was weathered and looked in danger of falling apart, but it might hold together long enough to lift it out of the well.

"Okay, I've got it." She looked up at the opening and waved the flashlight. Jack was peering over the edge, watching her. "The casket's secure; pull it up."

"What about you?"

"Get the box first, then drop the rope back down to me. I'll help get it started."

"Good idea." His face disappeared from view. A few seconds later the small casket started to rise toward the opening. Ssabra helped it along until she could no longer reach it, making sure that it didn't bang against the stone walls. Once out of reach, she kept the light shining on the tiny coffin as she watched its progress to the surface.

The casket paused for a moment at the opening, as Jack struggled to get it over the lip. Then it disappeared from view. A few moments later the rope fell into the well like an uncoiling snake.

"Remember how I tied the rope around you?" Jack called from above.

"I think so." Ssabra tied the rope around her waist and legs, trying to remember how he had done it. Her harness may not have been perfect, but it was secure and the knots were tight, so she probably wouldn't slip out. "Okay, all set. Go ahead."

"Here we go."

Ssabra felt a tug on the rope and then she began to slowly rise off the floor of the well. She slipped the flashlight back into her belt so she could use her hands to grab the rope, and keep her body from banging against the stone walls. She was almost to the top when she heard a loud crash, followed by a shout.

"Hold it right there!"

A scant second later the rope went slack in her hands and she found herself plummeting to the bottom of the well.

Ssabra screamed and tried to catch hold of something to stop her fall, but there was nothing to grab. The stones that made up the walls of the ancient well were tightly fitted together, and there were no handholds. She tried to grab the wall, but all she accomplished was breaking off two of her fingernails. She hit the floor hard, her ankle twisting painfully beneath her, falling backward to crash into the opposite wall.

The world flashed white hot, and a searing pain ripped through her body. Ssabra thought she was going to pass out, but remained conscious and painfully aware of the damage she had done to her ankle, back, shoulders, neck and head. She lay on her side, having bounced off the wall, staring at the stones in front of her. The flashlight was still tucked into the front of her pants, and, luckily, had not been damaged in the fall.

She had the wind knocked out of her, so several minutes elapsed before she could even think about moving. She was also fearful that she had broken her leg in the fall, but was able to straighten out both of her legs without too much pain or difficulty. Her legs weren't broken, but she wasn't so sure about her right ankle. If it wasn't broken, then it was badly sprained.

As she lay there, she slowly began to check her other body parts, inspecting what kind of damage had been done in the fall. Her legs appeared to be working, and so were her arms. At least she could move them. She gingerly touched the back of her head with her fingertips, feeling wetness beneath her hair. Removing her fingers, she studied them under the beam of the flashlight. They were red with blood.

Her head was bleeding, but she couldn't be sure how badly she was hurt. It might only be a small scalp laceration, or it might be a cut deep enough to require stitches. For all she knew, she might even have a concussion, or a skull fracture. One thing for sure, she needed to get out of the well and to a hospital.

Ssabra looked up at the opening. What the hell happened? Why had Jack let go of the rope? Had someone seen their flashlight and called the cops? Maybe the owner had showed up, or perhaps the manager or one of the employees had returned. They might have surprised Jack, causing him to let go of the rope. Maybe they even hit him over the head with something. He had been facing the well, his back to the doorway.

She also remembered hearing someone shout. It might have been Jack who yelled, or it might have been a police officer or security guard. Maybe someone pulled a gun on the detective, and he had to let go of the rope to keep from getting shot.

"Jack?" Ssabra cleared her throat and called up to the opening. Her voice wasn't loud, and she had probably not been heard. She coughed and tried again. "Jack, are you there? What happened?"

Detective Colvin did not answer, and the silence seemed to close in around her. She tried again. "Jack, can you hear me?"

A few more seconds passed, but there was no answer from above. Something had happened to Jack, but she wasn't sure what. He might have been arrested and taken out of the building. Maybe he felt it was better to drop her than run the risk of having her also getting arrested.

"Nice guy. Remind me to send him a thank you card from the hospital."

One thing for sure, she was getting nowhere fast just sitting there. Whatever had happened, Jack was not answering her calls. Nor was he pulling on the other end of the rope. That meant it was up to her to get herself out of the well. Of course, she could stay where she was until help came along. At the very worst she would only have to stay the night, but she didn't like the idea of remaining in the well for a minute longer than she had to. It was creepy and dark, and it was the place where a casket had rested for many years. Also, her flashlight might not last until morning, and there was no way in hell she was going to spend the night in the dark.

"I guess it's just you and me, kid," she said, talking to herself for reassurance. "And maybe Tolomato."

She looked around. "Tolomato, are you here?"

There was no answer.

"Great. He's gone again. Probably not around because of my rules about dating. Some date, definitely ended on a high note."

Wiping her hands off on her pants, she got to her knees. "Okay, here goes nothing."

Trying to favor her injured ankle, Ssabra pushed herself off the floor and slowly got to her feet. As she stood up a wave of pain and nausea washed over her and she almost passed out. Had it not been for the nearby wall she would have fallen over backward.

"Damn, that hurts." She again put her weight on her injured ankle, biting her lower lip to keep from crying out.

The pain wasn't as bad the second time, and she was able to move her foot, so the ankle was probably only sprained. Still, it was a bad sprain and extremely painful, and her ankle would soon swell up to where she couldn't put weight on it. That meant she had to get out of the well while she was still able to stand.

Hobbling over to the opposite wall, Ssabra took the climbing rope in both hands. She stood there holding the rope, hoping the dizziness would soon pass. But the dizziness and nausea refused to leave, and it was all she could do to stay on her feet.

Determined not to remain in the well for another moment, she took a firm grip on the rope. She had been a pretty good rope climber in high school, one of the best in girls' gym class, but that had been a long time ago. And she hadn't been injured then. Saying a short prayer for courage and strength, she grabbed the rope tight and pulled herself off the floor.

A burning pain shot like a bullet between her shoulder blades, and she suspected that she might have hurt her back in the fall. But she refused to let go of the rope, or give up. Instead, she slid her hand carefully up the rope and pulled herself even higher.

Hand over hand she went, slowly pulling herself out of the well. Every muscle in her body screamed for her to stop, and her head swam in a sea of dizziness. Three times she had to pause to catch her breath, forcing herself to go on. Finally she was at the top of the well, reaching up with her right hand to grab the lip. She almost screamed in surprise when a hand reached down from above to take hers, pulling her from the well. At first she thought it was Jack, but he wore a brown suit and this hand protruded from a blue sleeve. It wasn't a uniform, so it probably wasn't a cop who reached down to help her out of the well.

It didn't matter who it was that offered a helping hand. Ssabra was close to exhaustion, and she was grateful for any assistance, even if it meant having to explain why she had broken into the restaurant. A night in jail didn't seem so bad after all the things that had happened to her in the past twenty-four hours.

The man who pulled her from the well was about six feet tall, with a full beard and sandy brown hair. He was dressed in blue jeans, boots, a black shirt, and a faded denim jacket. There was something vaguely familiar about him, but she couldn't place his face. He might have been someone who had taken one of her tours, or maybe just one of the locals she had seen in passing.

He helped her out of the well, but didn't let go of her hand. Perhaps he was worried she might tumble backward into the opening. Or maybe he could tell that she was hurt and somewhat unsteady on her feet. It was a good thing he didn't let go of her right away, for another wave of dizziness washed through her and she almost fell flat on her face.

Despite the dizziness, and the pain of her injuries, Ssabra managed to remain standing, carefully balancing most of her weight on her uninjured ankle. She got her thoughts together enough to glance past the man who held her, but there was no one else in the storage room. Jack had either left on his own, or had been escorted out. She couldn't understand why he would leave her at the bottom of a well, and suspected something bad had happened to him.

"Thank you," she said, finally finding her voice. "I think I'm okay now, but I may need a doctor. Where's Jack? What happened to him?"

The man did not release her hand. Instead, he stood looking at her with a half smile on his face. She was just about to say something else, when she noticed a slight rippling beneath his jacket.

That's odd. There's something moving under his jacket. A pet perhaps. Something small.

Much to her surprise, a thin black eel suddenly appeared out of the top of the man's shirt and crawled slowly toward his face.

What the hell is that? A snake? No, not a snake. Much too shiny. It's an eel. What kind of man carries an eel around under his jacket?

A second eel appeared from beneath the bottom of his jacket; it slithered down his left leg and over the top of his boot, crawling across the concrete floor toward her.

Jesus, there's another one.

Ssabra tried to step back, but her hand was still being held. She wanted to stomp on the eel crawling toward her, but then she realized it wasn't an eel at all. It was a tentacle, and it was attached to the man who held her hand.

No. It can't be possible.

All at once, she remembered where she had seen

the man before. She had seen him in a dark alley, running away after he had attacked, and nearly killed, Detective Colvin. The man she had seen then, and who stood before her now, wasn't really a man at all. His features were only a disguise, worn by a dark god to walk undetected among humans.

"Oh, dear God. No."

The Shiru had found her, and she knew what it wanted. Ssabra looked down, horrified to see that the bearded man had an erection.

"No. Please . . . no."

And then the Shiru spoke to her, a voice coming from deep within his throat, the way a parrot mimics words, a crackled imitation of human speech. "You are mine, female. You are the two-legs I will breed with."

She didn't know if it was the voice that terrified her, its crackling hiss so inhuman and uncaring, or the words that were spoken. Either way, Ssabra suddenly found a little more strength than she had a few moments before, enough to tear her hand free from the Shiru's grasp.

Ignoring the pain of her injured ankle, she attempted to hobble toward the door. But the Shiru jumped to the right and cut her off, blocking her flight from the room. Ssabra turned and tried to circle the well, hoping to get past the monster from a different direction, but she slipped on a wet spot and her feet went out from under her.

She hit the concrete floor hard enough to cause her teeth to clack together, sending pain shooting through her head. The patch of floor she landed on was wet and slippery, littered with small pieces of fabric. Most of the fabric pieces had once been dark brown in color, but a few of them might have been white. It was hard to tell their original color, because they were now stained crimson. Mixed in with the fabric were tiny pieces of leather, flesh, and bone.

The storeroom had once been clean enough to pass inspection by the local Health Department, but a ten-foot area of floor was now covered with blood and gore. A shudder of revulsion shook through Ssabra as she realized the blood, fabric, bits of flesh, and tiny pieces of bone were all that was left of Jack Colvin. The detective had not been arrested by the police, apprehended by a security guard, or hit over the head by the restaurant's manager. Nothing as nice as that. Instead he had ended up as the Shiru's latest victim, his body looking like it had passed through a food processor.

Ssabra pressed her fist against her lips to keep from gagging, and tried to look away from the horror scattered around her. But there was no escaping the nightmare. Turning her head to the right, she was shocked to see Jack's face. Just his face: no body, no legs, no arms, no head, or even eyes. The detective's face had been peeled off his skull and stuck to the side of an empty cardboard beer case.

She screamed.

Blackness tried to overcome her, but she fought to stay conscious. If Ssabra passed out, then she could not escape, and she desperately wanted to flee the storeroom. She bit down on her fist, biting hard enough to draw blood. The pain pushed the blackness back, saved her from unconsciousness. Jack's face came back into clear focus; it was still looking at her.

No. No. Please God, no. Jack. Sweet, kind Jack. Why didn't you go down in the well? You might still be alive. She could still taste his kiss upon her lips, which made his death all the more painful.

Ssabra turned and looked across the room. The Shiru still stood between her and the doorway, but it was no longer worried about maintaining its human disguise. As she watched, the bearded man seemed to shimmer and go slightly transparent. And then his flesh began to ripple and stretch, pulling itself apart as it took on a new shape and identity.

She had seen the Shiru in its true identity once before, but that was in a dark alleyway. Now she was witnessing the transformation from man to monster beneath the glow of a hundred-watt lightbulb, the change taking only a few seconds to complete. Once complete, the sight of the Shiru in all its terrifying glory sent her mind reeling and threatened her sanity.

Ssabra screamed again.

The monster's head was large and triangular, reminding her of a cockroach or a beetle. It had six black eyes, the same color as its skin, two vertical rows of three eyes each. Beneath the eyes was a large, beaked mouth lined with a double row of teeth. The mouth opened and closed in a constant motion, the teeth clicking and grinding together.

The head was attached to an enormous saggy black body, looking like a clustering of overfilled trash bags. The underside of the Shiru's body was covered with dozens of tiny, reddish-brown, crablike creatures. These crab creatures scurried around, crawling over each other, feeding on a yellowish pus that oozed from the dark god's skin in thick droplets.

On the monster's back were hundreds of pencil-thick hairs that moved about as if alive. There were also several long tubelike appendages sticking from the Shiru's rear that opened and closed when it exhaled, making a strange woofing-hooting sound.

The Shiru crouched on six large, multijointed legs similar to those of a crustacean. In addition to the six legs, the creature had several dozen long tentacles that whirled about its body in constant motion. The tentacles served as arms and fingers, always touching, feeling, and probing. They also served to feed the Shiru, for each tentacle was tipped with a tiny mouth lined with sharp teeth.

When one of the tentacles came in contact with a piece of flesh, or a droplet of blood, there was a hungry slurping sound as the morsel of food was sucked up by the tiny mouth. And when a tentacle came upon a morsel too big to inhale, it would pick up the piece of food and shove it into the Shiru's main mouth. The item was then chewed and regurgitated in liquid form, to be sucked up again by the ever-feeding tentacles.

She stared at the Shiru in stark terror, too scared to even move. The creature was so alien to anything she had ever seen that its ancestral origin could not possibly be of this earth. Primitive people had looked upon the Shirus as dark gods, creatures to be feared and perhaps worshiped. Ssabra could understand the fear, for she was truly terrified, but she could not understand how someone might come to worship such a beast.

As she sat there, trembling with fear, Ssabra Onih saw the final feature that nearly brought her insanity. Beneath the Shiru's sagging belly hung a penis as thick as a man's forearm, and close to two feet in length, mottled gray in color and heavily veined. The penis was fully erect, and pulsed with a rhythmic throb, yellow semen dripping from the tip like mayonnaise gone bad.

Ssabra pushed herself up off the floor, trying desperately to get her good leg under her. She planned on hobbling for the door, but the monster reacted to her movement by scurrying closer to her. No way she could outrun a creature with six legs when she only had one good one.

Realizing that direct flight was not an option, she looked around the room for something to defend herself with. She was hoping to find Jack's pistol, but the gun was nowhere in sight. She was wondering if the firearm had been shredded and eaten with the rest of the body.

The situation seemed hopeless, then she happened to spot something on the opposite side of the room. Lying there in the shadows was the small wooden casket Jack had pulled from the well. The Shiru hadn't noticed the casket, or, if he had, then the creature didn't look upon it as a threat. Maybe the monster was too excited sexually to worry about such things. Not only was the casket there, but its lid had already been pried up and set to the side. The detective must have pried the lid off before lowering the rope back down to her.

Now the problem was getting to the casket without being stopped by the Shiru. The monster was not between her and the casket, but it might move to stop her if she tried to reach it. But maybe the Shiru was only guarding the doorway, blocking her from escaping the room. Maybe it didn't recognize the threat the casket contained, if it contained anything at all.

Don't think that. It can't be empty.

Fearful that any sudden movement might result in an attack, Ssabra started inching slowly toward the casket. She kept her eyes on the Shiru and walked backward. But for every step she took the monster also took a step, maintaining the distance between the two of them.

The Shiru paused when it reached the spot where she had just been sitting, one of the creature's tentacles reaching out to peel Jack's face off the beer carton. The face came loose with a wet sucking sound that made Ssabra go cold inside. Peeling it off the carton, the tentacle stuffed the detective's face into the Shiru's beaked mouth. A few moments later the face was regurgitated along with a puddle of digestive fluid, to be sucked up by several of the tentacles.

Straws. It's drinking Jack's face with a straw.

Ssabra nearly passed out from the sight of Jack Colvin's face being eaten, but she stayed on her feet and used the moment to move next to the casket. Looking down into the open box, she almost shouted with joy when she saw the yellowed skeleton of a hideously deformed child. The head of the offspring was long and triangular, and there were four eye sockets instead of the normal two. The skeleton also had an extra set of arms and legs, as well as a few other bony protuberances that definitely were not human.

The offspring had apparently been born without feet, the leg bones ending in points where the ankles should have been. Deciding that the pointed leg bones would make the best weapons, Ssabra reached down and broke off two of the offspring's legs just below the knees. She slipped one of the bones through her belt, wearing it like a sword; the other she kept clutched tightly in her right hand.

She should have felt better now that she was armed, but the leg bones looked mighty puny when compared to the size of the Shiru. Nor did she know if the bones really possessed some kind of magical quality that could kill the monster. But the bones were all she had, the only protection against a fate far worse than death.

"Tolomato, where are you?" The chief had been absent throughout her ordeal.

"Looks like I'm on my own." She stepped back from the casket and looked across the room. The Shiru had finished slurping up the remains of Jack's face, and was now back to watching her. How long would it be before the monster made his move? Lover boy was obviously growing more sexually agitated by the minute, the throbbing of his penis becoming more pronounced.

Maybe the Shiru was working itself up to a sexual frenzy. Or perhaps it wanted to take its sweet time about things in order to make the moment last. One thing for sure, Ssabra wasn't going to stick around to see what was about to happen. She was going to get the hell out of there, or she was going to die trying.

Looking for an opening move, something to put the monster off guard, she grabbed the offspring's skull and threw it at the Shiru. The skull hit the dark god square in the head, causing it to scurry back a couple of steps.

It was the break she was hoping for. When the Shiru stepped back, it moved farther away from the door. It also stepped into the center of the blood and gore that had once been Jack Colvin. The tentacles might be delighted with the opportunity to feed some more, but the slippery floor would provide a less than perfect footing for the monster.

No sooner had she thrown the skull than Ssabra started hobbling toward the doorway. The exit was less than twenty feet away, but her injured ankle was already starting to swell and she could barely stand to put her weight fully upon it. It was all she could do to walk, let alone run.

There was a loud hissing, woofing-hooting noise as the Shiru realized what she was doing and started after her. Even on the slippery concrete floor, the monster was surefooted and could move a lot faster than she could. The race was on, but even with a head start the advantage was not hers.

She reached the doorway a few feet ahead of the Shiru, but her lead was worthless because she had not taken into consideration the reach of the monster's tentacles. As she tried to flee from the storeroom, one of the tentacles grabbed her around the waist and jerked her back into the room. Two more tentacles grabbed her legs, ripping her pants off as easily as someone would peel the skin from a banana.

She was down to panties, shoes, socks, and shirt, and had a feeling she wouldn't have those articles of clothing for much longer. A few more tentacles had already wrapped themselves around her legs, mouths sniffing at the edges of her cotton underwear and probing up under her shirt. She was disgusted by the touch of the tentacles, her skin breaking out in goosebumps, but she was even more sickened by what those tentacles were attached to.

Instead of trying to pull away, Ssabra turned and lunged toward the Shiru, intent on driving the leg bone she held deep into the monster's body. She almost made it, but another one of the tentacles shot out and grabbed the bone, tearing it from her grasp.

Unarmed, she screamed and struggled, but her efforts were futile. She was a helpless fly trapped in a sticky web, and the spider was coming closer for the kill. She screamed again as she was pushed to the floor, the monster crawling over the top of her.

Ssabra heard the sound of fabric ripping, and felt the clothing being torn from her body. She was completely naked now, except for her shoes and socks, unable to struggle against the tentacles that held her legs and waist. She would have beat at the monster with her fists, but she could not bring herself to touch its pus-covered underside. Nor did she want to touch any of the crab creatures that scurried around beneath the Shiru like bloated ticks.

Her shoulders were pushed down against the cold concrete floor, and then her hips were lifted by the tentacles and her legs spread. The Shiru shuffled forward a little more, aligning its penis for the penetrating thrust. Ssabra screamed and tried to get free, but she was like a fish out of water and unable to move. She closed her eyes and awaited a pain that would undoubtedly send her mind to the brink of madness.

Then a voice spoke to her. "I am here, child."

Ssabra thought she had only imagined the voice, but she heard it again.

"Fear not."

She opened her eyes and looked around, but saw nothing but the hideous underside of the Shiru. The monster had stopped its forward movement and stood hovering over her, penis poised to strike like a thickly veined spear.

And then she saw Tolomato. The spirit of the Indian chief stood a few feet in front of the Shiru, glowing brightly as if he had been dipped in phosphorescent paint. He was almost solid in appearance, and Ssabra knew that Tolomato was using a lot of energy to appear in such a state.

The Shiru must have been able to see Tolomato, because it began to make an angry hissing sound. The creature was not happy with having its lovemaking interrupted, and was letting the Indian know about it. Ssabra wasn't sure how or why the Shiru could see the chief. Maybe it was because they were both from the spirit world, or perhaps the monster had qualities that normal people did not possess. Either way, Tolomato's sudden appearance had distracted the monster from what it had intended to do to her. She still hung spread-eagle beneath the Shiru, naked and unable to move, but she had not yet been mounted.

Not knowing how long Tolomato could continue distracting the monster, Ssabra looked around in desperation for something she could use as a weapon. The leg bone she once held in her right hand had been knocked across the room, and now lay in pieces. The other leg bone, however, was still stuck through her belt, even though her pants had been torn from her. The pants, and the leg bone, lay only a foot or two away from her.

The Shiru knew that it was much stronger than the woman it intended on breeding with, so it had not used any of its tentacles to hold her arms. Once she had been disarmed, it had grabbed only her legs and waist for the mating. Her arms had been left free. Big mistake.

Reaching out with her right arm, Ssabra snatched the pointed leg bone from her belt. She gripped the bone tightly in her right fist and directed her attention upward, looking for a vital spot on the monster's underbelly. She didn't know if the creature had a heart, or where it would be located. She only had one chance to inflict a wound, and she wanted to cause maximum damage.

And then she saw what she was looking for: the Shiru's penis hung almost directly above her. The heavily veined muscle had lost some of its frantic throbbing, due to Tolomato's interruption, but it was still fully erect. It was also the perfect target.

"This is for every woman who has ever been raped." Ssabra thrust upward with all of her strength, driving the pointed bone through the center of the Shiru's penis. From above her came a scream that defied description, sounding like metallic gears being ripped from the transmission of heavy machinery. She ignored the scream and pushed harder, stabbing the leg bone through the penis and deep into the monster's belly.

She continued pushing until only a few inches of bone were still visible, and then she grabbed those few inches and jerked back and forth, stirring the leg bone deep inside the monster's stomach, destroying tissue and vital organs.

The tentacles released their hold on her, whipping around in a mad frenzy. They tried to grab the leg bone and pull it free, but could not get a good grip on it. The bone, which held the penis impaled to the stomach, was slick with blood and seminal fluid.

Ssabra rolled free of the monster and got to her feet. She thought the Shiru would attempt to grab her again, but it was far too preoccupied with its injury. She watched as the blood pouring out of its belly grew from a trickle to a stream, and then into a flood.

She must have done more damage than she hoped, because the Shiru's stomach suddenly split open and dumped its internal organs on the floor in a great putrid mess. Maybe the offspring's bones really were magical, or perhaps poisonous to the creature. Whatever the reason, she watched in absolute delight as the monster staggered back from her, dragging intestines and vital body parts behind it. The Shiru only made it a few feet, however, before succumbing to death. Legs collapsing beneath it, the monster gave a final hiss and died.

"You did well, young one."

She turned at the sound of the voice. Tolomato still stood in the same place, but he no longer glowed quite so brightly. She barely heard what he had said, her system in too much shock to concentrate on the words that sounded in her head, and could only nod in reply.

Ssabra looked down and saw that she was naked, but she did not feel cold. She felt nothing but numbness, and heartache over the loss of a friend.

The Indian chief stuttered, as if at a loss for words. "I would have been here sooner, but I . . . your rules."

Again she nodded, tears forming at the corners of her eyes. "I know. From now on, no more rules."

She turned and looked at the Shiru. "What about that, will others like it be able to come into this world through the opening?"

"I do not know," Tolomato answered, shaking his head.

Ssabra hobbled slowly across the room to the little casket. Reaching down, she broke off the remaining leg and arm bones of the offspring, carrying them back to where Tolomato stood. "If more come, we'll be ready for them."

"Yes, we will be ready, but the fight is over for now. Let us leave this place. There are uniforms in the other room that you can wear."

Ssabra was too drained from her ordeal to think clearly, and could barely concentrate on what was being said. She allowed Tolomato to lead her to the doorway, pausing to give a final glance at the contents of the storeroom: empty boxes, tattered fabric, blood and tiny pieces of gore, all that was left of someone who might have become much more than just a friend.

There was also the Shiru. The monster's body appeared to be melting, a puddle of liquid spreading out around it. Maybe by morning it would be nothing more than a large stain on the floor.

Turning her back on the Shiru, she staggered out of the storeroom. As she stepped through the doorway, Ssabra turned off the light, allowing a blanket of darkness to cover the nightmare.

EPILOGUE

A light rain fell from the sky that morning, but it was not unusual for the time of year. Maybe it was the way things were supposed to be, rain and cloudy skies for solemn occasions. Ssabra didn't really mind the rain, but it did make the grass rather slick. To avoid slipping, she had left her crutches in the car. It still pained her to walk on her badly sprained ankle, but she would rather have the pain than risk a fall.

She stood back from the others, listening to the words being spoken by a man in a white collar. Jack's family was Catholic, so his funeral service was being conducted by a priest. Beyond the rows of mourners and fellow officers, a man dressed in a kilt and a blue jacket was playing a set of bagpipes. The haunting melody drifted across the cemetery, bringing tears to the eyes of all who heard it.

Ssabra reached into her purse and removed a handkerchief, dabbing at the corners of her eyes. She didn't want to cry, but she couldn't help it. Every time the bagpipes started, so too did the tears.

Detective Jack Colvin's remains had been found, and positively identified through DNA testing, after an anonymous female caller had telephoned the St. Augustine Police Station to report that something terrible had happened at The Sword and Cross Restaurant. The investigating officers had found what was left of the detective in a back storeroom. They had also found a small casket, containing a partial skeleton, and a melting mass that had yet to be properly identified.

Putting the handkerchief back into her purse, she tried to keep from crying as she watched the graveside ceremony. It had been a closed casket service, and she doubted if even a small piece of Jack was really inside the coffin. It probably just contained a few items of clothing, or maybe a pair of shoes. Perhaps all it held was empty space, or a few bricks to give it weight.

The casket had been covered with an American flag, but two police officers in dress uniform were removing the flag and folding it into a triangle. As the flag was being folded, seven officers standing in a single line raised rifles into the air and fired. They repeated the gesture three times, giving a twenty-one-gun salute for a fallen comrade. Once the volley was fired, the officers brought their rifles to their sides and stood at attention as the casket was slowly lowered into the ground.

Ssabra watched the coffin being lowered, again feeling an empty pain deep inside her heart. Why did all the good ones have to die? Why did she always lose those she cared about? It just wasn't fair.

Blinking back tears, she watched as one of the police officers stepped forward and tossed a shovelful of dirt down on the coffin. Another officer, a woman, stepped up to the grave and tossed in a yellow rose. Ssabra watched the others file past the opening, saying their final good-byes. She would have also approached the opening, but her legs had gone all rubbery. Instead, she stood where she was and whispered a few words.

"Good-bye, Jack. I will miss you." She reached back into her purse and retrieved the handkerchief, dabbing once more at the corners of her eyes.

"Jack says good-bye."

She spun around, startled by the voice. Tolomato stood beside her. The Indian had disappeared shortly after she had gone to the hospital to have her injuries treated. Dressed in a chef's jacket and pants, she had hobbled into the emergency room to have her ankle wrapped, the cut on her head cleaned, and to get something for the pain.

She hadn't seen Tolomato since that night, and was starting to believe he might be gone for good. But his disappearance was apparently only temporary, for the chief stood beside her now.

Ssabra looked around to make sure she wouldn't be overheard. "What did you say?"

"I said, Jack says good-bye to you." Tolomato grinned. "See for yourself."

The Indian pointed away from the burial service to a clustering of oak trees on a nearby hillside. There stood Detective Jack Colvin, dressed exactly as she had last seen him. He was there, big as life, but he was also somewhat transparent. For it wasn't Jack Colvin in the flesh, but his spirit that stood on the hill, looking down at her.

Ssabra felt tears flood her eyes and roll down her cheeks. She wanted to run up the hill and hug him, but knew that it would be impossible. He had already crossed over to the other side, a place where pain and suffering no longer existed. She was of the flesh, and he of the spirit, and, while the two worlds could sometimes walk hand in hand, there could never be a permanent bonding between them.

Instead of running up the hill to visit with the detective one last time, or calling out his name, Ssabra stood silent and watched as Jack raised fingers to his lips and blew her a final kiss. A moment later his image faded and blew apart, like mist on the morning wind, disappearing into nothingness.

"He's gone," Tolomato said. "I'm sorry."

Ssabra nodded. "I know. But he'll never be truly gone." She touched her heart. "He will always be here."

She turned and slowly walked away from the memorial service, heading back toward her car.